Luvin' Him
Wasn't Enough

Luvin' Him
Wasn't Enough

Racquel Williams

www.urbanbooks.net

Urban Books, LLC
300 Farmingdale Road, N.Y.-Route 109
Farmingdale, NY 11735

Luvin' Him Wasn't Enough
Copyright © 2024 Racquel Williams

ISBN 13: 978-1-64556-577-2
EBOOK ISBN: 978-1-64556-578-9

First Trade Paperback Printing May 2024
Printed in the United States of America

10 9 8 7 6 5 4 3 2 1

Distributed by Kensington Publishing Corp.
Submit Orders to:
Customer Service
400 Hahn Road
Westminster, MD 21157-4627
Phone: 1-800-733-3000
Fax: 1-800-659-2436

Luvin' Him
Wasn't Enough

by

Racquel Williams

ACKNOWLEDGMENTS

First and foremost, I will continue to give all praises to Allah. This has definitely been a journey, and I'm forever grateful that He keeps on blessing me.

To my readers, too many to name: I really appreciate the support y'all have shown me since the very first book. You all are the real MVP, and I hope that I can continue to live up to y'all's standard. I love y'all for real.

PROLOGUE

Amoy Simpson

I learned a long time ago that if I, Amoy Simpson, wanted something out of life, I had to go after it. See, I wasn't your regular bitch who sat on her ass hoping that shit was going to happen, and I damn sure wasn't going to sit around waiting on no damn check every first of the month.

I was born and raised in Mount Vernon, New York, otherwise known as Money Earnin' Mount Vernon. I grew up in an apartment building on the corner of East Third Street and Fourth Avenue. In my hood, there were hustlers slinging them rocks or dealing powder, and the bitches stayed on their grind either selling pussy or boosting hair bundles or designer clothes.

I spent most of my days hanging on the basketball court, watching the guys play, or hanging with my friends on Fourth Avenue. I hated living at home with my ol' tri-fling-ass mama. See, this bitch gave me life, and for that I was grateful, but other than that, her ass wasn't worth shit. I thought that bitch only had us so that she could get the government checks, which, by the way, we didn't get a dime of. She would buy food when the food stamps first hit her card, and then she would sell the rest to the dope boys in exchange for crack. She tried her best to hide the fact that she was a crackhead, but I wasn't no fool. At the age of 15, I found out after I walked in on her smoking that shit. She tried to convince me that it wasn't what I thought it was, but I brushed that off and walked out of the bathroom.

Over time, her behavior got worse. She started bringing different niggas home at all times of the night. I was old enough to deal with the shit, but I felt bad for my little sister, Shari. Her room was closest to Mama's room, and she was often awakened by moans and groans from that bitch and them tricks. That bitch didn't respect herself, and she damn sure didn't respect her daughters.

I started fucking early due to the fact that Mama never bought me clothes, soap, or even tampons for that matter. Most of the clothes my sister and I had were hand-me-downs from the Salvation Army or Goodwill. That kind of shit caused us to get teased, which resulted in me getting into fights, and I was finally expelled from Mount Vernon High School.

If I thought getting kicked out of school was bad, I had a rude awakening coming up.

"Amoy! Amoy!" I heard Mama yelling my name.

I grabbed my cell phone and checked the time. *Damn, it's only 7:30 in the fucking morning. What the hell does this woman want?*

"I know damn well you hear me calling your ass. Ain't no sleeping in my house after seven. Your ass needs to get up out of the bed. Your grown behind didn't want to stay in school, so you need to get a damn job!" she yelled.

"I told you I was going to look for a job. Now can you quit yelling and close my door?"

"Your door? Little bitch, this is my motherfucking house. You're grown now, so yo' ass can definitely sell some pussy to help pay these bills up in here. Ain't no need for you to be out there, lying on your back, fucking these random-ass niggas, and not getting paid," she said with a smirk on her face.

I looked at this bitch. She sounded stupid as fuck. *Did this bitch just tell her child to sell her pussy to help her pay the bills?*

"You know what? You are a poor excuse for a mother. How dare you talk to me like that?" I asked in a disgusted manner.

"Watch your mouth, you slut. I brought you in this world, and I damn sure will take you out of it. Don't think because your pussy is growing a little hair on it that you can talk to me like you've lost your damn mind."

Blap. Blap. Blap.

She slapped me in my face three times. My face started burning, and tears welled up in my eyes.

I grabbed her hand and pushed her ass back with force. "I hate you with everything in me. I wish you would fucking die, bitch." I stared her dead in the eyes.

She stood there, looking shocked. After a few seconds, she turned around and walked out of my room.

I locked my door and jumped into my bed. I pulled the cover over my head and started crying. I wasn't crying because that bitch had hit me or talked crazy to me. I had been going through that my whole life. I cried because I was tired of this fucked-up life, and I wanted more. I cried until I dozed off into a fantasy world, which was easier to deal with.

CHAPTER ONE

Amoy Simpson

I was fast, but I wasn't no dummy. I decided to go to night classes so I could get my GED. I knew it wasn't much, but it was better than nothing. I also did it to prove to Mama that I wasn't the "worthless bitch" she often called me. My goal was to save up enough money to try to go to college. If it was the last thing I did, I would prove this bitch wrong.

At the age of 18, I was eager to get the fuck on. I didn't need that bitch's permission because I was grown. Over the years, I had gained some experience by braiding the dope boys' hair and the chicks who needed their hair braided. I didn't have a cosmetology license, but I had to admit, I was a beast with my hands. I could braid any length hair and do any style my customers wanted. I hooked it up. My homeboy knew my skills and offered me a job in his barbershop on Third Street.

The money that I made at the shop wasn't a lot, but it was enough to help me get by. I managed to rent a room in a rooming house. I wasn't fussy. I just needed something clean.

I woke up with a heavy heart because I had to leave my sister behind. I wished there was a way I could get her away from this evil bitch, but she was only 16. The bitch was getting a welfare check from the State, and I knew she wasn't going to give that up.

I knocked on my sister's door and went in. She was sitting up in her bed, listening to music. Whenever you saw my sister, best believe she had some headphones on her head. I thought she used music to block out all the bullshit that was going on in her life.

"What's up, sis?"

I sat on the edge of the bed. I took her hand and rubbed it. "Baby, you know I keep telling you that I can't wait to leave this hellhole. Well, today is that day. I'm leaving."

She looked at me strangely. "Sissy, you can't leave me here with her." She snatched her hand away from me.

"Listen to me, Shari. I've got to go so I can make a life and come back for you. I'm a phone call away and over on the next block. You know I got you." I grabbed her and pulled her to me. I hugged her tight. I really didn't want to leave. I wiped the tears from her eyes. "I love you, baby girl. You hear me? I promise, this will be over soon." I kissed her face.

"Love you too," she managed to say.

I got up off her bed and walked out of her room. I was tearing up on the inside and couldn't hold it in any longer. My little sister was my heart and the only person who could make me shed a tear. I walked into my room and grabbed the plastic bags of clothes I owned. The cab I had called earlier was outside, honking its horn.

I was about to open the front door when I was stopped in my tracks. "You think you're grown now, bitch? Trust me, your stanking ass will be back, beggin' Mama to take you in. You goin' to always need me, you little slut."

I turned around to face her. I was about to address her, but I shook my head and opened the door. She was still hollering some shit, but I was gone. I put the bags into the cab, and it pulled off.

That day, a new woman was born. I was a force to be reckoned with, and no one was exempt. I was that bitch!

This was my first time alone, so I was nervous. I couldn't sleep, so I lay awake most of the night. I kept replaying Mama's evil words in my head. Even though I was lonely and kind of scared, I sucked it up and put my big girl panties on. I was determined not to grant her her wishes. She would never have to say, "I told you so."

CHAPTER TWO

Amoy

I'd been out of her house for about three months. and if I said it was easy, my ass would be lying. I busted my ass at the barbershop every day, trying to make sure I could pay for my room every Friday. Sometimes I would work ten or more hours, depending on how late the shop stayed open.

My hard work was finally paying off, because I had saved up enough money to move out of the rooming house and get a one-bedroom apartment. It wasn't no big, pretty apartment, but it was enough for me.

I didn't believe in coincidences, so when I met Devon, it was definitely in the making. I was at work one day at the shop when this tall brown-skinned brother with dreads walked in. I was doing another dude's hair, but my focus was more on the stranger who had walked in. He had some big brown eyes that seemed like they could see through my soul. I tried to break my stare, but I was unsuccessful.

"May I help you?" said Janice, the receptionist, breaking my stare.

I was kind of embarrassed and hoped he didn't notice. I went back to taking care of business, but I was still being nosy.

"Yes, I need to get my dreads washed and retwisted."

"Well, you came to the right place. Sign in right here and have a seat."

I pretended like I didn't see Janice walking toward my booth. After all, I was the only braider in here, so who else was going to take care of this stranger's dreads?

"Well, love, you can stop staring right now." She burst out laughing.

"Girl, bye. What are you talking about?" I played stupid.

"Mm-hmm. I saw how you were staring him down."

"What's he trying to get done?" I said, trying to get off the subject.

"He wants a wash and twist."

"Okay, I've got him after I'm finished with this guy." I smiled at her.

She shot me a dirty look and walked off. I took a second to regroup.

After I was finished with my client's head, he paid me and left. I washed my hands and walked over to where the stranger was sitting.

"Hello, my name is Amoy. Please follow me."

"Whaddup, B?" he greeted me in a sexy, sultry voice.

He followed me and took a seat in the chair. I took the hair holder out of his dreads and shampooed his locks. I stared down on his face as he closed his eyes. I started feeling tingling between my legs, but I ignored the feeling and continued doing my job.

I finished washing his hair and dried it with a towel.

"Come on over here."

"Your wish is my command."

I smiled but remained quiet. I knew he was trying to flirt with me, but I didn't want to come off as being thirsty, so I played it cool. We exchanged a few words, nothing major.

"Look in the mirror and tell me if you like it."

He stood up and looked around into the mirror. He had a fresh lineup, which made him look extra sexy.

"You did a good job, B. How much is it?" he inquired.

"It's sixty dollars. You can pay the receptionist."

"A'ight, bet. See you, shawty."

"Thank you." I smiled at him while I turned away to clean up my work area.

I still tried to peek at him through the corners of my eyes. He paid Janice, said something to her, and walked out.

I watched as she hurried toward me, smiling like she had just won the lottery.

"Girl, what did you say to his ass?"

"What are you talking about now?" I was getting tired of her nosy ass for real.

"Hmm, here you go. Looks like the nigga is checking for your ass." She handed me a $100 bill with a white piece of paper.

"What's this for?"

"That nigga said that's your tip, and he left his number for you."

"What? I don't need his money." I behaved like I was shocked.

"Child, you better take this money and take this paper so you can call that nigga. A nigga throwing money at you without even knowing you is a keeper. Why y'all chicks always get lucky?" She rolled her eyes.

I snatched the money out of her hand, along with the paper. I stared down at the number that was jotted down.

"Thank you, boo," I said. That was her cue to scram, which she did.

I sat down to rest my feet and to let my mind wander around a little. Who was this dude? This was my first time seeing him around here. Whoever he was, I could tell he had a few dollars. I grabbed my phone, put the number in, then put **Potential Boo** and pressed **Save**.

Another client walked in, and it was back to the money. But who was I fooling? I couldn't get this stranger out of my head. I wasn't really looking for a man—or was I? Anyway, back to the situation at hand. I could definitely use some good fucking and sucking. Shit, I felt my pussy tingling as the thought left my mind and took control of my body.

After braiding five heads and retwisting ol' boy's dreads, I was done for the night. I cleaned up my work area and left.

"Girl, don't forget to call him," Janice yelled out with her big-ass mouth.

I waved her off because I didn't have the energy to entertain her ass.

I was tired as hell and hungry. I stopped at the Golden Krust on Fourth Avenue and grabbed me a bite and then headed home. I was starving, so I dug into the Jamaican beef patty and coco bread and took a few sips of my pineapple soda to wash the food down.

My feet were hurting from walking. I watched as the cars sped past me. *I definitely need a car. I'm tired of walking or catching a cab,* I thought as I walked down the street toward my block.

Just then, I heard a car honking its horn. I kept walking without looking. This was New York, and crazies were always trying to holla. However, the horn kept going. "Look, leave me the hell alone," I turned toward the street and yelled.

I stopped immediately when I noticed it was none other than Mr. . . . .

"Damn, shawty, I've been trying to get your attention," he said as he pulled over to the side.

"And you think this is the way to get my attention? By the way, what is your name?"

"Nah, but it worked. Come on, get in, and I will tell you my name."

I kept walking, and he kept driving slowly beside me. "I don't ride with strangers. It's dangerous out in these streets," I said sarcastically.

"Ma, stop tripping. We're not strangers. Matter of fact, you're my stylist."

I really needed the damn ride because my feet were killing me, but I really didn't know this nigga. I had only met him a few hours ago. "You better tell me yo' damn name if you want me to get in." I stopped and gritted my teeth at him.

He smiled, showing his pearly white teeth. "It's Devon."

I stared at him. I figured he wasn't going to give up anytime soon. I reluctantly got into his black Chrysler 300. Instantly, the smell of new leather hit my nose. This was my first time riding in something this nice, but I didn't show my excitement.

"My apartment is right around the corner," I quickly said.

I was second-guessing my decision to get in his car. For all I knew, he could have been a killer or rapist. I looked around, trying to see where I could jump out.

"Why are you so quiet?" He reached over and touched me.

"I'm always quiet," I mumbled under my breath.

I was more focused on his hand that remained on my leg. I felt my body temperature slowly rising, and my clit started to tingle. I was about to say something, but the words wouldn't come out. I gently moved his hand off my leg.

I looked up and noticed we were going the wrong way. "Ay, what are you doing? My house is in the other direction."

"Relax, ma. I'm about to take you out to eat if you don't mind."

I looked at him and kept quiet. I ain't goin' to lie. His in-control attitude turned me on in a major way.

"All right, but you ask me first. You just don't make the decision," I spat.

"Damn, I love your attitude. Let a nigga know how to treat you. Well, let's try this again, Miss Amoy. Can I take you out to eat?" He smiled.

"Sure." I folded my arms.

He took me to Bronx Diner on Baychester Road. We sat down and ordered our food. I was kind of nervous because he sat there staring at me.

"So, Amoy, where's yo' man at?"

"What gave you the impression that I have one of those?"

"Shit, you're a cute chick with a fat ass, so I know some nigga done already bagged you."

"Hmmm. Interesting observation." I laughed aloud.

"Yeah, when I see something I like, I waste no time in small talk."

"Do you have a woman?"

"Nah."

I wondered why a fine-ass man like that was single. *Hmmm* . . . Shit, I wasn't going to worry about all that. He looked like the kind of nigga I could definitely fuck with, and he appeared to have money. I wondered what he did for a living. These were all questions I wanted to ask, but it was too early to be prying in the man's life.

Our food finally came, and I dug in. I wasn't worried about him watching me eat because I was still hungry. That patty and coco bread didn't even fill the gap in my stomach. We shared stories about our lives, nothing too deep, and when we were finished, he paid the waitress, and we left.

After dinner, we got back into the car. I was full as hell, and the wine he ordered me kind of made me tipsy. That was my first time eating in a fancy restaurant like that, and I hoped it wasn't the last. A bitch could definitely get used to this kind of special treatment. It was so different from when I dated Marquise. The only place he took me was to Kentucky Fried Chicken or to the Chinese spot on Gramatan Avenue.

"The night is still early. Do you wanna chill with me?" he asked after he pulled off.

"I 'on't know. I'm kind of tired," I said, hoping he would say something to convince me to chill with him.

"Come on, ma. I'll give you a massage and rub your feet." He looked at me and smiled.

Damn, that shit sounded enticing. My mind was telling me no, but my body was in full control and wasn't trying to hear that bullshit I was talking. "Well, we can chill, but only for a little while," I cautioned him.

I was grown, so why was I pretending like I didn't want to chill with him? I was curious to find out more about his life, and this was the perfect way to find out. "God, please don't let this man be no rapist," I whispered under my breath. I closed my eyes as he drove, nervous as hell. I counted from ten to one, trying to calm my nerves.

He pulled up at a house on the nicer side of Mount Vernon. Only people with money stayed in that section. I stayed seated as he pulled into the driveway. He got out of the car and walked over to my side.

"Come on, B." He opened the car door for me.

"Whose house is this?"

"This is my shit, B," he answered like he was annoyed with me asking that question.

He opened the door and showed me the way in. He followed me inside and locked the door behind us. I was starstruck at the sight of the house. The house was nicely decorated, with big leather couches and a large rug in the middle of the floor. The television was huge and sat nicely over the fireplace. I knew then that I was dealing with a nigga with some money.

"Don't be scared. Come in and get relaxed."

I gave him that "yeah, right, nigga" look.

"Here you go." He walked out of the kitchen and handed me a glass of wine.

"Thanks, but don't try to get me drunk," I jokingly said.

"Nah, B. It ain't like that. I just think you might need something to relax you a little."

I liked him already. I stared at his features. Baby boy was definitely blessed in the looks department. I still wondered why his ass was single. The wine was taking its effect on me because I went from admiring his face to looking at his crotch. The print of his dick was visible because of the Nike sweatpants he was wearing. I took another gulp of the wine to calm my nerves. *Bitch, stop trippin'*, a little voice in my head warned.

"You good, shawty?" He moved closer to me.

"Shit, I'll feel better if I lie in your arms," I said bluntly.

"What you waiting on then?"

He had big, strong arms. He pulled me closer and wrapped them around me. He used his hands to turn my face around to him, his lips then locking in on mine. The smell of alcohol reeked through his breathing, but that didn't bother me. He started to passionately kiss me, and I stuck my tongue in his mouth. The influence of alcohol clouded my judgment and caused me to act aggressively. He ran his masculine hand across my breast, gently massaging it. I grabbed his dick into my palm and gently stroked it. This nigga had one of those horse dicks. It was long and thick. Whoever his daddy was, he had definitely blessed him.

He aggressively started to rip my clothes off. I helped him out by unbuttoning my shorts and stepping out of my drawers. I felt a gush of juice dripping down my legs. He picked me up and carried me upstairs to his king-sized bed. My body temperature was on fire as he parted my legs and dove head-deep into my pussy.

"Aweee," I moaned out in ecstasy. He applied more pressure as he locked his tongue on to my clit. My body tightened, and my legs trembled as I busted into his mouth. I wanted to get fucked now, so I pulled him up toward me. He got on top of me and eased his dick inside. I cringed as his dick made its way all the way inside of me. The pain was unbearable, but the feeling was lovely. He slowly ground on top of me, and I held him close as I had multiple orgasms. I wanted him as bad as he wanted me. I knew then that I had to make him my man one way or another.

CHAPTER THREE

Amoy

Everything started moving so fast between us. I was definitely digging him, and I knew he was digging me also because he was showing lots of interest in me. I would go to work in the barbershop, and he would go to work, wherever that was. I thought about asking him where exactly he worked, but I didn't want to pry any further than I did already.

I was kind of skeptical at first because things were moving too fast, and I didn't want to be used and end up getting dumped. But the more time we spent together, the deeper my feelings for him got, and my goal was to make him my man. Even though we were spending time together and he was taking me shopping, he still hadn't come out and said we were going steady. I wanted to ask him, but I was kind of scared of what his answer may have been, so I kept quiet and just rolled with the flow.

I figured that he was a street nigga because his phone was constantly ringing throughout the night. Sometimes, while we were in bed, he would get up and walk out to answer it. At first, I thought it was a woman, but I quickly dismissed that idea because of the amount of time we were spending together.

I wasn't a fool though. I knew that if he was a dope boy, there were plenty of bitches lined up trying to get him. I had to admit, he made me feel special because he chose to be with me. I wasn't worried about no bitch though. In my eyes, I was his woman, and he was my man. Until I saw differently, that was what it was.

Things were still going good between us, but I started noticing a few things. Like, after that first night at his house, we never went back. Also, after a month of us going together, he started leaving at night but would come back early in the morning to take me to work.

One morning, while he was dropping me off at work, I decided to ask him what was going on. "Babe, why don't you ever stay over anymore?"

"Why you say that?"

"Because it's been a while since you spent the night, so I'm just curious."

"Ain't nothing, baby girl. Just been handling business, and when I'm finished, I be beat."

I didn't think he was telling the truth, but I had no proof that he was lying, so I dropped the subject.

He pulled up at my workplace. I kissed him as usual and watched him pull off. I had a bad feeling deep inside of me that had me bothered.

As soon as I got to work, I started feeling sick. Numerous times, I had to run to the bathroom to throw up. I figured it was that cheese sandwich I had earlier doing a number on my stomach. I made myself a cup of soup, thinking it would settle my stomach, but the smell sent me back to the bathroom. I decided to call a cab and go home. I tried to sleep, but I couldn't, and I was feeling really sick. I called Devon to see if he could take me to the hospital.

"Hey, babe, can you take me to the hospital?"

"What's wrong?"

"I've been throwing up all day, and I drank some soup, but I still feel sick. I had to take a cab home."

"A'ight, bet. I'll be there."

I dragged myself out of bed and changed from my jeans into a pair of sweatpants and a wife beater along with my Aeropostale slippers. Today was definitely not my day, and I didn't give a damn about my looks.

I lay across the bed, trying to block out the bad feelings. I was no longer throwing up, but my stomach felt queasy. I heard my phone ringing, so I reached for it. I looked at the caller ID, and it was my little sister.

"Hey, sissy," I answered, but I was weak.

"Damn, bitch. Why you sound like you're dying and shit?" She giggled.

She had no idea how true that statement was.

"I've been throwing up all day. Devon is on his way to take me to the ER."

"Devon? Who the fuck is this Devon, and why is this the first time I'm hearing about him?"

"This dude I've been dating for a while now. I didn't know how it was going to turn out, so I didn't say anything."

"So now we're keeping secrets and shit?"

"Nah, but, sis, just know he makes me happy, and I think I love him."

"That nigga must've fucked you real good for you to be bragging on him like that."

"Uh-huh, and he's got some money. Anyway, sis, I'll update you on my love life once I'm not feeling this sick. I've been throwing up all morning."

"Your ass might be knocked up."

"You're tripping. I'm not pregnant."

"Hmm. I'm ready to be an auntie anyway. Plus, from what you just told me, that nigga's paid, so you should be straight if you are pregnant."

"Please stop. I'm not ready to be a mother. I've got plans and shit, plus I don't know how serious we are as of yet." I noticed he was beeping in on the other line. "Sis,

I've got to go. That's Devon on the other line. I will call you later." I hung up and answered the other line. "Hello."

"I'm outside. Come on."

"Okay." I hung the phone up, grabbed my purse, and walked out the door.

Every time I saw him, my heart skipped a couple of beats. This was my first time in love, and it felt really good. Whenever I was around him, I got this bubbly feeling in my stomach, and then when I wasn't, I felt all alone.

I got into the car and sat down. "You straight, ma?" He reached over and rubbed my hand.

"Yeah, I'm good. Just want to know what's going on with me."

"Which hospital?"

"Lady of Mercy on 233rd."

He held my hand, and I lay back into my seat and closed my eyes. My little sister's voice popped up in my head, talking about how I was pregnant. I wasn't worried about being pregnant because I was on the pill and made sure I took it religiously.

I thought he was only dropping me off, but he surprised me and walked in with me. "Yes, ma'am, how can I help you?" the receptionist asked.

"Hello, I need to see a doctor. I've been throwing up all day."

"Okay, name and date of birth."

I gave her the info, and she put a band on my wrist. She then asked me to take a seat. We sat down, and he wrapped his arms around me. I felt so protected by him. My only wish was for this closeness between us to last. I leaned my head on his shoulder as I dozed off.

"Amoy Simpson." I heard someone yelling my name.

I jumped up and walked toward the nurse. "Here I come."

"I'm going to take your vitals and ask you a few questions."

"Okay."

When she was finished, she led me to a room and gave me a gown. "Here, I need a urine sample from you. Put it in the window when you're finished."

"Thanks."

I sat on the bed, waiting to be seen by the doctor. This was one of the reasons why I hated the hospital. They took their own sweet time to examine a person. I patiently waited until a nurse practitioner walked in.

"Miss Simpson, I'm Dr. Donahue, and I'm your physician's assistant today."

"Hello."

"Well, I see you're complaining of excessive vomiting and stomach pain. How long has this been going on?" He took his glasses off and looked at me.

"I started feeling queasy a few days ago, but the vomiting started this morning."

"I see. When was your last menstrual flow?"

"Umm, last week. The fourteenth." I tried to drag my memory.

"Are you sexually active, and if so, do you use protection?"

"Yes, I am, and no, I don't use protection, but I'm on the pill."

"I believe the nurse already got a urine sample, and I'm going to run a few tests for STDs."

I looked at him when he mentioned STDs. This bitch was tripping, because even though I used to sell pussy when I was younger, I was sure I didn't have any diseases because I got tested faithfully. Since my last test, six months ago, I had only fucked with Marquise and now Devon. If I had anything, it was one of these niggas, but I didn't say anything. I just needed to know what was wrong with me. He left and then came back and collected a specimen from inside of me. This was my second time getting one of those cold metal objects inserted inside of me. I cringed as he widened my pussy.

After he was gone, I sat up in the bed. I hoped this was just a stomach virus and nothing major. For the first time in my life, everything was going great, and I didn't want anything to mess it up for me. I grabbed my phone and texted Devon to let him know what was going on with me.

After waiting for over an hour and a half, I heard the door open. It was the doctor entering the room. "Well, Miss Simpson, your tests are back from the lab. You tested negative for gonorrhea, chlamydia, and tricho-monas. However, it's confirmed that you're pregnant."

It was like he was no longer the doctor but an animal with two heads standing in front of me. *Me, pregnant?* This had to be a cruel joke the doctor was playing on me.

"Doctor, how is that possible? I'm on the pill, and I take them consistently."

"I've always told my patients that the pill is not one hundred percent foolproof. Even with the pill, you still need to protect yourself if you don't want to get pregnant. So with that said, congratulations. Also, because you're feeling pain in your stomach, I want to send you up to see the gynecologist. That way, we can be sure that everything is fine with this pregnancy."

"All right." I let out a long sigh. I thought about Devon instantly and how I was going to break the news to him.

I sat there waiting impatiently for my turn to go to the second floor for the sonogram test. I never understood why the emergency room was one of the slowest fucking places. "Miss Simpson, my name is Carlos, and I'm going to take you to the second floor to get your ultrasound," the aide said to me.

"All right."

He put a wheelchair in front of me, and I got up and sat in it. All I could do was breathe hard because I wasn't sure what this test might show.

The feeling that I experienced when I heard my baby's heartbeat changed my perception really fast. A minute ago, I was scared, but now I was overwhelmed with joy.

I went back to the room and waited again. This time, though, I wasn't feeling down. I just kept thinking about the image that I saw earlier. It was small but beautiful nonetheless.

Dr. Donahue walked in the room, interrupting my thoughts. "Thanks for having patience. Today is a very busy day for us."

"No problem."

"All right, so your sonogram looks normal. You're about six weeks pregnant. I'm going to give you an IV because of all the vomiting. You might be dehydrated."

What the fuck? I was ready to get up out of there, and now I had to lie down for an IV. I remained quiet as he schooled me on what I needed to do in order to have a great pregnancy. To be honest, I could hear his voice, but I wasn't really paying attention. My mind was on my man and what his reaction was going to be.

The nurse came in and hooked me up to an IV.

"Can I get a blanket please?"

"Sure."

After she handed the blanket to me, I lay there with my eyes closed. My mind was speeding with all kinds of different thoughts popping up in my head. I heard the door open, but I thought it was the nurse, so I didn't bother to open my eyes.

"Yo, you good?" Devon's voice startled me.

I opened my eyes and saw him standing over me. My tongue tied up on me. I had no idea how I was going to tell him that he was going to be a daddy.

"Yes, I'm fine," I said in a slight whisper.

"What they say, and why you hooked up to that?"

I took a few seconds to breathe in and out. "The doctor said I'm pregnant. . . ." My voice trailed off.

"Really?" he asked.

I immediately regretted telling him. I mean, we hadn't been together for that long, and here I was telling this nigga I was pregnant with his child.

He walked over to me, took my hand, and kissed me on the forehead. "Babe, listen, I'm sorry. I didn't mean for this to happen. But know you've got a real nigga, and I'm gonna stand up and take care of what's mine."

I closed my eyes as tears rolled down my face. A part of me was happy, but another part of me was hurting inside. I wasn't ready to be a mother. Plus, the situation I was in was definitely a fucked-up one. While he hugged me close to him, my mind traveled back to six weeks ago when I bumped into my ex-boyfriend, Marquise. I had always had a weakness for him ever since we used to fuck around. We broke up because he didn't know how to keep his dick in his pants, and I stayed busting bitches in their heads over him. I got sick of shit after I checked his cell phone and saw several naked pictures of different bitches he was fucking. I was crushed by his behavior, but I decided I had to let him go.

Six weeks ago, when Marquise asked if we could chill, I quickly said yes because Marquise's ass had that fire tongue that could touch my soul when he inserted it inside. I ended up going to his house, and we drank and fucked. This was a few days before Devon and I first started talking. Now here I was hearing that I was pregnant.

"Oh, God," I whispered when a cold fact hit me in the face.

"Babe, what's wrong? I know you're scared, but I got you." He hugged me tighter as I allowed the tears to flow loosely.

While he thought that I was crying because I was pregnant, it was bigger than that. I had a child, and I had no idea who my baby daddy was.

I was discharged from the hospital with instructions from the doctor to do a follow-up with an ob-gyn. I sat in the car, staring out the window as my mind wandered. I used to watch *Paternity Court,* and I saw the bitches on there getting different niggas tested. I used to turn up my nose at them and often wondered how the fuck they didn't know their baby daddies. In a million years, I would have never thought it would be me.

CHAPTER FOUR

Amoy

As time progressed, it became hard for me to stand up on my feet for long hours. My stomach was starting to show, and the morning sickness was killing me. To be honest, this pregnancy was putting a strain on me physically and emotionally. I tried my best to act like I was happy that I was pregnant. No one knew that I was in a fucked-up situation because I had no one to confide in. The only person I had was my little sister, but I was older and didn't want to put that kind of strain on her. Plus, I didn't want anyone to think I was a whore or anything like that.

I was almost six months pregnant when I decided to quit the salon for a while. Devon and I were still seeing each other, but it kind of threw me off that, even though we had been going steady, he didn't invite me to move in with him. Other than the one time I had been to his house, I had never been. His attitude was getting horrible, too. We would get into petty-ass fights, and he would storm out. I would blame myself because I knew I was pregnant, and my hormones were all over the place. I would cry many nights when he would leave, and when I called his phone, the voicemail would come on. I knew I wasn't tripping. Something was definitely going on.

We were lying in my bed one night after he had come over only minutes to eleven. "Hey, boo, can I ask you a question?"

"Yeah, what's good?" he answered with an attitude.

"How come you didn't ask me to move in with you?"

"Why would I do that when you've got yo' own crib?" he quizzed.

I was kind of thrown off by his response. Lately, he wasn't as loving as he used to be with me. I sat my fat ass up in the bed and grabbed his arm.

"What the fuck is your problem, yo? Lately, you've been short with me. Shit, you barely talk to me. All you want to do is eat, fuck, and sleep," I lashed out with tears gathered in my eyes.

"Yo, B, don't you ever put your fucking hands on me again. you hear me?" He grabbed my hand and squeezed it real hard.

"Let go of my hand, nigga." I tried to use my left hand to swing on that nigga. That must've angered him more, because he pushed me back on the bed, got over me, and grabbed my neck.

I couldn't breathe, and all I could think about was my baby. I tried to say a few words, but the pressure on my throat totally stopped me from saying a word.

"Listen, bitch. Don't fucking question me or raise your fucking hands at me again. You must not know who the fuck I am. I will kill you, bitch," he spat with venom in his voice.

At that point, I knew I was going to die. My eyes were getting blurry as I kicked my feet, trying to get him off me. All I knew was that I had to fight for my unborn child and myself. I might've brought this on myself, but my baby didn't deserve this. I tried to fight, but I had no strength compared to his.

God must've heard my cries, because Devon released his hand from around my neck and stood up. I lay there. I couldn't move. I watched as he put his clothes on and grabbed his keys. In the blink of an eye, he was gone. He didn't even check on me to see if I was all right.

I rolled over and buried my head into my pillow. I was pissed the fuck off, but worse than that, I was hurt because before now I had never seen that side of him. I finally got my tears under control and then jumped up and locked my door. I thought about calling the police, but as sad as it sounded, I was in love with him. It was a possibility that he was my child's father, and I didn't want him behind bars. I just cried until I couldn't cry anymore. I was mentally and physically drained. On top of that, I checked my neck in the mirror, and there was a big bruise on it.

That night, before I fell asleep, I made a mental note to get myself a gun. There was no way I was going to keep allowing him to do this to me. I was the wrong bitch. Yes, true, he got me this first time because I wasn't prepared, but on my unborn seed, that shit wouldn't happen again. Those were the last thoughts I had before I dozed off.

I hadn't heard from Devon in a week, since the day of the incident. So many times, I picked up my phone to call him but quickly dismissed it. I was no longer hurt, and I was missing him. I was silently praying that he would slide through and apologize for the shit he did to me. I quickly snapped out of that mind frame. Even though I was still in love with him, there was no way I could forgive him for what he did to me.

I quickly remembered that I needed to get a gun for protection. I lay there racking my brain, trying to figure out where I could get one from. That was when my mind ran on my ex-man, possibly my baby's father. He was also in the streets, and I recalled him bragging about how he could get guns. I let out a long sigh. He was the last person I wanted to deal with. I hadn't seen him since the last day we fucked, and now that I had a big stomach, I really didn't want to see him. I didn't want him questioning if he was my child's father.

Fuck it. I didn't have too much of a choice. I wasn't no gun bitch, but I needed to get one. At least if a nigga knew I had one, they would think twice about putting their goddamn hands on me. I grabbed my phone and dialed Marquise's phone number. I rolled my eyes as the phone rang out. I was about to hang up when he answered.

"What's up, boo?"

"Boy, whatever. I'm far from being yo' boo," I replied with a slight attitude.

"Damn, ma, it's like that? You know you miss daddy."

I was going to respond to that, but instead, I chuckled. "Hey, I need a favor from you."

"Hmmm, what? You need me to come tear that pussy up for you?"

"Nah, I'm good in that area, but I can't ask you on the phone. Can you come through later?"

"Hell yeah. You know I won't turn down seeing my baby girl."

"A'ight, I'll text you my address." I hung the phone up and texted it to him.

It wasn't a good move to invite him here, over to the house. Even though I hadn't heard from Devon in a few days, I knew he could pop up at any second without warning. I grabbed the phone to tell Marquise not to bother, but I threw the phone down. I wasn't too worried over a nigga who wasn't too worried about me. Shit, I could've been dead, and his ass wouldn't have given two fucks about me.

I took a quick shower and put on a pair of tights and a wife beater. I would be happy when I was not pregnant anymore because lately I couldn't fit into any of my clothing. And the things I could fit into were not very comfortable. I brushed my hair in a bun and put a little cream on my face. This baby was taking a toll on my mind, body, and soul. I heard my doorbell ringing. I took one last look in the mirror, walked out of the bathroom, and opened the door.

Marquise stood in the doorway, looking at me with his mouth wide open. "What . . . tha fuck? You pregnant?" He stood there, staring at my stomach as if this were the first time he had ever seen a pregnant bitch.

My mind quickly went into overdrive. There was no way I could tell him that he was possibly the father. "Yes, I am, but don't worry. You're not the daddy," I blurted out.

I could tell he was thrown off. He stood there, staring at my stomach.

"Are you gonna come in, or you gonna stand there?" I said with a slight attitude. God knows I didn't want to go there with this nigga today. He stepped inside, and I closed the door behind us.

"Whose baby is this?"

"Why? All you need to know is that it's not yours."

"How you know? We fucked not so long ago, and if I remember correctly, I busted all up in you."

I cringed as I heard the words that were coming out of his mouth. He was right, and I wasn't 100 percent sure that he wasn't my child's father.

"Listen, Marquise, I know who my baby daddy is, so don't worry about it. I didn't call you over here for all this. I need you to get me a little gun," I came straight out and said.

"A gun? You're joking, right? This ain't the same chick who hates to be around guns and shit."

"I know, but you know I'm here by myself, and anything can happen. I just want to protect me and my baby."

"I got you. So what size gun are you looking for?"

"I don't know. Something small that I can possibly hold in my purse."

"Uh-huh. You sure you're good?" he quizzed.

I wanted to break down and let him know what Devon did to me, but I knew how bad Marquise's temper was. The last thing I needed was for him to approach Devon, who wasn't no punk either.

We ended up sitting there, talking for about an hour. It was amazing how things changed. When we were together, we didn't get along, but the minute we broke up, we could actually sit down and talk.

"A'ight, B, I'm 'bout to bounce. Give me 'til tomorrow to bring you that."

"So how much is it?"

"You're good. You know you owe me a good fuck after you drop the baby." He laughed.

"Whatever, boy." I poked him in the arm and laughed.

He walked out the door, and I locked it. I smiled as I thought about what that fool said. I really liked the new and improved him. I entertained the idea of getting back with him, but who was I fooling? I was in love with Devon and not him.

The next day, he brought me a cute pink gun. He said it was a .25 nickel finish.

"I hope you ain't did no shit wit' this." I looked at him with an attitude.

"Come on, Amoy. I ain't that dirty, B."

"I'm just saying. Don't want to get caught up in no shit, for real."

"You good. Anyway, I got to bounce."

After he left, I sat there, examining the gun. I ran my hand across the barrel. Surprisingly, I felt my clit tingling. I stuck my hand down in my pants and stuck my finger inside. I was wet. I quickly brought my finger to my face and examined it. I breathed out when I realized it was pussy juice and not blood. I was feeling horny as fuck. I rubbed the gun across my face, opened my legs wide, and started grinding on my index finger. I didn't realize how backed up I was until then.

"Awee, awe," I screamed out as I ground harder on my finger. I put the gun down and grabbed the side of the sofa with my hand. I held on for dear life as I exploded all over my finger.

"Damn!" I said as I fell back on the sofa. That was definitely needed to release some of this juice I had built up in me.

After I rested, I got up, went into my room, and placed the gun under my bed. I then went to take a bath. I lit two candles and ran my water. My mind was all over the place. I was hoping this water could relax my mind a little. All this stress wasn't good for me or my baby.

CHAPTER FIVE

Amoy

I was up bright and early. I needed to do something to make my situation better. My baby was due in three more months, and I had no idea what I was going to do. I only had a few hundred dollars saved up from when I was working at the salon. I knew I would need some money to pay my bills and shit. I grabbed my phone and dialed Devon's number. After the first ring, I thought about hanging up, but before I could press the end button, he picked up.

"Hey, bae," he sang into my ear.

The sound of his voice was like a sweet melody to my ears. My body tensed up as my legs shivered. There was something about this man's voice that woke up everything inside of me.

"Whatever, Devon. You must've forgotten that you have a child on the way," I said sarcastically. I was trying my best not to let him know how I was really feeling.

"Damn, ma. Calm down wit' all that yelling and shit. I thought you were still upset wit' a nigga, so I was giving you time to blow off some of that steam."

"Really? You fucking choked me and left me for dead. I can't believe this is how you treat me, the bitch you claim to love." I couldn't stop the tears from flowing.

"Ma, I swear, I'm fucking sorry. I don't know what the fuck happened to me, because I've never put my hands on no chick before."

I was engulfed in tears. I couldn't respond to the bullshit that he was feeding me.

"I'm so sorry, bae. I promise that shit won't happen again. Damn, that's my nigga beeping in on my line. Listen, I've got to run, but I'll be over there later on."

Before I could respond, the phone hung up. I fell back on the bed, clinging to the phone. I wanted to believe him. I needed to believe that he was sorry, but I wasn't sure. My mind was telling me, *Bitch, fuck that nigga.* But my heart and my pussy were telling me quite the opposite. It had been a minute since I had my pussy eaten, and I could have definitely used a good pussy whipping. The thought of him entering me sent chills through my body and tingling through my clit. In that split second, I forgot how mad I was at him. I missed his smell and his touch, and most importantly, I missed him telling me how much he loved me. It may have seemed like I was crazy, but shit, I loved my man. Even though he did that fucked-up shit the other day, I knew he loved me.

I heard the doorbell ringing. I glanced at my phone, and it was a little after 11:00 p.m. By the time I got up, my phone was buzzing. "Yeah."

"I'm at the door. Hurry up, man. You know I don't like to be out here like that."

Boy, shut up with your whining ass, I thought as I waddled to the door. I unlocked the door, and he walked in. I melted as I caught the first glimpse of the nigga I fell for. His hair was neatly done, and he looked like he had just gotten a shape-up. I felt a bit of jealousy rush over me. I used to be the one who kept his hair done. Now he walked up in here with his shit all put together. I made a mental note to revisit that situation later. I was too happy to see him at the moment and didn't want to start an argument.

"Hey, bae. What's good?" He hugged me as tight as he could.

"Nothing," I said.

"Man, I've got some good news for ya. I found a two-bedroom crib for you and the baby. It's over there on Fifth Avenue. My boy owns the complex, and I gave him the deposit and money for the first five months. That will give you enough time to have the baby and get back on yo' feet." He kept running his mouth.

"What? So you don't even ask me what the fuck I want to do? You just up and make that decision for me? Last time I checked, I'm fucking grown." I was too annoyed with him.

"Damn, my bad, B. I thought you wanted a bigger and better place. Just the other day, you were asking about moving out."

"Don't be twisting my words. I asked you why you didn't ask me to move in with you. That's not moving in with you. That's me living by my damn self," I lashed out.

"Damn, B, you are never fucking happy! I'm trying my fucking best to be here for you and my seed. Quit nagging so fucking much."

I was about to respond to him, but I remembered what had happened the other day. I didn't want to put my baby in harm's way, so I shot him a fucking look and went back to browsing Facebook.

"I need to jump in the shower. A nigga's been in the streets all day and shit. Nuts musty," he said as he walked toward my bedroom.

"Why didn't you bathe at home?" I asked, annoyed.

"Damn, 'cause I didn't want to go home and then come back out. Just give me a washcloth and towel."

There was something about the way he said that that raised my suspicions. I was starting to feel like he was living a double life, but I had no proof. The one time I did visit his house, I really didn't see any evidence of a female living there, but then again, I was intoxicated and was more worried about getting fucked.

I walked over to the closet in my room, grabbed a towel and washcloth, and threw them at him. I watched as he slid out of his clothes and walked off into the shower. Lord, the sight of his naked body had my head all fucked up. Whew, God knew how I was going to behave. My thoughts were interrupted by the ringing of his cell phone.

The antennae in my head quickly stood alert. I looked around, but I decided not to snoop around. I sat down on the bed, feeling torn, but the phone wouldn't stop ringing. I got up and tiptoed to the bathroom door and placed my ear by the door. The shower was still running, so I was sure he was still bathing. I quickly picked his pants up and searched for the phone. I looked at the caller ID. It read Wifey.

Wifey? Without thinking twice, I picked it up. "Hello." I almost choked up.

"Who is this answering my husband's phone?" A woman's voice echoed through my ear.

"Your wh . . . who?" I stuttered.

"I don't know who you are, lady, but please put my husband, Devon, on the phone," this smart-ass bitch yelled in my ear.

"First off, bitch, if he were your husband, he wouldn't be over here fucking me and I wouldn't be carrying his child," I snapped back at this ho without thinking.

I didn't hear anything else but silence when she hung up. I guessed I hit a nerve with that one. I stood there shaking with his phone still in my hand. It was like I was frozen.

"What the fuck are you doing with my phone?" Devon's voice startled me.

I looked down at the phone still in my hand. I then looked at this nigga with tears rolling down my face. "You're married?" I said between sobs.

"Nah, I ain't married. What the fuck you talkin' 'bout, B?"

"You're a fucking liar. I just got off the phone with some bitch who claims she is your wife."

"You did what?" His eyes widened as he stepped outside of the bathroom with his dick hanging and all. "Answer me, bitch. What the fuck did you do?" The veins in his forehead popped out as spit flew out of his mouth.

I knew then that I was in trouble. My first instinct was to get to my gun, which I'd placed under the mattress. I started to run, but he grabbed me by my hair and threw me up against the wall. "Let me go, you fucking bastard. You lied to me," I cried out as I tried to get away from his tight grip.

"Bitch, what did you say to her?"

He squeezed me up against the wall. I started bawling. I looked at him and knew that he was a desperate man willing to do anything to me.

He looked at me, laughed, and then said, "You know what's crazy? I fucking love you, B. I was going to tell you about her, but e'erything between us happened so fast, and by then I was too caught up with you."

The sick bastard tried to stick his tongue down my throat while squeezing my neck and pushing himself on me.

"Stop! You're fucking sick," I mumbled while holding my lips tight together. He looked at me, laughed, and loosened his grip. I didn't stick around to listen to him sing the blues.

I dashed over to my bed and grabbed my gun from underneath my mattress. I walked over to where he was putting his dirty drawers back on. "Get your shit and get out of my fucking house."

"Man, what the fuck you call yourself doing, B?" he asked with a smirk written on his face.

"You heard what the fuck I said! Get your shit and get out of my fucking house." I fired a shot in the ceiling, scaring my damn self. I jumped but managed to get my feelings under control.

"Damn, B, chill out. I'm about to go."

I kept my eyes on him the entire time. "Yo, hurry up and get up out of my shit. You fucking lying-ass nigga."

"Yo, B, you know I'm a killa, right? I do this shit for fun. Rule number one, don't pull a gun on a nigga you have no intention of using it on." He grabbed my arm and pulled my wrist back. I tried to hold on for dear life, but he wrestled the gun out of my hand. I started saying a silent prayer to God because I knew he was going to kill me. Fear for my baby's life took control. I closed my eyes, held on to my stomach, and waited, but nothing happened. I slowly opened them only to see him walking away and out of the room. I got up and ran after him.

"I fucking hate you for what you did to me. You hear me? I fucking hate you," I screamed out and fell to my knees as the door closed behind him. "Nooo. Oh, my God. How could he do this to me? I fucking love him, God. I love him," I screamed out.

I felt an excruciating pain in my stomach. I grabbed my stomach and screamed out in agony.

I hope my baby is okay.

CHAPTER SIX

Kennedy

I'd always known that men, or should I say overgrown boys, weren't worth shit, not even the damn toilet paper I used to wipe my ass. However, I wasn't thinking with my head. I was so caught up in emotions that I had allowed myself to fall for the bullshit. Devon was a young goon out in them streets, and I was attracted to his young ass. There was nothing like a young nigga tearing my pussy up. Yes, I was a cougar who had my own money, owned a house, and was retired from being a Wall Street investor. The only thing I was missing was getting fucked on the regular. When I met Devon, the young boy ate on this pussy like he was about to lose his life.

It wasn't hard to woo him. Shit, these young bitches didn't have anything on me. Matter of fact, my pussy game was all the way turned up. I hadn't fucked anything since my husband, Travis, had passed away three years ago. At first, I mourned his passing, but that didn't stop me from wanting this pussy serviced.

It was mere coincidence when I bumped into this young, handsome man. I was coming out of the bank, and he was going in. I was looking at my receipt, and by the time I picked my head up, we collided.

"I'm sorry, sir," I apologized.

"Nah, you're good, ma," he said in a sexy Barry White voice with a smile that gripped my internal organs immediately.

"Hmm. I love your voice. If you don't mind me asking, do you sing?"

"Nah, I 'on't do no singing," his cocky ass replied.

"Well, you should." I smiled at him.

We stood there chatting for a few minutes before we parted ways, but not before numbers were exchanged. I got into my car, smiling. I still had my game on point. Being 59 was nothing but a number because I was willing and able to do every- and anything that these young bitches could possibly do.

Approximately two weeks later, we were out on our first date. It was then that I learned that he was out in the streets. I had never had a goon before and was eager to find out what his fuck game was like. That night, I took him back to my house. I ran the bathwater and washed this nigga from head to toe. Then I dried him off and oiled him down with my African oil. I took his big cock into my mouth. It had been years since I sucked a cock, and I'd never sucked one that big, but I was a beast at pleasing a man. I licked the tip of his cock while I gently massaged his balls with my hand. I took every inch all the way into my mouth. I loved the feeling of it touching my throat. That inspired me to suck harder on his pretty manhood. I felt his veins enlarge, so I sucked harder. Within minutes, he exploded in my mouth. "Aargh," he groaned.

"Damn, B. You're a beast at sucking dick," he said.

I didn't know if that was a compliment or an insult, but either way, I was on a mission. He surprised me when he flipped me on my stomach and entered my wet pussy. Using a condom crossed my mind, but it was too late, and I was too gone over the way he was working my pussy from the back. This young nigga was doing all sorts of unimaginable things. I felt something shift inside, like he moved my womb. I didn't have time to investigate because I was too busy getting fucked. God knows, by the time he was done, my pussy was burning, and I could barely walk. Needless to say, the shower didn't help anything. It only made it worse. I took my washcloth and patted between my legs, trying to ease the pain.

When I got out of the shower, he was lying back on my bed, looking as cool as the summer breeze. "You a'ight, shawty?" His voice startled me.

"Yes, dear. I've never been better." I smiled at him.

I didn't care how much I was hurting. I wasn't going to show him. I was the head bitch in charge, and I had to play my position.

The young man fucked me so good that one night turned into two nights, and before we knew it, he was over at the house seven days a week. I felt guilty at first that I was screwing around in my dead husband's bed, but what the hell? He was gone and wasn't coming back. I knew he was probably looking down on me right now, smiling at how well I performed.

In no time, I bought my new love a car and a new wardrobe. I knew he was from the streets, but whenever he was going out with me, he had to leave that street shit alone. What the hell would I look like having a street thug on my arm when I went to functions with my aristocratic friends? I wasn't no fool and couldn't bear to be embarrassed. I also asked him to leave the streets alone. At first, he refused, but with a little convincing, he finally decided to give that thug life up. In return, I gave him his own debit card.

He surprised me when he asked me to marry him, and even though we hadn't known each other that long, I said yes. A few of my friends said I was moving too fast, but I ignored their comments. Devon was making me happy, and that was all that mattered. Life was too short, and who knew how long I would be there? Even though I was moving fast, I wasn't stupid. Before our wedding, we went to my lawyer, and he drew up a prenup. I worked too hard and sucked too many dicks to get where the hell I was at, and I wasn't gonna let anyone—and I meant anyone—come in and snatch it up.

The ringing of my cell phone startled me and brought me back to reality. I glanced at the caller ID and noticed it was Christopher, the private investigator I hired to follow my husband. See, even though I loved the dick, I wasn't a fool. A few months ago, I noticed my husband's behavior had changed. He was no longer the sweet and doting husband I married. Matter of fact, even the sex wasn't up to par anymore. He wasn't into it. He barely ate my pussy, and when he did, the nigga rushed. So you know I was fuming with anger inside. I noticed he also stopped coming home every night. When I asked him, he got irritated with me and accused me of keeping tabs on him. Nonsense. I wasn't trying to hear that, and my woman's intuition was telling me he was up to no good. I had been around long enough to know when a nigga was getting fresh pussy.

"Hello, Christopher. Tell me you've got something for me." I was nervous as hell. Even though I had hired him, I still didn't know what I was getting myself into.

"Mrs. Guthrie, I followed your husband as you requested, and I have to tell you, he is one busy man."

I pulled the phone closer to my ear. He had my full attention now. "Talk to me, Christopher. Did you catch him with another woman?"

"I didn't really catch him, but without a doubt, I'm telling you he is having an affair. I followed him, and late at night he goes into the same building and leaves in the morning. Also, I stayed behind one morning after he drove off, and a pregnant woman came out of the same apartment."

"A pregnant what?" I choked on my words.

"A young woman in her twenties. She seems to be around six months pregnant."

"Did you manage to get pictures?"

"Yes, ma'am. I got pictures of your husband and the woman."

"All right, Christopher. Send those pictures to my email and stay on top of your job."

I hung up before he could respond. I felt my blood pressure rising as I thought about a bitch being pregnant by my husband. I got up and stumbled to the bathroom. I turned the pipe on and splashed water over my face. I hoped it was a dream, but I realized it wasn't when I looked into the mirror. Tears welled up in my eyes as I stared at myself. "God, this can't be. I swear, it can't be," I whispered as I wiped my face dry.

I threw the towel in the dirty basket and rushed over to my computer. I nervously put in my password and went straight to my email. I was nervous but curious. I wanted to see the bitch who was bold enough to fuck my husband. I opened the email from Christopher, and there it was—numerous pics of my husband coming and going into that building. I opened the pics of this bitch! I stared into her young, dumb-ass eyes as if I were standing in front of her. Jealousy and rage filled my veins. I had no idea who this bitch was, but she was my enemy and would be treated as such.

I saved the pictures and logged out of the computer. I got up, walked over to my bed, and grabbed my cell phone. I dialed my husband's phone.

At first he didn't answer, so I continued calling, and then a female voice answered his phone. It wasn't the fact that he was careless enough to let someone else answer his phone. It was what the bitch said after I asked for my husband. *Pregnant? Having his baby?* Those words kept replaying in my head. I quickly hung up on the bitch. I was angry, but I wasn't going to let that whore know that. After about ten minutes of trying to calm my ass down and drinking three glasses of wine, I dialed his number again.

"Hey, babe," he answered in an upbeat tone.

"Devon, are you fucking around on me?" I got straight to the point.

"Hell nah, what would make you ask me something crazy like that?" this lying-ass bastard asked me.

"Who was that bitch who answered your phone a few minutes ago?"

"Babe, ain't no woman answer my phone. You must've called the wrong number."

"Devon, I'm telling you right now, if you're out there slinging your dick all over the place, I'm going to cut you off from everything and divorce your ass. I'm too old to be out here chasing after a boy who don't want to be kept."

"But b—"

I cut him off before he could get another word out. If I was correct, he would be walking in these doors soon.

Just like a fucking puppet. Exactly thirty minutes later, I heard the front door opening. I sat up in bed and braced myself for the lies this bastard was getting ready to let out. He dashed into the room and sat beside me.

"Yo, B, what the fuck you talking 'bout?"

"I'm way older than you, so you should know that I'm not young, dumb, and full of cum. With that said, I know a lying-ass nigga when I see one." I stared that nigga down.

"Babe, come on now. I've never been with no other woman outside of you. What the fuck would I get out of cheating on you? Your pussy is the best, and you take care of a nigga."

"Good pussy never stopped a dog from throwing his dick around. You ain't the first nigga a woman helped before they turned around and cheated on her. Some niggas are dumb enough to leave their good woman at home and go fuck with one of those dumb-ass young bitches," I spat.

I was sick of sitting here listening to this nigga. I saw that he wasn't going to confess, and as much as I would have loved to pull out the email, I decided not to because I didn't want him to know he was being followed—not yet.

"I'm warning you, Devon! Whoever that bitch is, you better get rid of her before I divorce you and take all your shit."

"Yo, B, there ain't no bitch, and another thing, don't fucking act like you're handling me. I'm a man, and I was making my own damn money before you came along. So don't keep threatening me and shit."

Without saying another word, he walked out of the room. I really didn't care about his attitude toward me. This was no game. I meant what I said. *He'd better get rid of that bitch before he pays dearly.*

CHAPTER SEVEN

Amoy

Two Months Later

After all the stress I'd been through these last three months arguing and fighting with Devon, I was ready to give birth to my baby boy. I wasn't working, and money started to get tight. Keeping up with the rent at my place was putting more stress on me, so I decided to move into the apartment that he paid for, just until I had the baby and got back on my feet. I soon realized that was a big mistake because he felt like he could pop up whenever he wanted to. The more I thought about it, the more I realized that we were not going to work out because he was a fucking liar and a cheater. On the good days, he was loving me and was ready for his family, but as soon as I mentioned his bitch, he would snap. I couldn't blame anyone but my damn self.

I was just getting out of the shower when I felt a gush of water coming down my legs. I also rushed to the toilet bowl and started vomiting. I knew what time it was. I tried to stay calm as I wiped the fluid from between my legs and slipped on my panties. I rushed as fast as I could to my room and called 911. I thought about driving, but the pain was hitting me really hard. I then called Devon, but his phone just rang out. I decided to text him. I then called my sister and let her know it was time. She was very happy and told me that she was on the way to the hospital. I knew that if I couldn't count on anyone else, I could count on her to be there for me.

"Push," a nurse's voice echoed.

I was feeling weak and really didn't have any strength to push, but I needed to get this baby out of me.

"Come on, baby. You can do it," said my little sister, holding my hand.

"Ughhhh," I screamed out as I used all of my might and pushed.

"There you go. He's here," the doctor said.

I then heard a baby crying. Not just any baby, but my son.

I'm a mommy.

"Here you go, Mommy." The nurse handed him to me a few minutes later.

I wasn't ready mentally, but I took him and smiled. While everyone around me was cooing and saying how beautiful he was, my mind was on something else. I sat there staring at him to see who he resembled. The fact was, I wasn't sure who my baby's daddy was, but I needed him to be Devon's child. Just looking at him, I couldn't tell.

"E'erything all right, sis?" Shari's voice startled me, bringing me back to reality.

"Yes, I'm good, sissy. Just stunned by how much my baby resembles his daddy."

"Speaking of Daddy, where is his ass at?" my little sister blurted out with her big-ass mouth.

"Not now, okay?" I gave her a dirty look. She saw how irate I was and quickly dropped the subject.

The nurse took my baby out of my arms and cleaned him off. That gave me a quick second to get my mind right. I reached for my phone on the nightstand and checked to see if he had called or texted. My heart sank when I realized that he didn't text, call, or show his face. This nigga promised to be here for his firstborn. His son was here, and he was MIA. I said "his son" because he didn't know that there was a possibility that he wasn't the daddy, and truthfully, that was something I planned on taking to my grave with me.

Hatred filled my veins as I remembered the bitch who claimed she was his wife. I knew she was the reason why his behavior had changed toward me and my child. I couldn't wait to get out of there so I could really address this nigga. It was one thing to treat me like shit, but it was not cool to treat my child like that.

"Miss Simpson, we are going to take your precious baby with us. We will bring him back in a few."

"A'ight," I said in an annoyed tone. I was kind of irritated that the bitch interrupted my thoughts.

After the nurse and doctors left the room, the nurse's aide entered the room. She was ready to help me to the bathroom.

"Nah, I can help her," Shari said.

"Are you sure?"

"Yes, we got it," I replied.

She handed me a couple of pads and soap and walked out of the room. I was in so much pain that I really didn't want to get out of bed, but I mustered up the energy and hopped my pained-up ass to the bathroom.

I finally got back into bed, and the first thing I did was check my phone. Shari must've peeped that shit, because she gave me a strange look.

"What?"

"You tell me. Ever since you had my nephew, you've been checking your phone, so I figured you're looking for Devon."

I let out a long sigh. "I texted him and called him, but I have not heard from him."

"You want me to call him?"

"Nah, you're good. I just wish he had been here to witness the birth of his son, that's all," I lied. There was so much more than that. Who I thought was my knight in shining armor turned out to be a two-timing-ass nigga.

"Sis, don't even worry yourself. You're gonna make one great mother, and my nephew will know how much you love him." She took my hand into hers and rubbed it.

"Yeah," I barely murmured.

I heard the door push open, and someone entered. My heart skipped a few beats, and my face lit up because I hoped it was Devon. My facial expression quickly changed when I realized who the fuck was standing in front of me. It was the bitch who gave birth to me, the same one who degraded me when I was growing up. I wasted no time to address this bitch. "What the fuck are you doing in my room? How did you know where I . . ." I turned to my sister before I finished my sentence. "You invited this bitch up here?"

"Calm down, sis. She is our mother, and you were giving birth to her first grandchild, so I figured you needed the support."

"Support? Where was this bitch when I was on my period and needed pads? Where was this bitch when I was hungry, shit, when you were hungry, and I had to sell my pussy to buy us food? But now that I'm a grown-ass woman, you're talking about support. I don't need this bitch for nothing, nada. You hear me?"

"I didn't come here to hear your ass throw my past in my face. You're grown, like you said, so get the fuck over it. I knew I shouldn't have come. I see you're still the same selfish little bitch you always were."

"Guys, guys, stop it! This is not the place to be airing out y'all's dirty laundry. I'm sorry. I thought I was helping." Shari burst out crying.

I didn't feel bad for her ass. She knew how I felt toward this bitch, so why the fuck would she come up with this not-so-brilliant idea?

"Get your ass out of my room. Bitch, you're dead to me, and I never want to see your face again," I spat.

"Ha-ha. I hope you know who yo' baby daddy is, 'cause from the look of things, he's nowhere around here."

"I know more than you know about your fucking sperm donors. Now get your sorry ass out of here before I let security throw your ass out."

The bitch looked at me, hissed through her teeth, and walked out.

"Really? Was all that necessary?" Shari yelled.

"I don't owe your ass no explanation. Matter of fact, you need to carry yo' ass, too. Go comfort your ho-ass mama," I said through clenched teeth.

"You know what, Amoy? You can't keep living like this. You need to let go of some of this anger that you have built up. You're now a mother, and you never know if you might make some of the same mistakes—"

Before she could finish her sentence, I cut her ass off. "I will never be anything like that bitch. I'm gonna make sure my seed never wants for anything, and I mean anything, as long as I'm breathing. I don't want to beef with you because you my little sister, but please leave."

She looked at me for confirmation, and the look on my face let her know how serious I really was. "All right. It really doesn't have to be this way. I'll be here tomorrow to check on you and my nephew." She grabbed her purse and stomped out of the room.

I fell back on the bed and let out a long sigh. What the fuck was my dumb-ass sister thinking, bringing this bitch up in here? Then that bitch had the nerve to call me selfish. I was far from being selfish, but I wouldn't forget how terrible of a parent she was and how horrible she made my childhood. Tears welled up in my eyes. This was too much. I had just given birth to my son, and his daddy was probably lying up with his bitch. Now this old dopehead-ass bitch walked her ass up in here like shit was good. *This must be "let's fuck with Amoy" day.*

"Are you okay, dear? I'm here to check your vitals," the little old nurse said.

I quickly wiped my tears and shot her a smile. I tried to hold everything inside until she was gone, and then it all flowed out. I was feeling alone and hurt. What was supposed to be the happiest day of my life turned out to be a fucking sad day. I was happy that I gave birth to my son, but when I thought of what was ahead, my heart ached.

I had just finished feeding my son and placed him back in his bassinet. I was kind of excited that we were going home today. I was tired of being in the hospital, and I needed some damn food. My phone started ringing, and reluctantly, I reached over and grabbed it. My sister was calling nonstop, but I was still angry with her and really didn't feel like talking. "Hello," I answered without looking at the caller ID.

"Yo, what's good?"

"What's good? Did you get my damn messages?"

"Nah, I ain't get no message. Matter of fact, I just got bonded out the county jail and shit."

"Yeah, whatever, Devon. You're such a fucking liar. That's the lamest shit I've ever heard in my life."

"Come on, B. I'm for real. So what's good though? You said you were calling and texting me."

"What's up?" I took a pause because my blood was boiling. "What's up is your motherfucking son is here, and you were nowhere to be found."

"What you talking about, B? You had the baby?"

"You heard me, nigga. Yes, I had your son," I spat.

"Damn, what hospital you at?"

"I'm at Sound Shore in New Rochelle."

"A'ight, I'm on the way."

I shouldn't have told him shit, but part of me wanted him here.

I was kind of nervous about him seeing his son. I paced the room as I anticipated his arrival. All kinds of emotions, even anger, were trying to creep up on me, but I tried my best to tune them out. My phone started ringing, and I jumped to get it. It was Devon.

Wait, what does he want? Is he trying to tell me he can't make it up here? My palms started sweating as I looked down at the telephone, which was still ringing. "Hello."

"Yo, what floor you on?"

I let out a long sigh. "I'm on the third floor. Room number 312."

I ran my fingers through my hair. I knew I looked a hot mess, but still, I tried to straighten myself up a little bit. I picked my son up and held him closely. I wanted his father to see me holding his firstborn.

"Yo, what's good?" he said as he walked in. His facial expression wasn't screaming excitement like I hoped it would.

"Hey, wash your hands. Come get your son."

He seemed as if he caught an attitude by me saying that, but the truth was I didn't give a damn about that. He walked out of the bathroom and walked to the chair that I was sitting in. He stood there staring down at little man. I started to panic. I wondered if he was looking to see a resemblance.

"Here, hold your son. He looks just like you," I said nervously.

He took the baby and continued staring at him. "What's his name?"

"I named him after you. Devon Jamal Guthrie Jr. I thought that since this is your first seed, it would be nice for him to carry your name."

He didn't respond, but his facial expression spoke volumes. "I wish you'd have asked me first."

"When was I supposed to ask you? I can barely reach you, and whenever I do talk to you, you're always ripping and running."

"B, I didn't come up here to fight with you. I'm just saying maybe I wanted to give him a different name. I ain't never tell you, but I hate my name."

Yeah, right. I wasn't buying that bullshit he was selling. I could tell he was deeply bothered by my baby's name.

"Okay, you ready to go?" he quizzed.

"Yes, I have my discharge paper, and we're all set. There is his car seat in the corner." I pointed.

I pressed the buzzer to let the nurse know I was ready to go. He placed little man into the car seat, I grabbed his diaper bag, and we walked out. While he walked off to go get the car, I couldn't help being bothered. This nigga should be happy that I named his child after him. Instead, he was walking around with his face balled up like it was the worst thing that could have happened to him.

CHAPTER EIGHT

Kennedy

I may have been older in age, but I was far from dumb. I pretended like I was asleep when he answered his phone. He walked toward the kitchen, whispering all along. I chuckled to myself because this young nigga really thought he had one up on me. See, he had no idea that yesterday, while he was in the shower, I checked his phone. I used to not touch his phone, but since I realized that my husband had lots of secrets lately, I didn't mind running his motherfucking phone.

Where are you? I'm on my way to the hospital. Our baby is comin'. This message was in his phone from an unknown number. I quickly pulled the number up and put it in my phone. Before anything could register in my head, I heard the water stop running. I quickly placed his phone back into his pocket and rushed back to my room.

I watched him get out of the shower and get dressed. "You leaving, babe?"

"Yeah, I've got a few errands to run. I won't be long." He then placed a kiss on my cheek.

I didn't respond. I pretended like I was paying attention to the TV, and funny enough, *Wives with Knives* was on the ID channel.

As soon as the garage went up, I got up and rushed to the window. I watched as he slowly pulled out of the driveway and sped off down the street. I made sure he was out of sight before I called Christopher's phone. "Are you still out there? Because he just left in a hurry. Please stay on his ass and make sure you get close pictures of wherever he goes and whatever he does."

"Yes, boss lady. I've got you!"

I hung up without saying another word. The message that I read kept playing over and over in my head. *So my husband got a bitch pregnant?* Then my memory took me back to what that little bitch said to me on the phone about having his baby. Also, Christopher sent me pictures of him and a pregnant whore. *Coincidence? I think not.* That dirty bastard had the nerve to be cheating and running up in these little bitches without a condom. I was damn well near old, and my pussy never burned before. So I'd be damned if I would let this young, dumb-ass nigga bring anything home to me.

I was nervous and was tempted to call Christopher, but I knew he needed to do his job, and my interruption might hinder his progress. The anticipation was killing me. I decided to pour a glass of gin. I needed something strong that would numb the pain. I poured my first glass and took it directly to the head. The liquor stung my throat, but it wasn't enough for me to stop. I poured a few more glasses, and like a pro, I drank that liquor down in big gulps. "Aweee, damn you, Devon! How could you do this to me? A fucking baby? How can you bring a bastard into our lives?" I screamed out in agony. I banged my hand up against the cupboard a few times.

This pain was burning my soul. I gave that nigga everything. I fucked him good, brought him in my world, showed him how the other side lived, and this was how he repaid me? By going off and fucking one of these $2, cheap-pussy bitches? *Bitch probably can't afford soap to wash her ass. Pussy worn out worse than my grand-*

ma's old drawers. What was this nigga thinking? Nah, fuck that. He couldn't have been thinking at all.

Tears continued flowing like a river, and I couldn't stop them. I was crying because I was a fool. I was a well-established woman who could've gotten a lawyer, doctor, or a fucking pastor. But no, I listened to my pussy and went after this young nigga, and I was paying the price for my foolish decision.

I scooted down on the floor, resting my head on my knees. I was really hoping that this time it would work out well for me because I wanted to be a better person. One husband had to learn the hard way. God knows husband number two was going to learn that I was the wrong woman to cheat on.

"Yes." I quickly answered the phone. I took a quick glance at my surroundings. Last thing I remembered, I was on the kitchen floor.

"It's me." Christopher's voice echoed through my phone.

"What do you have for me?" I asked eagerly.

"It's too much to explain, so I'm sending it to you in an email. I have to tell you, your husband's ass is in some big trouble."

"All right, send me the email." I hung up the phone. I wasn't in the mood. The bottom line was that I just wanted to see the damn pictures.

My heart rate sped up as I grabbed my laptop. I quickly put in my password and logged into my Yahoo account. It was like a hammer beating on my chest. That was how I was feeling as I stared at picture after picture of my husband and his whore walking out of the hospital. He was carrying a baby, and she followed closely behind him. Then there were pictures of them in the car, the car that I bought his ass.

I stared at the picture of them getting out of the car and walking into an apartment building. Altogether, there were over twenty pictures from every angle. By the time I got up from the computer, the tears were gone. I was no longer feeling weak and hurt. Matter of fact, I felt a surge of energy flowing through my body. I smiled at myself because I knew I was stronger than this, and I knew what I was capable of.

CHAPTER NINE

Amoy

It felt so good to be back home in my apartment. There was something about hospitals that I hated. "Come here, little man," I said to Devon Jr. as I picked him up out of his car seat. I grabbed his diaper bag and walked off into his room. I changed him quickly and laid him in his crib.

I walked out of the baby's room and into the living room, where Devon was. I was kind of thrown off because he didn't even come in the room to see his child. He seemed so standoffish, and I was eager to find out what the fuck his problem was.

I noticed he was still standing up with his car keys in his hand. "Ay, what's going on with you? You didn't even come check on your son."

"Ain't nothing going on. I've got to run some errands real quick. I'll be back later to check on y'all."

"Are you fucking serious? We just came home from the hospital, and you've got errands to run? Nah, what the fuck is the real issue? Is it that bitch who claims y'all are married? Yeah, let's talk about that. Do you remember telling me you were single and shit? Do you remember telling me how much you wanted this baby? So what the fuck changed?"

He stood there, staring at me, and then scratched his head. "Yo, B, ain't nothing changed. I didn't tell you I was married because I didn't know how. I met you, and everything between us happened so fast. As far as my son, I still want him. I just need time to let this process. Everything just seems to be happening too fast."

"Yo, what the fuck you mean, you need time? You had nine motherfucking months to figure out shit. I told yo' ass from day one I wasn't tryin'a be in no damn drama. I damn sure didn't want to be no nigga's side bitch. I can't believe I let you fool me like this. I believed you. When you stood in front of me, lying, I believed you," I screamed as tears welled up in my eyes.

He stepped closer to me and tried to touch me.

"Don't fucking touch me. If it was pussy you wanted, I would've fucked you and sent you on your way. But you hung around here and played me like a dumb bitch. Everything you told me was a lie. Every goddamn thing," I hollered.

"Baby, calm down! I swear to you it wasn't no game. I fell in love with you. It's just that shawty ain't tryin'a let a nigga go. Every time I try to leave her, she's talkin' 'bout killing herself and shit."

"I don't give a fuck about that bitch trying to kill herself. I'm the one hurting, and that's all I give two fucks about. I need you. Shit, your motherfucking son needs you."

"I know y'all need me, but I need a little more time. I promise I'm gonna make this right for you, for us."

I looked him directly in his eyes, and all I saw were lies. I could tell the nigga was desperate and would say anything to leave up out of there.

"Devon, you think I'm a fucking fool. This ain't about just me and you anymore. My son needs his daddy in his life. I grew up without a daddy. Shit, I ain't have a mama, and I'll be damned if I'm gonna allow my son to go through this same shit," I warned.

"Amoy, chill out wit' all that. I ain't no deadbeat. You and my little man ain't going to want for shit as long as I'm breathing. Listen, I've really got to run, but I promise I'll be back later, B."

Before I could respond, he was by the door, opening it up. I wanted to stop him from going, but physically my body wasn't able to. So I just stood there, looking as he walked out and slammed the door behind him. I walked over to the door and locked it. Disappointed was an understatement for the way I was feeling. I really thought he would be happy to be with me and his son, but that bitch had a hold on him. In a way, the nigga was behaving like a scared bitch.

CHAPTER TEN

Shari

Ever since I was growing up, that bitch always acted like she was the head bitch in charge. But really, I was just playing my position as the little sister until the time was right. Don't get me wrong. I fucked with my sister to a certain level. Shit, I had to give the bitch credit. Many days while Mama was strung out on drugs, Amoy would go out and get money by any means necessary. I was young, but I wasn't a fool. I knew her ass was selling pussy, and that was why she had all that money. It was then that I decided that I was gonna get money, and I didn't give a fuck how I got it.

I was definitely blessed with a cute little shape, and I weighed about 121 pounds. Yes, I was a skinny bitch, but a bitch knew how to work this skinny pussy and make a nigga feel like he was a king. Over the years, I perfected my craft and kept my shit on the low-low. The only person who knew that I was doing it was my ace, Kaysia, because we had tricked a couple of niggas before. She was my bitch and the only bitch I fooled with.

Anyway, enough of all that. Let me address the situation at hand—my dear sister. I had been mad at that bitch since the day she up and packed her shit, leaving me at home with Mama. She was the oldest, and I depended on her to protect me from Mama and all her shenanigans, but that selfish bitch was all for self. She didn't care that Mama's man was gonna be fucking me when she was no longer in the house. Yes, I got fucked every night for a year straight. I used to cry, but after a while the tears would no longer come and I would just lie there. Every night when that nigga's dick entered me, I lay there, plotting how to get my sister back. For years that was all I could think about. See, I couldn't really blame Mama 'cause she was on drugs. Therefore, she wasn't responsible for that shit, but my sister was capable and just didn't give a fuck about me.

So she came bragging to me about this dope boy she met. Like the good sister I portrayed to be, I listened attentively. At first, I just sat on the phone listening, but I really didn't give a fuck about who she was fucking. That wasn't anything new. She'd been fucking since her eyes were at her knees. The few times we hung out, I couldn't help but notice the way she was dressed. She had on name brands from head to toe, and the bitch even kept a hairdo. I could tell that she had those expensive bundles in. The bitch smelled like money from a mile away. I looked at her, and every bit of jealousy and envy that I had for this bitch was awakened. That should have been me, not her. I longed for a nigga who would lace me out like that. Shit, I deserved to be happy, not that bitch.

I was tired of hearing about this nigga and decided that I needed to know who Mr. Devon was and what his pockets were hitting for. I started to ask her a few questions about who this nigga was. I was very careful not to go overboard with it because I didn't want to raise her suspicion. At first, she was happy to share how much paper he was spending on her and how good he ate her pussy. I took in everything like a good student while, all along, I was dreaming of a nigga like Devon.

"What are you over there thinking about?" my ace asked.

"Girl, how to take my sister's man away from her," I said with an evil grin plastered across my face.

"Huh? Did I hear you right? You're talking about Amoy, your sister, right?"

"Yes, I'm talkin' 'bout that bitch. Her man-slash-baby-daddy gonna be my next victim. I told you nobody was safe from me, and I know for a fact that this nigga is paiddddd," I emphasized.

"Damn, bitch. What the fuck did she do to you?" She looked up at me.

"What didn't she do? I don't really fuck with that ho. Truth is, you're my only sister."

"Well, you know I've got your back in whatever. So if he's next, I say get it then, bitch."

See, that was the reason why I fucked with her. It didn't take much for her to support me. I continued sipping on my Cîroc I had ordered. It was my bitch's birthday, and the turnup was real.

The rest of the evening I was lost in my thoughts. I had been waiting on the day to really pay that bitch back. I just hoped everything worked out the way I planned for it to.

Things must've started to get sour between them because she no longer bragged about him like she used to, and I knew shit really hit rock bottom when she went into labor and the nigga wasn't present. I was kind of disappointed because I was hoping to finally meet up with my brother in-law.

I had another plan though. I knew how much Amoy hated Mama, so I decided to invite her to the hospital. See, at first Mama didn't want to go, but after about twenty minutes of coercing and telling her I'd give her a few dollars, she decided to show up. After being in the room for a while, I started to think that Mama had taken my money and wasn't going to show her face. But as soon as I heard someone enter the room, I held my breath, hoping it was her. I looked at my sister's face to see how she would react. It wasn't even a full minute before they started going at each other. I stood there and watched as they went in on each other, almost to the point where blows were going to be thrown. I was cracking up inside. I had to try hard not to let it show, but I was really enjoying myself a little too much. It was hard to hide. I was irritated that she was calling Mama all those fucked-up names, but Mama held her own. It got so loud that I had to intervene. I wanted to go on with the show, but Mama showing her face was enough. Miss High and Mighty sure didn't give a fuck how she handled people, especially her mama, but I swore that, one day, her ass would be down from that high seat. *She better not forget she is one of us regular bitches.*

I didn't have time to get in my feelings after she put our asses out of the hospital, unlike Mama, who was spitting fire. She cursed all the way down to the elevator. Me, on the other hand, I was calm, cool, and collected. I had accomplished everything that I set out to do.

The next day, I called my sister to check on her. I wasn't trying to hear that shit that she was upset. At the end of the day, I was the only family that bitch had, so I knew she could only stay mad for so long.

"Hey, sissy," I greeted her when she picked up her phone.

"Hey, what do you want? I told you, I'm mad with yo' ass. I still can't believe that you pulled that bullshit yesterday."

"Come on, sissy. I told you I'm sorry. I thought that it would be nice if you had some support, that's all. I was only tryin'a cheer up my big sissy."

"You know how I feel about her ass. I don't ever want to see that bitch again."

"Okay, look, I admit I should've asked you first. I am so sorry, sissy. You know I can't live with you being mad with me," I pleaded in my fake voice.

"Man, whatever. You know I love you and you're my heart. Don't let her ass manipulate you to do no shit like that no mo'."

"Aw, thanks, sissy. I was so stressed out. You know I don't like when we beef. Anyway, how is my nephew doing?"

"He is doing great. We are going home today, so I'm excited."

"How are you getting home? Do you want me to pick you up?"

"Nah, I'm good. Devon is coming to get us."

"Oh, okay. He finally decided to show up," I said sarcastically.

"Girl, yes. Anyway, let me get my stuff together. I'll call you later." She hurriedly got me off the phone.

I hung the phone up and busted a U-turn in the middle of the street. I was heading to my sister's apartment. I needed to see what this nigga looked like once and for all. I parked across the street from her apartment and waited. I wasn't sure how long it was going to take them to get here, but it was definitely worth the wait.

I cut the music on and scooted down in my seat. I parked at an angle where I could see everyone who entered her apartment building. To fight boredom, I logged on to Facebook. I let out a sigh. It was the same shit, just a different day—a bunch of bitches lying about who they were fucking with and these niggas lying about how much money they were making. I continued scrolling through, trying to catch up on the latest gossip. Mount Vernon was a little town, but it damn sure had a lot of drama popping off.

Damn, twenty-five minutes had passed, and they still were not there. I thought about calling her to see where the fuck she was at, but that would be kind of suspicious, so I laid my head back on the seat, taking in the sultry voice of Adele singing "Hello."

I must've dozed off because I was startled by a car alarm. It took me a quick second to get myself together. I quickly noticed my sister and a dude getting out of a car. I scooted back down, just lifting my head enough to see what was going on. I watched as they walked into her building. Out of the corner of my eye, I saw a dude snapping pictures of the couple as they walked in. It was kind of strange for someone to take pictures of my sister. I tried to get a glimpse of the person's face, but I couldn't. I decided not to worry about that and to go back to minding my own business.

I hope this doesn't take too long. God must've heard my prayer. Dude walked out of the building and toward his car. The dude in the car started snapping more pictures. It was confusing because I had no idea what was going on. Was this the police taking pictures of him? And if so, what was this dude involved in? I continued watching what was taking place. I watched as dude got in his car and pulled off, and then, seconds later, the other dude pulled off in a black sedan with tinted windows. I scooted all the way down as they drove past me. I waited a minute, and then I started my car and pulled off. I tried not to get too close to the sedan because I didn't want to be involved in anything.

About two blocks down, the sedan took a left turn and disappeared. I was happy because now I was directly behind Devon's car. I sped up, and without putting much thought into it, I rear-ended his car. I did it a little too hard, because my head almost hit the steering wheel. He stopped, and I prepared myself for the role I was about to play. I cut my car off and got out. I walked toward his car and almost bumped into him.

"Lady, you just hit me!" he said in an upset tone.

"Oh, my God, I'm so sorry. I didn't mean to. My phone was ringing, so I tried to reach for it, and when I looked up, I tapped your bumper," I said while batting my eyes at the nigga.

"Do you have insurance?"

"Let me see how bad it is," I said, walking over to his car to examine his back bumper. I made sure my fat ass was showing when I bent over. "It doesn't seem so bad."

"Do you have insurance?"

"No, I don't, and please don't call the police. I can't go to jail." I burst out crying.

"Police? I 'on't do them, and why are you crying? It's just an accident. Wait, do you have a warrant or something?" He looked at me suspiciously.

"I just got a warrant for fighting some girls, and I don't wanna go to jail." I cried harder.

"Baby girl, don't do all that. You ain't going nowhere 'cause I ain't calling no police."

"Are you sure? I can give you a few dollars, but I don't have much," I said between sobs.

"Man, chill out for real. You good. Matter of fact, dry them tears."

"Aweee, you're such a sweetheart. Your wife must be one lucky woman to have a man like you. What's your name, sweetie?"

"Wife? What gave you the impression that I'm married? And my name is Devon." He smiled at me.

"Nothing. I was only assuming since guys like you are often cuffed by a chick."

"Anyway, enough about me. Where's your man at while you're out here by yourself?"

"I'm single." I changed the expression on my face.

"Look, you can make it up to me by letting me take you to dinner."

"I don't know . . ." I pretended like I was in deep thought.

"Look, I ain't going to do nothing to you. Just dinner—nothing more, nothing less."

"All right, you seem pretty cool. I guess I can follow you."

"All right. Cool."

I jumped back in my car and quickly wiped my tears. *Damn, that was pretty easy,* I thought as I followed him. I couldn't help but think about how fine this nigga was. I loved niggas with nice teeth, and he had those pearly white teeth with a pair of sexy, thick lips, the kind that made me want to kiss that nigga ASAP. He was bow-legged and seemed like he was packing a good-sized dick. The thoughts of me riding that dick sent a thrill through my body. I reached between my legs and massaged my clit with my left hand as I drove closely behind him. The honking of a horn quickly jolted my memory to reality. Shit, I couldn't wait until I got the chance to ride this nigga. The ride was going to be extra special. I chuckled to myself as I thought about my sister and what her reaction might be if she found out her baby sister was boning her baby daddy.

Dinner was great. He took me to this nice Italian restaurant. I wasn't a fan of Italian food, but a bitch was trying to make a good first impression, so I looked on the menu and ordered some chicken Alfredo. I fucked that shit up like it wasn't my first time eating it. I sat across from this nigga and tried to size him up.

"So, Miss Lady, what's your name?"

"Shari."

"That's a beautiful name."

"Thank you." I smiled seductively.

"Your skin is so radiant." He reached over, took my hand, and rubbed it.

My pussy tingled as his masculine touch sent electrical energy through my body.

"You a'ight? I'm not making you scared, am I?"

"Scared? You do realize I'm a grown woman, right? Devon, let's cut to the chase. Why are we here?"

"What do you mean? I think you're a beautiful woman, and I don't believe in coincidences. I think it was fate that brought us together tonight."

His long dreadlocks up against his caramel-looking skin made him the apple of any woman's eyes.

"Well, Devon, I have my own damn money if I wanted to eat out. I'm going to cut straight to the point. I think you're a fine-ass nigga, and to be honest, I would love to fuck you," I said without blinking.

"Damn, ma, you're bold as fuck, but I ain't gonna lie—it's sexy as hell." He smiled.

"So what are we waiting on? Pay the waiter and let's get out of here."

After he paid the waiter, we left. "So where are we going?"

"You can come to my place. How about you follow me this time, daddy?" I said and rubbed his chest.

"A'ight, ma. I'll follow anywhere you lead." He licked his lips and walked off to his car.

As I was getting into my car, I spotted the car from earlier. *What the fuck? Who the fuck is this, and why are they still following us?* I thought about approaching the car, but in these crazy days, that wasn't a wise idea. I took one last look and hurriedly got into my car. I pulled off, and as I drove past the car, I tried to peep inside, but the windows were up and tinted pitch-black. I tried to shake the feeling, but I knew it wasn't a coincidence. I wasn't tripping. It was the same car that was at my sister's apartment.

I pulled up at my apartment complex and parked. Devon pulled up in the parking space next to me. I got out of the car, and he did the same. I tried to look around to see if I saw that damn car again, but I didn't see anything but three cars in the parking lot.

"You a'ight? You're looking all nervous and shit," he giggled.

"I'm good."

"You sure? I don't need to be watching my back for no boyfriend or husband, right?"

"No, but seriously, did you see a car following you when we left the restaurant?"

"Nah, I ain't see no car, and I always pay attention to my surroundings. Ma, you sure you're just not paranoid?"

"Nah. Earlier . . ." *Fuck,* I thought as I caught myself. I had almost blurted out that I saw the same car earlier when I was at my sister's apartment.

"What were you gonna say?"

"Nothing. I just thought I saw that same car earlier, but you're right. I'm probably just paranoid. Let's go." I grabbed his hand and led him into my building.

We weren't in the apartment a quick second before I started kissing on that nigga. He didn't waste any time either. He started unbuttoning my shirt. He kissed me passionately on my neck while fondling my breasts with his hand. He used his other hand to grab my butt cheeks. I wanted him in a way that I couldn't explain. There was something about his swagger that made me feel relaxed. I could smell his cologne and taste his cool mint breath as I pushed my tongue down his throat.

He kissed my inner ear and then sucked on my earlobe. A chilling sensation traveled through my spine and between my legs. "Aweeee," I moaned out.

He gripped my D-sized breasts, twirling his long, slim fingers around my nipples, which were harder than a rock. I was ready, ready to ride that dick. My body felt awkward, hypnotized by his slithering hands, which traveled to my hot spots.

"Bitch, what are you doing?" I could hear my sister's voice in the back of my head, but fuck that. I couldn't resist his touch. Quite frankly, I wasn't trying to elude his strong, aggressive hands, which were in full control of my body.

He stared into my eyes as our tongues wrestled. His hands palmed my ass like a basketball. I felt my feet gradually being lifted off the ground. His strength was unbearably strong. I locked my legs around his waist as we traveled into darkness. My skin flickered with goosebumps as he placed me onto my sofa. He continued to place small, gentle, passionate kisses around my ears, neck, and face.

Instinctively, my chill bumps became heat bumps. "Damn, I want you so bad," I screamed out, exhaling and making circular motions with my fingers through his long dreads.

He traced the outline of my face with his tongue, slowly and steadily, sending my body into ecstasy. I tensed up after his long, wet tongue slithered between my cleavage. I was so caught up with his affectionate tongue that I didn't realize he had unwrapped my dress until a cool breeze caressed my skin.

What am I doing? my subconscious mind questioned, but his affection had my body craving his touch. I played with his ears, twirling my fingers around them.

In one motion, he cocked both of my legs up in the air with his hands. A mixture of cool air from the air conditioner and his hot breath over my open slit made me quiver. My sweet nectar was purring like a cat each time he planted wet kisses around my womanhood.

"Awee, baby." I sizzled when his lips connected with my sweetness. His tongue toyed with my clit. He kissed passionately around my walls, and I dug my nails deep into his back as he applied pressure on my clit.

I ground my hips with the motion of his tongue. My juices continued to flow like a faucet, dripping hot liquid. He held my leg up with his forearm, and with his free hand, he inserted two fingers into my wetness. I ground on them as if I were riding his dick.

The rhythm of his fingers increased in speed, thrusting against my clit.

"Damn, baby, fuck me, pleasseeeee," I cried out, feeling my blood ready to explode.

Suddenly, he paused. *What is he doing? Don't stop right now,* I wanted to shout, but when his mouth acted as a suction cup, plunging away on my nectar, I was ready to explode.

"Such a teaser," I grumbled, gyrating my hips. Still on the edge of reaching my climax, I continued to dig deeper into his back as if I were trying to find his soul.

His tongue was dancing in the name of love around my clit. My hormones raced with joy as I reached my climax. I squealed like a worm as he sucked me dry like a vacuum. I looked down as he looked up, making sure I was satisfied. His glossy lips glowed with my cum in the dark. I gave him a look as if I had had better. Without speaking, his tongue plunged into my brown eye.

"Oh, shit," I screamed out in feel-good pain as his tongue dug deeper. "Oh, my gosh." I felt fingers enter back into my love box.

Double penetration sent shockwaves through my body. The way he worked my body was like no other. He slowly thrust his hard dick inside of me. Pain and pleasure had me in pure bliss. This nigga was playing a sweet melody with every string of my soul. I exploded over his dick, back-to-back, as I dug my fingernails into his skin. I felt his dick harden as he exploded inside of me.

"Arghhhhhh," he groaned.

Fuck, I'm happy I'm on the shot.

After the sex session was over, I was mentally drained. I'd been with quite a few niggas, but there were none I could compare this nigga to. I got up off the sofa, and cum rolled down on my legs as I rushed to the bathroom.

I stuck my finger in my wet pussy and licked it off. I looked in the mirror and smiled. *So this is what had my dear sister wide open over this nigga?* I was enjoying myself a little too much until I heard him talking on his phone. I cut the water off and leaned my ear toward the door.

"Man, I told you I would be back over there tonight!" he yelled.

Hmmm, if I could guess who's on the other end, I would have to say it's my dumb-ass sister.

I hurriedly washed myself off with warm water and soap. I then walked out of the bathroom butt-ass naked. I was ready for another round if my stallion was up for it. I was disappointed to see him dressed and standing up. "Don't tell me you're leaving me already," I said, pretending like I gave two fucks.

"Yeah, I got a few runs to make. You know how it is." He smiled.

"Well, do you think I'm going to see you again?" I pouted.

"Hell yeah. After the fuck you just gave me, B, I've got to get some more of that shit. You had a nigga weak and shit." He walked over to me and rubbed his hand all over my face.

"Make sure, 'cause I definitely ain't finished wit' you." I licked my lips and gently stroked his dick in his pants.

"A'ight, I'm out. Take my number and hit me up tomorrow."

"Okay." I took his number and stored it in my phone under Bae. In the blink of an eye, he was gone through the door.

I walked to my window and watched as he walked to his car. Homeboy's swag was definitely turned all the way up. I watched as he pulled off. I was about to walk away from the window when I glanced back through it and saw that same sedan pulling out behind him. I closed the curtains but still wondered who the fuck that person was following him around.

I was worn out from busting a nut back-to-back. I decided to crawl in my bed and rest my body.

I checked my phone and realized that I had three missed calls from my sister. Hmm, whatever the hell she wanted had to wait until the morning time. Thanks to her baby daddy, me and my pussy were dead tired. I smiled to myself as I dozed off.

CHAPTER ELEVEN

Amoy

I couldn't believe this nigga had talked to me the way he just did, especially after I just gave birth to his baby. All I wanted to know was if he was going to come through as he had promised. I really didn't understand any of this. One minute, he loved me, and the next minute, it was like he fucking hated me. After I hung the phone up in his ear, I dialed my sister's number, but that bitch's phone just rang out. I really needed someone to talk to, and she was the closest to me, the only person I could talk to without being judged. I was disappointed that she didn't answer, but her ass was probably asleep. I wiped my tears, took my son out of his crib, and laid him on my chest. No matter what I was going through, I vowed to make sure my little man was all right.

As I listened to his heartbeat, reality kicked in. I really didn't know who my baby's daddy was, and God help me if he started looking like Marquise and not Devon. I knew my ass was in some hot shit, and I had no idea how I was going to get myself out. Tears welled up in my eyes. I could just leave here, maybe go out of town and run away from it all, but that was just a stupid idea because I was down to my last couple hundred dollars and I had nowhere to go.

"God, please help me figure this out," I whispered as I rubbed my baby on his back. "Don't worry about it, baby boy. Mama's gonna make sure everything works out."

It was then that I decided that, when I woke up in the morning, I was going to call Marquise and talk to him. If I could get him to take a paternity test without anyone knowing, then I would know for sure who the daddy was.

I was so brokenhearted that I wished that Devon would show up and comfort me. I missed his smell, his kind words, and just the good times we had spent together. I just wished he would see that he belonged here with his child and me.

I was up bright and early. I had so much shit on my brain that I was surprised it hadn't exploded. After I bathed little man and fed him, I grabbed the phone and dialed Marquise's phone. I was nervous, but I was desperate. Plus, I needed to know who the hell my baby daddy was. The phone rang out, and his voicemail came on. I was happy because I really wasn't ready.

Before I could put my phone down, it started ringing. I looked at the caller ID and noticed it was Marquise. I swallowed hard and answered. "Hey," I said shyly.

"What's good, ma? Long time, no hear from you. You 'on't fuck wit' a nigga no mo'?"

"Nah, it ain't that. Just been going through some things, that's all. Anyway, I need to talk to you."

"Shit sounds serious." He chuckled.

"Nothing serious. Can you come for a minute?"

"A'ight. I'm all the way downtown right now. I'll be back on your side soon."

After I hung up the phone, I felt like a big burden was lifted off my shoulders, but who was I fooling? Soon, I would be face-to-face with him, telling him there was a possibility that he was my child's father. I decided to clean up real quick, even though I wasn't feeling my best. Ever since I had my son, I had been feeling kind of weak, along with having bad headaches. I'd been taking Advil, but that shit wasn't working. I figured I'd been stressing too much. *One day, this has to get better. I swear it has to,* I thought as I vacuumed my carpet.

By the time I finished cleaning, I realized it had been over an hour. I jumped in the shower and took a quick wash off. I put on a pair of sweats and a wife beater and brushed my hair in a ponytail. I was always conscious of how I looked whenever I was around him. I never wanted the nigga to think that I fell off after I stopped fucking with him.

I heard my doorbell ringing, so I put the brush down and walked over. I looked through the peephole and saw Marquise standing out there. I quickly opened the door.

"Hey, come in."

"Whaddup, ma?" He gave me a quick hug. The scent of this man always gave me a mental high and physical arousal. He finally let me go, and I closed the door. He walked over and sat on the couch.

"Damn, you had the baby?"

"Yup, a few days ago," I said nervously, not knowing what his next set of questions might be.

"Oh, okay. What you have, boy or girl?"

"A boy, and that is the reason I wanted you to come over here."

"What you mean, and why the fuck are you acting all nervous and shit?" he said as he pulled out a blunt and started rolling it up.

I took a seat close to him and made up my mind to just let it out. "Listen, Marquise, remember when you asked me whose baby it was, and I said it wasn't yours?"

"Yeah, and?" he asked in a not-so-friendly tone.

"Well, I'm not sure if it's your baby or the other dude I was messing wit' after you."

"Yo, B, I 'on't know what you're tryin'a pull, but that's not my seed. Matter of fact, you told me that yourself."

"I know, but a few days after you and I had sex, I met dude and I started sleeping with him. To be honest, I'm not sure whose baby he is."

"So what the fuck the other nigga say about it? He's not claiming him? That's why you decided to put it on me?" He looked me dead in my eyes.

"Marquise, just shut the fuck up. You know me better than this. I'm not on no bullshit. I didn't plan on being in this situation, and I'm not looking for no nigga to just put my child on. All I'm asking for you to do is take a blood test and see if he's your baby. That's all." I was very irritated that he would even try me like this. Like for real, I was hoping it was not his baby.

"Calm down, B. I didn't mean to upset you. I would love to have a seed with you, but you told me it wasn't mine. I just don't want to be no fool, you feel me?" He stared at me.

"Yes, I—" Before I could finish my sentence, I heard my phone ringing. I jumped up and ran into the bedroom to get it. It was Devon. I couldn't answer it, not now anyway. I walked out of the room with the phone in my hand, and it continued ringing.

"Damn, yo' nigga looking for you, B," he joked.

I didn't say anything—or I didn't have time to say anything—when I heard the doorbell ringing. My heart jumped as I stared at the ringing telephone.

"Yo, you expecting somebody?"

"Nah, not really."

I tiptoed over to the door and peeped out the peephole. Devon was standing out there with boxes of Pampers in his hands. *I have to think fast.*

"Who is that at the door?" Marquise stood up and took his gun out of his waistband.

I hurriedly walked over to him. "Please put that away. It's the other dude I've been messing with."

"Man, what the fuck? I ain't got time to be laying a nigga out over no bitch. I knew I should've never come over here. What kind of shit are you on?"

"I didn't know he was coming over here. I would never put you in no fucked-up situation, for real. I swear, please put your gun away. I'm just gonna tell him that you're one of my sister's friends and you stopped by to say hello."

"Man, I don't give a fuck what you tell that fool as long as he don't pop off at the mouth."

This wasn't a good situation. I wished the ground would open up and take me in this minute. Devon was now banging on the door while continuously calling my phone. I breathed hard and walked over to the door. Before I opened it, I mouthed, "Please don't say anything to him." I could tell he was aggravated, but there was nothing I could do about it right now.

I opened the door, and instead of this nigga greeting me, he pushed his way in, cursing. "What the fuck took you so long?" He stopped in the middle of the living room. "And who the fuck is this nigga up in here?"

"This is my little sister's friend. He just stopped by to check on me for her," I lied.

"Really? And that's what the fuck took you so long to answer the door?"

"Devon, please don't start. I was in the room and didn't hear you knocking."

"Bitch, you better not be playing with me, having no other nigga up in here around my son."

"Yo, my nigga, you ain't got to disrespect the lady like that."

I wished like hell Marquise hadn't said a word.

"What the fuck you say to me, my nigga? This is my bitch. I talk to her any fucking way I please, and while you're running yo' motherfucking mouth, tell me, are you the nigga she's fucking?"

"Devon, stop!" I shouted. "I just had my baby, so how can I be fucking anybody? I told yo' ass, he's my sister's friend, so drop it."

"Ay, fuck nigga, this pussy was mine before she started fucking wit' yo' old punk ass. So technically, you got my leftovers. When you're kissing her, fuck nigga, that's the flavor of my dick, and when you're fucking her, I done left my DNA all up through there," Marquise spat and took a step closer to Devon.

"Nigga, I'll blow yo' motherfucking brains out up in here! This is my bitch and my pussy now, so get the fuck up outta here."

Marquise didn't say another word, but he pulled out his gun and slapped the shit out of Devon's face. Blap! Blap!

Devon stumbled and fell backward. "No! Stop. Please just go," I started screaming at Marquise. "Are you okay?" I ran over to Devon.

"Bitch, don't touch me. My nigga, you're a dead nigga! You hear me? You're dead, bitch-ass nigga!" Devon yelled as he wiped the blood away from his face.

"Pussy nigga, I should just blow yo' motherfucking brains out, but then I'ma have to body shawty, too. Nigga, you'll see me around though," Marquise said before he walked out the door.

I thought about grabbing my baby and running out also, but before I had time to gather my thoughts, whap! Whap! Whap! My face stung as I felt his hands connect to my skin. I grabbed my face and backed up from him. He lunged toward me and grabbed me. "You cheating on me, bitch?"

"Let me go, nigga! Cheating on you? How can I cheat on a nigga who's married? Huh? Tell me that."

I must've angered him, because he started punching me in my face. "Get off of me," I screamed. "I'm gonna get your ass locked up for a long time," I said in between blows.

"Bitch, I made you, and this is how you repay me, huh? Having this fuck nigga up in here around my seed?" He punched me in my eyes.

"Noooooo! Noooooo," I screamed out some more.

Pain trickled through my body as I tried to fight off this woman beater. I mustered up the strength and reached between his legs and grabbed his balls. I wrapped them around my tiny hand and squeezed with everything in me. I squeezed and squeezed until it was like soft dough in my palms.

"You bitch," he yelled out.

I didn't ease up any. I squeezed like my life depended on it. It brought him to his knees. I then let go and ran as fast as I could to my room. I slammed the bedroom door and called the police and the ambulance. I couldn't see, and my head was throbbing.

"911, what's your emergency?" was all I heard before I fainted.

CHAPTER TWELVE

Kennedy

After seeing what my husband had been up to lately, I started thinking of a master plan. The nigga fucked me good, but that dick wasn't that damn good for me to keep dealing with his cheating behind. No, I wasn't going to just walk away from him—at least not yet. His ass was going to learn that I wasn't the one to be fucking with.

The first thing I did was go online and cancel his debit card that was on my account. There was no way he was going to keep spending my money while he couldn't keep his dick in his pants. I knew that he was going to be pissed the fuck off, but I really didn't give a damn.

I was in the kitchen fixing some steak and potatoes when I heard the garage door go up. I braced myself for the drama that was getting ready to kick off.

"Kennedy!" I heard him screaming my name while coming up the steps.

"Yes, darling? What's the matter?" I asked calmly.

"Why the fuck my debit card ain't working? I called the bank, and they said it was closed by the main account holder."

"Well, honey, I don't see why you're upset. You didn't think that I was going to allow you to keep spending my hard-earned money while you run around here with these little whores, did you? See, honey, you might have me a little gone over the dick, but I haven't lost my damn mind at all!"

"Man, what are you talking about? You keep accusing me of shit that I'm not out here doing. What the fuck do I look like, cheating when I've got you? You've got good pussy, and I've got money to spend. These young bitches can't do nothin' for a nigga. You hear me? Nothing."

Clap! Clap! Clap! "You sound pretty convincing, but please know I'm not no fool. Matter of fact, I have plenty of sense. Yes, I know about all your shit, and I know you got that little whore pregnant, too."

"What the fuck are you talking about, babe? You're really tripping now. My ass ain't got no kids, don't want no kids." He chuckled.

"Hmm, you will find out in due time. You can play pussy and get fucked. Not a cent of my hard-earned money will be used to finance your whore or your love child. You will leave this relationship the same way you came in it, with that old, raggedy-ass car and the few pieces of clothes you own." I went back to cutting the onion, all along pretending it was his ass that I was cutting up.

"Yo, B, I ain't tryin'a hear all that shit you're talkin' 'bout. Don't be coming at me like I ain't have shit when I started fooling around with you. I've been on my own since the age of fourteen and made plenty of money out in these streets. You were the one who begged me to leave the streets alone and settle down with you. Don't sit up here and act like you don't know. I ain't never depend on no broad, for real, so quit talking to me like I'm a flunky!" he yelled.

"I'm done talking. Get rid of that whore, or I'll get rid of your ass."

He looked at me and hissed. He then turned around and stormed out of the door. I continued cutting up my onion. See, this young nigga had no idea what I was capable of doing. Matter of fact, these niggas always slept on my ass, I guessed because I was a female. My late husband, Travis, thought the same damn thing.

See, he was a good provider, but that nigga couldn't keep his dick in his pants. For years, he fucked anything with a pussy. I begged him over and over and over. I cried and even tried to commit suicide one time because I was too embarrassed. All that shit ended one day, though, when I grew the balls to fire five shots into him without blinking. I was no fool. I made sure everyone knew I was going to be at our vacation home in Nyack.

Earlier that night, I spoke with my husband, and then I got in my car and headed back to our house. I was careful not to bring my cell phone along with me. See, watching the ID channel had its pros. I parked at the side of the house, where we had no neighbors, and I busted the window on the back door. See, if I was correct, I knew he never set the alarm when he was home by himself. I slowly crept up the stairs. Poor Travis was so caught up with whomever he was talking to on the phone that he didn't see when the first bullet hit him in the chest. I fired the other shots as a precaution to make sure he was dead.

I wasted no time. I turned around, walked down the stairs, and went out the door. I drove to the Hutchinson River and threw the gun in the water. This was a gun I had bought off a street thug about two years prior to me planning his murder. I got back to our vacation home without incident and waited.

Bright and early, I started calling my husband's phone, but it just kept ringing. I called his office and was told he didn't come in. "That's very strange. I spoke to him last night, and he said he was coming in early."

"I've been calling him also, Mrs. Campbell. Do you want me to go over and check on him?"

"Yes, dear. I'm still out here at our other home and will be leaving shortly. Please call my phone as soon as you get in touch with him."

"Okay, Mrs. Campbell."

I hung up without saying another word to that home-wrecking bitch. She was one of my husband's whores. The bitch was at the bottom of the barrel because she would laugh and talk in my face while screwing my husband behind my back. I was just as fake as that whore because I didn't let her or my husband know I was on to them.

About an hour later, I received a frantic call from her ass, telling me that they had found my husband shot to death in the home. I burst out crying and screaming.

"I'm on my way," I managed to say between screams.

It took me forty minutes to get there. The coroner, police, and newspeople swarmed my home. I got out of my car and ran toward my front door. They were taking him out on a gurney. I took one look and collapsed into the arms of one of the policemen. That day, I gave my best performance, like my life depended on it—shit, my life did depend on it. There was no way I could let them think I had anything to do with his death.

His death was ruled a homicide. The detectives told me an intruder had broken in, and they thought the motive was robbery. I buried his ass and played the grieving wife whenever I was among our friends, but behind closed doors, I slept well, knowing that bastard wasn't able to cheat on me anymore.

The sizzling of the frying pan jolted my mind to the situation at hand. I turned the stove down and went back to preparing my dinner. I poured a glass of red wine to help mellow out my mood. I was praying that this nigga did the right thing and wouldn't make me have to commit murder twice!

CHAPTER THIRTEEN

Shari

I was tired as hell. I had a long-ass day from ripping and running out in them streets. Me and my bitch did a little retail therapy, and then we got something to eat from the Jamaican spot on 241st Street.

"So, bitch, you've been blushing all day. Spill it," she said as she took a sip of her soda.

"Girl, I'm telling you, that nigga had some bomb-ass dick," I bragged.

"Wait! Slow down. Are we talking about Devon?"

"Yes, bitch, the one and only. My sister's baby daddy." I smiled.

"How the fuck did you pull that off? Where did you meet him?" She bombarded me with questions.

"Ho, slow down, and ain't none of that relevant. All you need to know is that nigga's dick game is on point. That nigga has my insides feeling gooddddddddd."

"Really?"

"Yes, bitch, really." I peeped the look on her face. "Bitch, don't tell me you're in your feelings. You know damn well these niggas don't mean shit to me. I just wanted to fuck him because my sister brags about him so much."

"Hmmm, oh, okay," she said.

I knew she was tight with me. See, Kaysia and I had been fooling around for a minute now. We were not in a relationship, but I ate her pussy occasionally, and she ate mine. This mostly happened late nights when we were high and fucked up. I did enjoy her, but I loved dick, and even though I lied to her that one day we would be together, I had no intention of being with her. I loved dick, and I didn't mean no plastic dick. I wanted the real thing up inside of me.

Speaking of dick, my mind was on ol' boy all day. I was tempted to call him, but being the bitch I was, I wasn't chasing no nigga. I knew with the fuck I gave him, he would definitely be hitting me up real soon.

After I dropped my bitch off, I headed home. I didn't like to be around her when she was moody. I was loving my life right now and had no time to deal with unhappy motherfuckers. I walked in the house and threw all my bags on the floor. I was hot and couldn't wait to get out of these damn clothes. I decided to jump in the shower and wash this pussy. Wasn't no better feeling than having a fresh-smelling pussy.

As soon as I got out of the shower, I heard my phone ringing. I ran to the living room and grabbed my purse. I snatched my cell out and looked at the caller ID. My face lit up as I noticed who it was. "Hello," I said in my sexy voice.

"Whaddup, ma?" His strong New York accent echoed in my ear.

"Hey, boo. I've been dying to hear from you." I cut straight to the chase.

"Really?" He chuckled.

"Hell yeah. I couldn't get you off my mind after that sweet fuck you gave me the other night."

"Damn, since you're talking like that, how would you love for me to come over and give you some more?"

"Well, what are you waiting on? Come on then."

"Bet! I'm on the way."

I smiled as I hung up the phone. Let me find out ol' boy was digging me as much as I was digging him. Hmmm, or was it the fact that my sister had just had her baby and couldn't fuck? Either way, it worked out for me.

I got myself a glass of chardonnay. I wanted to feel right when he got here. I couldn't wait to work my magic on Devon after googling how to give your man exclusive head. Shit, I wanted to suck dick like redheaded Becky. Lord knows them white girls started sucking dick at a young age.

"Ha-ha." I laughed at my damn self because I knew I was wrong for thinking that shit, but what the hell. *It is what it is.*

I heard the doorbell ringing, startling me from my train of thought. I leaped up and ran to the door, almost knocking over my glass.

"Hey, baby," Devon said as he walked in my door.

"Hey, daddy," I replied seductively.

Devon must've known I was mesmerized over his hot chocolate body, and I was truly in awe over his penis print, which stuck out like black ass.

"You miss me?" he asked with an "I'ma tear that pussy up" grin plastered on his face.

What the fuck? Is this a trick question? Stupid-good-dick motherfucker, I missed the hell outta your dick, I wanted to say, but I didn't. I didn't want to seem too desperate. "Yes, daddy. I missed you." I continued to role-play with the sexy innocent-little-girl voice.

"I can't tell that you miss me." He shook his head in disbelief.

I guessed I had to show him, because actions always spoke louder than words. With that said, I found myself rubbing on his chest. My fingers traced every curve from his chest to his ripped abs down to his oversized penis.

My hands were both gripped around his thick, hard chocolate dick. My dried mouth became wet, and I was ready to devour his chocolate king-sized Snickers bar.

"Damn, you must have missed daddy for real," Devon moaned as I took his diamond-shaped head into my moist, warm mouth.

"Ssssss, damn, babe," he hissed when I twirled my tongue ring around his dick head.

I couldn't front. His moans had my pussy dripping wet. It wasn't summertime for a Super Soaker. My wetness flowed down my inner thighs and wet my legs. My pussy tingled as I tried hard not to explode. My pussy was begging for my fingers, but my mouth was craving Devon's dick.

"Oh, shit, sssss," he moaned, grabbing the back of my weave and guiding my head back and forth in rhythm while he fucked my mouth. Another time and place, I would've flipped the fuck out because my Brazilian hair cost $300 a bundle, but the way my mouth was playing his instrument, he couldn't do anything except pay the bill.

I closed my eyes and went in for the kill. I felt Devon's nuts on my chin and his dick touching my tonsils. I had to pull back because I almost gagged.

"Don't stop," he begged, twirling my hair around his fingers and guiding me back to his head.

Devon's dick slid in and out of my wet mouth. The faster I sucked, the louder he became, and the wetter my pussy got.

I couldn't help myself. With my free hand, I inserted two fingers, working them in and out of my pussy. Both my hands and head were hard at work. Devon was moaning, groaning, and bouncing my head like a ball onto his dick. His veins started to get bigger, and I knew then that he was getting ready to cum. I locked my jaws around his dick as his juices spewed out into my mouth. I eagerly licked them up and swallowed every drop. I then used my tongue and cleaned his dick off.

"Damn, baby, come here." He pulled me up toward him.

The ringing of my cell phone interrupted my thoughts. *Fuck that. I'll call whoever that is back,* I thought as he lifted me in the air, but the phone was not easing up. It was ringing nonstop.

"Babe, hold on. Let me see who the fuck this is calling me like they've lost their damn mind," I grumbled as I went to get my phone.

"What the fuck? Is this bitch dying?" I said out loud. I had twenty missed calls from my sister's phone and a few from a strange phone number. I was pissed as fuck as I dialed back this bitch's number. I was just about to get my pussy eaten, and here this old jealous-ass bitch was calling.

"Hello," a strange voice answered.

"Who the hell is this, and why are you answering my sister's phone?"

"Hello, ma'am. My name is Sergeant Claiborne, and I'm with the Mount Vernon PD."

"Okay, and what are you doing with my sister's phone?"

"Your sister was beaten really badly earlier, and we were trying to get some information on who she really is. Your number is under 'sister,' so I assumed y'all are sisters."

"Is she dead or something?"

"No, ma'am, but she is in the ICU, fighting for her life."

"All right, so what do you want to know?" I was trying to get this nigga off the phone so I could go back to getting this pussy devoured.

"Her full name, age, and if you can shed any light on who might've done this to her."

"Well, I can give you that. Her name is Amoy Simpson, and she is twenty years old. I don't know who might've done this to her. My sister is kind of secretive, so I have no idea."

"What's your name?"

"My name is Shari."

"Okay, Shari. She's in the ICU at the Westchester Medical Center in Valhalla."

"A'ight, cool." I hung up the phone with an attitude. I walked back over to where Devon was, and he looked a bit agitated. "I'm so sorry, boo. That was the police calling."

"For what? You in some sort of trouble or something?"

"Nah." I paused. "Some nigga beat up my sister, and she's in the ICU."

His facial expression changed from pleasant to uneasy.

"You all right?" I asked.

"Yeah, I'm good. I never knew you had a sister. You never mention her."

"Yes, I do have a big sister, but we're not that close."

"Oh, okay. So what did the police say happened to her?"

"He really didn't say. He just said she's in the ICU, fighting for her life."

"Damn, that's fucked up. You tryin'a go see her?"

That question kind of knocked me off my square. *Hmm, that's not a bad idea. Maybe that bitch can see us together and finally decide to tap out on life.*

"Yes, do you want to come with me?"

"Sure. This sound serious if she's in ICU. What monster would put their hands on a woman like that?"

"I don't know, but my sister be fucking every- and any-thing, so only God knows who did that to her. I thought she would've changed her ways after she got pregnant with my nephew."

"Your sister had a baby?"

"Yes, my nephew is about a week old now. Anyway, let me put on some sweats and a tank top, and then I'll be ready."

I walked into the room and grabbed my clothes. I was irritated to the core. I wanted to get fucked real good tonight. *Shit, what the fuck are they calling me for? I'm not God. I can't save this bitch.*

I got dressed, and we walked outside to his car. The entire ride to the hospital was kind of quiet. The only music was Plies playing in the background.

As I listened to the lyrics of "Issues," I wondered who he was so angry with. I looked out the window as he drove. I knew I should have been feeling some kind of emotions about what was going on with my sister, but honestly, I didn't. Matter of fact, if this bitch was gone, I could really be with Devon without having to deal with her old dramatic ass.

"You good, babe?" he said as he reached over and grabbed my hand.

"Yes, I'm fine!"

All along in my head, I was wondering what the fuck was going on in his head. I knew he didn't know that Amoy was my sister and my nephew was his child.

We finally pulled into the parking lot, and we parked. I wasn't too pressed to go up there, but I knew that it would seem suspicious if I didn't act concerned. We walked into the lobby in a hurry. I walked to the desk while Devon stood by the elevator. I glanced back at him while he checked his phone.

"Hello, yes. I'm here to see Amoy Simpson."

"Hold on a second please. She is in the ICU on the fourth floor."

"Thanks." I then walked over to where Devon was standing. Devon massaged my shoulders as we waited for the elevator to come back down.

We took the elevator up to the fourth floor. I walked to the desk and gave them my name. "Come with me," the nurse said.

She led us to a room, and I stopped at the door. I wasn't sure if I wanted to go in.

"Your sister is in here. Whoever did this to her tried to hurt her badly, and the detective said her newborn baby was feet away. She's in a medically induced coma. She has swelling on the brain, so we are trying to get some of that swelling down."

I walked closer to the bed with Devon close behind me. "What the . . ." Devon's voice trailed off.

I turned around to face him. The nigga looked like he had just seen a ghost.

"What's wrong, babe?" I quizzed, all along playing the fool. I knew exactly what was wrong. He noticed that it was Amoy, his baby mama.

"This your sister, yo?"

"Yes, this is my big sister, Amoy."

"Man, fuck! I need to get the fuck up outta here! Yo, what kind of sick game are y'all playing?" he yelled.

"Lower your voice! What are you talking 'bout? Talk to me. What's wrong?"

"Yo, B, I'm out." He pushed past me and out the door. I was about to run out after him but was stopped by a uniformed police officer and a plainclothes detective.

"Miss Simpson, I'm Detective Munroe, and this is Sergeant Claiborne. We would like to ask you a few questions if you don't mind."

I backed up into the room. I took a long stare at Amoy's face. Her shit was swollen, and bandages were around her face.

"Miss Simpson, who was that man you were with? He left in a hurry, mumbling something under his breath."

"Yes, that's my friend. He was just upset that someone would do this to my sister, that's all," I lied.

They continued asking me questions about my sister and who she was involved with. I didn't mention Devon at all because I wasn't sure what was going on.

"Miss Simpson, your nephew is on the pediatric floor. He is unharmed, but we need to know if you can care for him until your sister feels better."

"What? Care for him? My ass ain't got no damn kids. How the hell I'ma care for a newborn baby?" I hated to sound so cold, but there was no way I was going to take on that responsibility.

"I'm sorry. Does your sister have any other family member who might be able to care for the baby? I'm only asking because our next option is going to be foster care until your sister is able to care for him, and that's if she pulls through."

"The only family we have is our mama, and Amoy and her don't get along. I doubt she would want her child with our mama."

"Okay, thank you. Here is my card. If you think of anything that can assist us with our investigation, please don't hesitate to call us, and I promise you, Miss Simpson, we are going to do our best to bring the guilty party to justice."

I didn't respond. Instead, I just nodded my head. They both walked out of the room, and I was face-to-face with my bitch-ass sister. "Well, what have you gotten yourself into, my dear sister?" I said sarcastically.

She couldn't reply, so there was no need to keep on talking to her. I dialed Mama's number. "Hey, Ma."

"Hey, baby. I tried calling you earlier. Remember, you were supposed to take me to the social security office today?"

"Shit, I totally forgot. Anyway, I'm up here at Valhalla. Somebody tried to kill your daughter."

"What daughter? You seem fine, and that other bitch is dead to me. You heard how she handled me the other day, like I was the ground she walks on."

"Yes, Mother, I know, but they're not sure if she's gonna make it, so I was only letting you know."

"So are you taking me tomorrow? I really need to go see about this money."

"I'll call you in the morning." I hung up the phone. I was sick of this old dysfunctional-ass family. Sometimes I wondered why I couldn't be born in a different family or something.

I got on the elevator. I grabbed my cell phone and dialed Devon's number.

"Yoooo!"

"Where are you at? I'm coming down."

"A'ight, cool."

I pressed End and put the phone into my purse. The elevator reached the lobby, and I got out. Devon was standing by the side. I tried to gather my thoughts of what I was going to say to him. "We need to talk," I said as I stormed out.

As soon as I got into the car, I didn't waste any time. "You want to tell me what all that was about?"

"Yo, B, just drop it, okay?"

"Fuck nah. You were good before you walked into that room and spotted my sister. So you better start explaining."

"Did you know that your sister is my baby mama?"

I sat there, staring at him like I'd seen a ghost also. I didn't know how long I could hold that expression on my face. "What the fuck did you just say to me?"

"Yes, the person in that room is my son's mother, Amoy." He rubbed his hand all over his head. He was breathing heavily and behaving like he was about to pass out.

"So you're fucking telling me that I'm fucking my sister's man?"

"I didn't say I was her man. I said she was my baby mama."

"Same shit. Oh, my God, how . . . how did this happen? Eww, me and my sister fucking the same nigga? This is fucking nasty." I started to cry.

"Ma, don't do this. Oh, man. I didn't know that was your sister. Remember, we met by accident. None of this was planned. Oh, my God."

I wasn't trying to hear none of that. I continued crying like I had just lost my best friend. He reached over and hugged me tight. "I'm sorry, babe. For what it's worth, shawty might be your sister, but she ain't got shit on you. For real. If I had a choice, I would choose you. I haven't known you that long, but you're cool as fuck, and you've got that good pussy," he tried to joke.

He had my full attention when he said that if he had to choose, he'd choose me. Shit, that was all I needed to hear. I was going to make him my man, whether my sister liked it or not.

He drove me home, and we continued what we had started earlier. Only this time, it wasn't no lovemaking. It was more like aggressive fucking. I wasn't in the apartment completely when he grabbed me up and started kissing me. He lifted me up and threw me on the couch. I pulled my sweatpants down and ripped my underwear off. He then slid his dick inside of me. Thank God I was wet because otherwise he would've ripped my insides. I was kind of loving the aggressive behavior, but I couldn't help but wonder what brought it on. I didn't have time to focus on that. He started tearing my pussy up. I grabbed him tight as I tried to throw this pussy on him. Homeboy was a beast, but I bet ain't nobody told him that I was a lioness in the bedroom.

After about an hour of fucking, he finally busted. Only thing was that this time he pulled out. I smiled inside because, just a few days ago, he wasn't worried when he came all up inside of me. Let me find out he was being cautious. *Ha-ha. Niggas are funny.*

"Where's the bathroom at, ma?" he asked.

"The first left." I pointed.

He walked off to the bathroom, and I walked to the kitchen to grab paper towels so that I could wipe between my legs. By the time I walked back into the living room, he was fully dressed. He still seemed agitated. "Babe, are you okay?" I decided to act like I cared about his mood.

"Yeah, ma, I'm good. I'm just a little irritated about all this, you know? I need to know who did this shit to my baby mama. And what did them doctors say? Is she gonna make it?"

I was kind of thrown off by his line of questioning. "I'm not sure. They said she had swelling on her brain. Why didn't you stay and ask them?"

"Man, I was too fucked up to stay in that room. I couldn't believe that somebody did that to her, and then it fucked me up that y'all are sisters. Man, all this shit is too much for real."

As soon as he said that, his phone started ringing. He looked at his caller ID and then looked at me. "Yo, I've got to bounce. I'ma hit you later on to check on your sister and see how you're doing."

"All right," I managed to say.

Truthfully, I was kind of happy he left. I needed a minute to get my thoughts together. Everything that happened over the last couple of hours had all happened so fast, and my head was spinning. It was kind of suspicious to me that Devon was acting all nonchalant about what had happened to Amoy. It was strange that this was the same dude she used to brag to me about. None of this made sense. This was his son's mother, and what was even more interesting was that not once did he ask me about his son. A regular nigga would be worried about his child, even if he didn't fool with the mother.

My brain was overloaded, and I needed a damn drink, a very strong one at that.

I decided to take a shower, and then I poured myself a drink. I checked, but I was out of weed, and it was too late to be hitting up the weed man.

CHAPTER FOURTEEN

Amoy

Ten Days Later

I was thirsty as hell. I felt like I could drink a gallon of water. I pressed the buzzer for the nurse.

"Yes, may I help you?"

"Can I please get some water?"

"Sure, give me a few seconds."

I was still trying to fathom everything that had happened to me in the last few days. The doctors informed me that I had swelling on my brain, but thank God they were able to bring the swelling down. All I was really concerned with was the well-being of my baby. I was told that he was in foster care until I felt better. My heart sank just thinking that I wasn't able to care for my child. Tears welled up in my eyes as I recalled what transpired the day that Devon came over to the house. As soon as I woke up, the nurse told me that the police wanted to talk with me. I felt a sharp pain ripping through my chest as tears flowed from my face. The physical pain was there, but it was the mental pain that hurt. I racked my brain, trying to figure out how the man I loved, the father of my child, could do this to me. What did I do for him to start hating me like this? I couldn't stop the tears from flowing, and honestly, I wasn't trying.

"Hello, Miss Simpson, my name is Detective Munroe, and this is Sergeant Claiborne. How are you feeling?"

"I'm feeling a little better." I tried to smile.

"Well, we spoke to the doctor, and he said you're one lucky young lady. Somebody did a number on you."

"Yeah, well, did y'all lock him up?"

"Him who? This is our first time getting to talk with you, and we're hoping you can give us a name and a motive."

"Devon Guthrie. He is my son's father."

"Can you give us an idea of how all of this went down?" I watched as the detective took his pen out of his pocket and started writing in his notebook.

I continued telling him how it all started out. I didn't mention Marquise's name. Instead, I said a friend was visiting. Tears rolled down my face as I told them what had happened that landed me in the hospital.

"Do you know his address?"

"Umm, yes. He lives with his wife over on California Road." I tried to remember the exact address.

"His wife? So this gentleman is married?" He looked at me suspiciously.

"Yes, he's got a wife." I wasn't in the mood to entertain any foolishness. I was really tired and stressed out about my damn child.

I gave them the address and answered a few more of their questions.

"Okay, Miss Simpson, we are going to get a warrant, so we can go pick up Mr. Guthrie and get him off the streets. In the meantime, please don't contact him, and if he contacts you, please call us immediately." He placed his card on the table beside the bed.

They stayed another five minutes, and then they left. My heart was hurting because I knew that Devon was going to be arrested, but there was no way I was going to lie for him. This wasn't the first time he had put his hands on me, but I was going to make sure this was the last time. Yeah, I loved his ass, but I knew he didn't love me because there was no way he would've tried to kill me. The thought of not being there to care for my child hurt really badly. I just hoped they caught him sooner rather than later.

I was about to lie down when I heard my room door open. I wished these nurses would just give me a break for a few hours. I was mentally drained and just wanted to rest.

"Hey, boo." My sissy walked in.

"Hey, I was just going to call you. I was wondering why I haven't heard from you. The nurse told me you came up here once."

"Yeah, I did. You were so fucked up. I broke down. I couldn't bear to see you like that anymore. Sis, you just don't know how I felt when I thought I was losing you," she said.

I looked at my sister, and something wasn't right. It was more like she was performing and wasn't sincere about what she was saying. I brushed it off. Maybe I was looking too deep into things. "Well, thank God you didn't lose me."

She walked over and gave me a hug. I hugged her as I fought back tears. I loved this girl right here. She and my son were the only two people I had in the world, and I was grateful that I had another chance with them.

"So listen, I was waiting for you to wake up so I could ask you, what the hell happened to you? Who did this shit to you?"

I thought about the question she had just asked, and I was embarrassed to tell my little sister that it was the nigga I had bragged so much about who had done this to me. She sat there, staring at me, and knowing my sister, she wasn't going to go for "I don't know."

"It was Devon!"

The room got so quiet that you could hear a pin drop!

"Come again? Did you say Devon?" She looked at me like she was disgusted.

"Yes, he is the one who beat my damn face in," I confirmed.

"I can't believe that shit. After how you told me he treats you all good and shit, why the fuck would he turn around and beat you the fuck up, right after you had his son?" Her tone wasn't so friendly anymore. I felt more like she was getting defensive and shit.

"Why would I lie to you? I am sitting here, telling you. He did this to me."

"Hmmm, well, tell me the full story. I want to know what the fuck happened that day."

I wasn't feeling her attitude. Something wasn't right. My sister seemed like she was more worried about Devon and not sympathetic about what had happened to me.

I sat there and told her about everything that went down, from me fucking Marquise in the beginning and not being sure if he was my son's daddy or if Devon was. I then went on to tell her about Devon coming to the apartment while Marquise was there.

"So did you tell the police all this?"

"All what?"

"Everything that you just told me."

"Yeah, I did. They're out there looking for him now."

"Damn, that's fucked up!" she blurted out.

"What's fucked up, Shari?"

"Oh, nothing. I was just thinking that, if he did this, he's fucked up for that."

"Why do you keep saying 'if'? I'm fucking telling you Devon is responsible for this, and he didn't give two fucks that his baby was in the other room. I hope they find him and lock his ass up." I was starting to get angry.

"Well, I'm happy you're feeling better, but I've got some errands to run. I'll call you later."

"Damn, bitch, you just got here."

"Yeah, but shit, I've got errands to run." She reached over, kissed me on the forehead, and out the door she went. No "love you, sis" or anything. Her behavior today was kind of strange, but shit, my sister was strange. I usually joked and said she was special in her own way. I closed my eyes and tried to doze off.

CHAPTER FIFTEEN

Kennedy

I turned over and looked at the time. The clock on my nightstand read 11:55 p.m. I looked at the other side of the bed and realized that my dear husband still hadn't made it home. This shit was definitely going from bad to worse. This bastard used to stay up with my ass twenty-four seven. Now all of a sudden he started disappearing. I thought about calling his phone but quickly dismissed that idea. I was not the woman who went around trying to see where this nigga was at. First off, I was pretty sure he knew where he lived, so if his ass wanted to come home, trust me, he would've brought his black ass home. I turned back over and tried to fall back asleep. I really hated this man trying to stir up my evil side. I really hated when men thought that they could do any old shit to a woman and we were just supposed to sit back and take that shit.

It was eight o'clock in the morning. I felt like I didn't get any sleep, and on top of that, my soul was irritated. I got up, brushed my teeth, and decided to make myself a cup of coffee. I had some serious decisions to make and definitely needed caffeine to start my day. I walked downstairs and immediately saw Devon's shoes at the door, so I went to investigate. There this nigga was, sprawled out on my damn expensive Italian-made couch. He knew damn well there was no sleeping allowed on my shit. I walked my happy ass over and poked him in the face. He didn't flinch, so I did it again, but this time, this fool jumped up.

"What the hell are you doing?"

"I don't think that's any way to greet your wife. What time did yo' ass sneak in here this morning?"

"Sneak? Kennedy, why the hell do you think I'm a little boy? I was out with my niggas, drinking, and didn't realize how late it was, that's all."

"Get yo' ass up off my damn couch. You should've stayed your ass over at that whore's house."

This man looked at me like he thought I was joking around. I stared him down and folded my arms so he could know I was dead-ass serious.

"Man, you're tripping, B." He stood up and looked at me. If looks could kill, I would be one dead bitch. He stormed off, mumbling some shit under his breath. I really didn't give a fuck about what he was saying. I spent good money on my furniture, and I didn't care who it was—I didn't want nobody sleeping on my shit.

"You better bathe ya ass before you get in my damn bed!" I yelled up the stairs.

"Man, fuck you, Kennedy! All this material shit that you worship ain't worth shit if I'm not here. Keep pushing and you'll lose a good nigga."

I walked up the stairs so I could properly address this fool. "A good nigga? You're fucking hilarious. You're a low-level nigga out here fucking these dirty-ass bitches. I took you in, thinking you wanted better, but it just goes to show that you can take the nigga out of the hood, but you can't take the hood out of the nigga. You think I'm weak 'cause I'm older, but you've got it wrong, baby boy.

I can fuck myself with these ten fingers, and I've got my own damn money, so don't you think for a minute that I need a man. Yes, it's good to have someone to spend my life with, but trust me, I'm far from happy. You're more of a liability to my happiness, and that's not good."

"I'm not going to sit here and listen to you talk to me like I'm beneath you. Growing up, I ain't have no mother. Matter of fact, I don't know that bitch, so I know damn well I don't need no bitch at all. If I make you so unhappy, why don't you leave me the fuck alone? Huh? Why are you still trying to keep me on a fucking leash? I know why. You don't really want me, but you're scared that one of these young bitches might scoop me up." He chuckled.

I was ready to throw his ass out of my house, but I heard the doorbell ring, which was strange. I rarely had visitors, and it was too damn early for Jehovah's Witnesses to be ringing my damn bell.

I shot him a dirty look to let him know that this was far from over. I stomped down the stairs. I took a peek through the peephole. *The police? What the fuck are the police doing here?* The only way to find out was to open the door.

"Good morning." I smiled at the fine officers. I meant fine literally.

"Good morning, ma'am. My name is Sergeant Claiborne, and this is Detective Munroe. We are looking for Devon Guthrie."

"That's my husband, and if you don't mind me asking, what is the problem, Sergeant?"

"Ma'am, is he here?" he asked in a not-so-friendly tone.

"Yes, Sergeant. Hold on a second."

"No, ma'am, call him down here. Who else is in the residence?"

"He is the only one in there."

"Ma'am, please step back," he said as he pulled his firearm while he and his partner pushed into the house.

I was shocked as hell. This was my house, and they had no respect for that. I would definitely make a complaint about this, but right now, there was a bigger issue at hand. I stepped inside to see what the hell was going on. "Put your hands up before I shoot you," I heard one officer holler.

"I ain't do shit. What the fuck y'all arresting me for? I've been in here, sleeping. Y'all can ask my wife. Kennedy, baby, tell them I've been here!" he screamed.

"Put your hands behind your back. I'm not going to tell you again," the detective yelled.

"Aaarrrrgh, you just stung me. Aaargghhh, baby, make sure you're recording this. We're going to sue they ass!" He screamed some more.

As a wife, I wanted to see what was going on with him, but part of me didn't give a fuck. The nigga was talking shit to me a few minutes ago, and now he was screaming for me. They dragged him down the stairs. All along, he was hollering and screaming, "Police brutality!"

They dragged him out of the house, and I followed them outside. They placed him in another police car that was waiting, and the detective walked over to his unmarked car. I walked over to his car. He was writing in a notepad.

"Detective, that's my husband, and I don't know what's going on."

"Mrs. Guthrie, we arrested your husband for battery and assault on a young lady."

"Say what? Are you sure? My husband was in here, sleeping."

"We are one hundred percent sure. He banged her up really bad, and she identified him."

"Thank you. Where are y'all taking him to?"

"The officer is taking him to jail. He will go in front of the magistrate for possible bond."

"Thank you."

"Have a good day, ma'am."

The police car had left a few minutes ago, and the detective pulled off. I looked around to see if my neighbors had seen what was going on. It was early, so chances were that they were still in bed. I breathed hard as I walked back up the driveway.

I closed the door behind me and leaned up against it. All of this was crazy as hell. Who the fuck did this man beat up? His ass might've signed a check that he couldn't cash this time. I walked up the stairs, still trying to gather my thoughts. I wished that I had someone to talk to, someone who could help me get a better understanding of what was going on.

I grabbed my phone and dialed Christopher's number. I knew it was early, and I had told him that he could take the day off, but shit, it was an emergency. I needed his ass to come over.

"Hey, boss lady," he answered.

"Christopher, it's early, I know, but the police just came here and arrested Devon for some sort of battery. I don't want to say too much on the phone, so I need you to come over."

"Wow! What the hell has he done now?"

"I don't know, so just come on over."

"All right, boss lady. Let me take a quick shower, and I'll be there."

I hung up the phone. I heard Devon's phone going off. I glanced around, but I didn't see it. I sat down on the bed, but the phone was becoming an annoyance. *Where the hell is this damn phone?* I pulled the sheet off the bed and grabbed the pillow when I heard it fall. I walked to his side of the bed and grabbed it off the carpet. I checked to see who was calling. There were over thirty missed calls. There was no name to the number, so I got curious. Who the hell was calling a married man over thirty times? I pulled the number up and called it. It rang a few times and then went to voicemail. Hmm, that was strange. Someone was desperate to talk to him, but now they didn't want to pick up. Before I could scroll through the phone, it started ringing again.

"Hello. Good morning."

There was a long pause and heavy breathing.

"Hello? Say something," I said.

"Can I speak to Devon?"

"Devon is not here, but you can leave a message."

"Nah, that's all right." She hung up the phone.

Hmm, I guess that was one of his hoes. The bitch sounded like she was scared or something. I threw the phone on the bed. I wasn't in the mood to entertain any foolishness this morning. I took a quick shower before Christopher came. I let the water beat down on my body as I allowed my thoughts to run freely. I had one thing on my mind, and that was murder.

I decided to make Christopher some breakfast. *Shit, I might even lay him down and put this pussy on him.* See, I knew Christopher had been checking for me ever since I hired him. He was always complimenting me, and oftentimes he threw out hints that he may be interested in me. I never really looked at him like that. Plus, I wasn't the kind of woman who fucked around with more than one man. I was really trying to be faithful to Devon, but his two-timing ass had proved that he couldn't be faithful and had no desire to be. The saying was true: you can fuck a nigga good, suck his dick, cook and clean for him, and he'll still find a reason to fuck another bitch. I knew one damn thing. I was not going to be a fool for this boy.

I heard the doorbell ringing. I knew it was Christopher, so I walked over and opened the door. "Good morning, sir."

"Good morning, beautiful."

"Come in here. I cooked you breakfast." I walked off into the kitchen.

"Uh-huh, it's smelling good up in here," he said in his Southern accent.

"Sit down." I placed a plate of bacon, eggs, and toast in front of him.

"Thank you, ma'am. You do know the way to a man's heart is through his stomach, right?"

"So I've heard, but I do know that you can feed a man and still not have his heart." I smiled at him as I took a seat across from him.

We sat there quietly as we ate, but I was curious about what could've happened between Devon and whoever.

"So what the hell happened? You followed him around this week. Did you see anything as far as him beating up somebody?"

"Nah, I ain't seen no shit like that. Matter of fact, I sent you all the pics that were taken this week. He frequents this one chick who lives in a building in Mount Vernon. He also went to this other female's house. She lives on Fulton Avenue. The other day, I did see him storm out of the building like a madman, but other than that, I haven't seen anything out of the ordinary."

"So you're telling me that he's not only screwing around with one bitch, but he's got another bitch somewhere out there?" I cut my bacon with an attitude.

"Yes, that's how it looks. I don't know why you don't let that boy go because, obviously, he is not trying to be a husband. There are good men out here who would love to get a chance with you, you know?"

I looked at him and smiled. "Like who, you?" I put some eggs into my mouth while staring at him seductively.

"Kennedy, you already know how I feel about you. There's nothing in this world I wouldn't do for you, but you already know that."

"Christopher, regardless of how my husband is out there behaving, believe it or not, I used to love him, but those days are gone. He disrespects me in the worst way. Not only is he cheating, but he didn't respect me enough to wear a goddamn condom. What if this little bitch had some kind of STD?" I sat there, looking out in space.

"Kennedy, you're a smart woman, and I'm not saying this because I want you. Hell, I would love to call you my woman, but I know you're a married woman. But like I was saying, he's young, and I'm not saying young niggas can't be faithful, but he's not. He is mooching off you, driving the car you bought, and is just out there, slinging dick. You're a woman of substance. You don't need that. You need a man who can love you the way you need to be loved. Hold you when you're hurting. A man to let you know you're the only woman who matters."

I sat there taking in each and every word he spilled out. Tears welled up in my eyes because I felt like a fool. I really thought Devon loved me and was really into me. I thought age didn't matter to him and that he was happy with me, but now I was seeing that I was all wrong. I was only a money machine to him.

"Don't cry, my love. We all play the fool at one time or another." He got up, walked over to me, and wrapped his big, muscular arms around me. I inhaled his masculine scent as I leaned my head on his shoulder. I needed this, someone to just hold me. On the outside, it seemed like I was strong, but deep down, I was hurting. I tried hard to hide it, but it was unbearable. I just gave in and let all my burdens out on his shoulder.

After minutes of him rubbing my back and kissing my face, I finally managed to get my crying under control. "Why are you single? What's your story, Mr. PI?"

He let me go and walked back to the table. "What's my story? What makes you think I've got one?"

"We all have a story."

"I was married for over twenty-five years. She was my high school sweetheart. But no matter what I did to please her, she was never happy. Eventually, she ran off with the lawn boy."

"Really? Just like that?"

"Just like that. No warning, no nothing. At first, I was bitter, and I wanted to kill that son of a bitch. But as time progressed, I started realizing that she did me a favor. I was now free."

"Wow! It's crazy how you can love a person, give them your all, and they're still not satisfied. I know one thing— this is my last time saying 'I do.' I'm done with marriage."

"I said the same thing un—"

"Hold that thought," I said as I cut him off. I heard my cell phone ringing. I walked into the hallway and grabbed it off the table where I had left it.

I looked at the number. I didn't recognize it, but I still answered it. "Hello?"

"Babe, it's me, Devon. I just went in front of the magistrate, and she gave me bond. It's twelve thousand."

"What I'm trying to comprehend is why the fuck you are calling me and not calling the bitch you're fucking."

"Man, babe, this ain't the time to be discussing this kind of thing. That bitch pressed bogus charges on me 'cause I told her I love you and want to be with you."

"Devon, to be honest, I don't give a fuck one way or the other. I want you out of my house and out of my life for good."

"Kennedy, baby, just come and get me, and we can talk about this when I get home. I love you."

"So you're telling me you beat up your mistress, and now you're on the phone, begging your wife to come bond you out? This is some funny shit," I spat.

"Kennedy, baby, I love you, and that bitch ain't my mis—"

I hung my phone up before he could finish telling me that lie. I let out a long sigh and walked back into the kitchen.

"That was Devon's ass, calling from lockup, trying to tell me that I need to come and get him."

"So are you going to get him?"

"Christopher, I'm far from dumb. You think I'm going to spend my money to bond him out so he can get out here and do the same shit he was doing?"

"Mrs. Guthrie, I know you're one tough cookie." He chuckled.

"Do you have the address of the whore with the baby?"

"Yes, I do, but it wouldn't be wise for you to go see her. She might not even know about you."

"Christopher, just text me the address. I'm grown, and I know what's wise for me and what's not," I said in a little more aggressive tone than I meant to.

"Yes, ma'am. You're the boss." He started searching his phone.

I got up and picked up his plate. It was time to clean up and get Christopher on his way. What he learned was that I didn't like a man telling me what to do. I danced to my own beat, and that was the way it would always be.

"I texted it to you. So now that your husband is locked up, what do you want me to do?"

"Do you know of any good divorce lawyers? One that knows what he's doing? I plan on taking every damn thing with me. His ass won't get not one dime of my

money. When I'm done with his ass, he will be on somebody's street, begging for donations."

"Well, I know quite a few. I will forward their information to you when I get to the office."

"Well, just sit tight. I am not bonding him out, so I
know he'll be in there for a while. I plan on serving him
divorce papers while he's there."

"Okay, I gotcha. Well, call me if you need me. Oh, yeah,
that breakfast was delicious."

I just looked at him and smiled. He walked through
the door, and I locked it behind him. I walked back to the
kitchen and placed the dirty dishes in the dishwasher.

CHAPTER SIXTEEN

Shari

I was literally losing control of my sanity. I knew I had just met Devon, but my feelings for him were growing very quickly. I'd never met a nigga who made me feel like this before. I hadn't been able to eat or drink for a whole day. I'd been calling his phone. I was trying to tell him that my sister pressed charges on him, but when he didn't answer, I knew something was up. I was even more surprised when an elderly woman answered his phone. I was curious to know who the hell she was, but I didn't ask because it might have just been his mama. I was thrown off because I hoped his grown behind didn't live at home. The bitch wasn't too friendly, so I just hung up.

I thought about calling my sister to see if she heard anything, but I knew that would have only triggered her suspicions. I picked up the phone to call the jail, but I remembered that I didn't know his last name. Shit, don't judge me. His last name didn't mean shit to me before now. I threw the phone down and lay across the bed.

"God, please let him be okay," I said out loud.

I heard my phone ringing, and I snatched it up without looking at the caller ID. "Hello."

"Bitch, I've been calling you," Kaysia spat.

"Okay, and? I was busy."

"Damn, what's up with the fucking attitude?"

"I don't have an attitude. I just don't have time to deal with your shit right now."

"Yo! What the fuck has gotten into you? You didn't start acting like this until you started fucking that boy."

"There you go, being fucking jealous and shit. This ain't got nothing to do with Devon. This is about you. Just because I gave you the pussy a few times don't mean you get to know my every move."

"You know what? I'm going to let what you just said fly because this is so not you. We were friends even before we started messing around, so all this doesn't make sense. I haven't heard from you, so I was just checking on you. That's all."

"All right, you checked on me. See? I'm good. Now bye." I hung up before she could say anything else. I threw the phone back on the bed. *God, why does she have to be like that? Why can't she just be my fucking friend when I need one?*

My phone started ringing again. "Man, I'ma cuss her ass out for real," I said as I reached for the phone. "Hello," I yelled into the phone.

"You have a collect call from Mount Vernon City Jail."

My heart sank. That bitch was serious when she said she had pressed charges. I hurried up and pressed five.

"Hey, boo," I yelled into the phone excitedly.

"Hey, babe."

"Man, what the fuck happened? I've been trying to call you, but I got no answer, and then yo' mama answered the phone."

"Listen, Shari, yo' sister lied to them people 'bout me being the one who beat her up. She knows damn well that I've been nowhere near her after I dropped her off the day she came home from the hospital. I need you to post my bond. I've got some money stashed away, but I can't get to it from in here, and I can't trust no one else right now."

I paused. *Where the fuck does he think I'm going to get money from?*

"Babe, you still there?"

"Yeah, I'm here. How much is your bond?"

"It's twelve thousand, but you only have to give the bondsman ten percent of that. I know this bond dude I used to deal with when I was in the streets. Shit, his name is Pete, but I can't remember his number, but google the business under Right Away Bails Bond. Just tell him it's for me, and he will bond me out once you give him the money."

"Uh, I . . ."

"Baby, come on, you've got to do this for me. I need you," he pleaded.

"All right, I got you. By the way, what's your last name?"

"It's Guthrie, and please, baby, get on it for me. I can't wait to get out of here so I can really treat you the way you deserve to be treated."

"Baby, calm down. I've got you. Give me a few hours."

"All right, baby. I have to go, but I'll be waiting."

He hung the phone up, but I still sat there, holding the phone to my ear. I was still yearning just to hear him call me baby. I finally put the phone down. My sister was a fucking bitch for doing that. She knew damn well that boy didn't beat her ass up. I bet you money she was just angry that he decided not to fuck with her anymore. *Old bitter-ass bitch better get her story right and tell who the fuck really did that shit to her.*

I quickly switched my thoughts to the issue at hand. I fucked with Devon, but how the fuck was I expected to get that money to bond him out? I knew I had some money stashed away in a shoebox under my bed. It was my rainy-day money that I had saved up. I swore I didn't want to touch it, but the more I thought about him being in that hellhole, the more I was leaning toward using it.

After all, he did say he would pay me back, and I had no reason to doubt him on that.

I got up and kneeled down on the floor. I pulled out the shoebox and opened it. I took a long sigh. After I got the money, I googled the business that he gave me. I got the phone number and dialed it. I hoped he was right that this dude would bond him out because a bitch didn't have a job, and most of these bond companies would need proof of one.

After I got off the phone with the bondsman, I called Mama. The bondsman agreed to bond him out but told me I needed a cosigner. Since Kaysia was upset with me, my only other option was Mama. I just hoped her ass was strung out today because God knows I didn't want to deal with her shenanigans.

"Hey, Mama," I said as soon as she answered the phone.

"Hey, baby. Why the hell you keep lying that you're going to take me to the social security office?"

I wanted to check her ass really quick, but I held my composure. I had to remind myself that I needed her right now. "Mama, I am so sorry. I promise you, I'll take you tomorrow morning. But I need your help right now."

"And what might that be with?"

"I need to bond a friend out, and I need another person's signature on it."

"Hell nah, you done lost your mind. I ain't putting my name on shit. You know how niggas have a way of not showing up for court. Shit, you shouldn't put your name on shit either."

"Mama, c'mon. I will pay." I knew she was a dopefiend, and there was no way she was going to let money slip by her.

"Hmmm, now you're talking. How much?"

"I'll give you fifty dollars."

"Fifty dollars. What the fuck you think I am, a junky?"

"Ma, no, I don't think that. How much do you want?" I asked reluctantly.

"Well, let's see. Hmmmm."

I was one inch from going off on her ass. This was very important, and she was playing fucking games with me.

"Man, c'mon wit' this bullshit."

"Damn, why you yelling? You needed my help, remember?"

"Mama, you're starting to piss me off. Let's see how you're going to get to the social security office tomorrow."

"I need two hundred fifty dollars."

This bitch done lost her fucking mind, but I didn't have the time to go back and forth with her. "A'ight, man. Get ready. I'm coming to pick you up."

"Okay, daughter."

I hung the phone up, feeling disgusted. I wished her ass would behave like a parent once in a while. Not every time, but at least once.

I jumped up off the bed. I needed to take a quick shower and get dressed. I had to meet the bondsman in an hour. I wasted no time washing my ass. I quickly put lotion on my body and put on a pair of tights with a wife beater along with my Michael Kors sandals. I took one last glance in the mirror before I sprayed myself with Amore for Women. I couldn't wait to grab my boo up in my arms.

Before you knew it, I was out the door and into my car. Damn, this car needed to be cleaned out. Shit, I planned on getting a better whip in a few 'cause this wasn't cutting it anymore, and to be blunt, I looked too damn good to be driving ugly Betsy. I pulled up at Mama's house and honked the horn. *God, I hope this lady is ready.*

I was parked out there a good minute before she came strolling out of her building. She looked a damn mess in that red dress and red hat. I just looked and shook my damn head. "You got your ID?"

"Yup, right here." She tapped her old red boot-ass purse.

I pulled off and headed to the jail. I hoped my baby knew that his baby was on her way to get him. I also hoped that he knew that, after I got him out, ain't no more fucking around with my sister. Matter of fact, he needed a damn DNA test 'cause he might not be her baby daddy either.

I almost acted a fool down at them people's jail. We sat out in the lobby, waiting damn near four hours for them to bring him down. I had no idea what was taking so long, and then the bitch at the window had the nerve to tell me to be patient. That bitch better be happy that I didn't show my black ass.

"Let me get my money now," Mama demanded from the back seat. I saw Devon give me a quick glance, so I grabbed my purse, took the money out, and handed it to her.

I dropped her off, and then we headed to my house. We were quiet the entire ride. There was so much I wanted to say, but I held it in because he looked like he was bothered. I parked, and we got out and walked into my building.

"Welcome home, baby," I said as I planted a kiss on his cheek.

"Damn, you have no idea how much a nigga appreciates you." He squeezed my ass and pulled me closer to him.

"Man, I can't believe my motherfucking sister did that shit to you."

"Man, I'm still trying to figure out why the fuck she would say that shit. I know she's mad and shit that I 'on't want to be wit' her, but to get a nigga locked up is just fucking evil. Did you talk to her?"

"Nah, I ain't got shit to say to that bitch, for real. I know her ass is a liar, but to get a nigga locked up, you just don't do shit like that. I thought about going over there, but if I did, I would've been down at the jail also 'cause I woulda torn that ass up."

"Man, I'ma need to talk to her. She's got to drop this fucking charge. I'ma get me a lawyer ASAP so I can get these charges dropped. Damn, I need some damn clothes. A nigga needs to bathe." He smelled his armpit.

"I can take you to get some clothes and pick up your car."

"Damn, B. I need to talk to you real quick. Sit down."

My heart dropped! The look on this nigga's face told me it was something serious. "What's up?" I stared him in the eyes.

"If we're going to be together, I've got to come clean to you."

"Oh, okay."

"Well, you know that I was messing with your sister, but I didn't tell you that I was married, and that woman you talked to wasn't my mother but my wife—"

Slap! Slap! Slap! Without thinking, I slapped him back-to-back out of anger. I was pissed the fuck off. Here I was thinking that I finally got him from my sister, only to find out this nigga was fucking married.

"Yo, when the fuck were you planning on telling me that you were married? Matter of fact, your ass should've told me that shit before you got my pussy."

"Man, chill out! I wanted to tell you, but I was so fucking gone over you that I didn't want to risk losing you."

"Boy, bye with that old lame-ass line."

"Listen, ma, I know I fucked up, but I didn't think it mattered. Shit, you know I'm the nigga your sister was fucking, and you still chose to fuck around with me."

That was low as fuck! How dare he try to compare the two? I never gave a fuck about my sister and still didn't give a fuck about that bitch!

"You're wrong for that shit, but just so you know, that ain't your fucking son, so you can shut up about being the baby daddy," I blurted out. *Now let's see how deep that shit cuts his ass.*

"Wha . . . what the fuck did you just say? I know you're upset, but don't play like that, B."

"Playing? Do I look like I'm playing? I'm dead-ass serious. That baby is not yours. He is her ex-boyfriend's baby."

"How the fuck do you know this?" he yelled.

"Because she's my damn sister, and she told me when I went up to the hospital."

"And what else did she tell you?"

"That you were the one who beat her up. So now that we're talking about it, did you do it?"

"Man, c'mon, do I look like a woman beater? I ain't never put my motherfucking hands on your sister. I should've, now that you're telling me that bullshit. I'm mad as fuck that the bitch played me. Had me giving her money and buying shit for a baby who's not mine."

"Well, calm down. You can always get a blood test to prove you're not the daddy 'cause you know her ass might try to get child support out of you."

"Man, fuck! I'm so fucking mad right now." His voice cracked.

I started rubbing his back. "Baby, listen, don't worry about that bitch. You've got me . . ." Before I could finish my statement, I remembered his wife. "By the way, where the fuck was your wife? Why didn't her ass bond you out? I mean, I'm just the bitch you're fucking on the side."

"Man, don't even mention her ass. Somehow, she found out about your sister, and now she's trippin' and shit. I called her ass when I first got locked up, and that bitch laughed in my face and hung up. That's all right though 'cause I've got something for that ass. Hey, babe, don't even worry 'bout yo' money. I have 'bout eighty grand stashed away in an account. Trust me, baby girl, you're good. I do need a ride over to the house, though, so I can get some clothes."

While he was talking, I was trying to figure out how I was going to get my hands on that eighty grand. See, yes, I was falling in love and shit, but pussy wasn't free, and I damn sure wasn't fucking for free.

"Okay, cool. I'll drop you off over there. I hope there's not no drama 'cause I'm petty as hell and don't give a fuck if that's your wife or not."

CHAPTER SEVENTEEN

Amoy

I was happy that I was finally released from the hospital, and a social worker brought my baby to me. I held him close to my chest while planting kisses all over him. It had only been weeks, but it seemed like I had been gone for years. I missed my little man so much that words couldn't even explain it.

The social worker was nice enough to drop us off at home, and she gave me her card just in case I needed her. That was very nice of her, considering my own damn family didn't give a fuck about me. I wasn't going to lie. It shocked the hell out of me that my sister was acting all stank toward me. Ever since I could remember, I'd been there for her, and the one time I needed her, she couldn't be there. Maybe I expected too much from people by expecting them to treat me the same way I treated them.

The first thing I did when I walked into the apartment was pop one of the Percocet pills that the doctor had prescribed. This headache was becoming a nuisance. The constant throbbing and blurred vision were really impacting my life. I tried my best to let the doctors know that I was feeling better because I wanted them to discharge me so I could get my baby. I didn't trust anyone taking care of little man. Plus, I knew he missed his mama.

I jumped in the shower after I straightened up my apartment. As soon as the water started pounding on my body, the tears started to flow down my face. My soul was tired from all the stress that I'd been through over the past month. I knew I'd done some fucked-up shit throughout my lifetime, but I didn't deserve what happened to me. I should've kept walking that day when Devon drove up beside me on the street. I didn't hold back the tears. I allowed them to flow while I washed, hoping that I would feel better when I got out.

I heard my doorbell ringing. I wasn't expecting anyone, at least not today. My heart jumped. *What if it's Devon?* No, I quickly dismissed that thought because he was locked up. The last time I checked, he was still there. I hurried up and put on a pair of shorts with a tank top. I walked over to the door, kind of cautious of who was on the other side. I took a peek through the peephole. I saw a nicely dressed lady standing there. "Who is it?" I yelled, but I got no response.

That was when I remembered the hospital telling me that a social worker would come by to talk to me, being that I was a victim of domestic abuse. *Damn, they didn't waste any time,* I thought as I opened the door.

"Hello, I didn't know you were coming by this soon." I smiled at the well-groomed woman.

"Hello, Miss Simpson," she said in the warmest voice I'd ever heard.

"Come on in. Excuse the messiness. As you know, I'm just coming home from the hospital and haven't had the time to clean up. Sit down."

"I prefer to stand up, Miss Simpson, and I'm sure you're mistaking me for someone else."

"What do you mean? You're with social services, right?" I turned around to face her.

"No, my name is Kennedy Guthrie." Her voice changed. It was no longer warm and friendly.

That name . . . that name, I pondered. That was when it hit me—that was Devon's last name. "I don't know you. Who are you?"

"I'm the wife of your baby daddy." She chuckled.

"I have no idea what you're talking about, but, lady, you've got the wrong one. Please get out of my house before I call the damn police."

"Sit your ass down and calm down!" she said in a motherly tone.

"Bitch, how dare you come up in my shit, talking crazy? I don't know who the fuck you think you are, but I tell you what, you've got the wrong one."

"Ha-ha. You know, you remind me of myself over twenty years ago. I was the one who cussed people out, quick to tear another woman down over a man. I had to grow up to realize that it's not the other woman's fault. Matter of fact, it's these old trifling-ass niggas who are playing us women, and we are dumb enough to fight each other over them."

"You can quit acting like you're Mother Teresa. I'm pretty sure you didn't come over to preach this holy shit to me. So, lady, why the fuck are you here? Did your husband ask you to come over and beg me to drop the charge? Because it ain't happening."

"My husband is locked up, and no, I came over here to talk to you on my own. I would never encourage you to drop the charge. If that bastard put his hands on you, his ass deserves to be behind bars. His ass called me, begging to get bonded out, but I hung up in his face. I'm far from being stupid."

I didn't know what to think about this bitch! My mind was on my gun in the room. I just prayed to God her ass didn't come in here on no bullshit 'cause, the way my mental state was set up, I could murder a bitch right now.

"So, lady, I'm asking you again, what the fuck do you want from me?"

"I just wanted to talk with you. I wanted to know how long my husband and you have been sleeping around."

"Sleeping around? You make it seem like it was a fling or something. No, we had a relationship. I went to his house and everything. He spent many nights here, and we were always with each other, so forgive me if I sound naive, but how the fuck do you fit in all of this? I mean, where were you when all of this was going down?"

"Hmm . . . I was wondering the same goddamn thing. So tell me, Miss Simpson, did my husband suck on your pussy also?"

"Excuse me? That ain't none of your business. You know what? I think it's time that you leave up out of here." I was pissed off by her intrusive question.

"You're right. I know I overstepped my boundaries. Excuse my rude behavior. I'm suggesting that you stay away from him. He's no good and will only drag you into his misery. Take my word for it." She turned around and walked toward the door. She opened the door and walked out without saying another word.

I slammed my door and locked it.

That was strange. What did she think she was going to accomplish by coming to my house? And then to ask me if he ate my pussy was off the wall. Man, this shit is definitely getting out of hand. That nigga is really good at hiding his dirt, and how stupid was I for not seeing through his lies?

The crying sounds of my baby interrupted my thoughts. I smiled as I ran to his room to get him. Even through this storm, he was the one who could make me smile.

CHAPTER EIGHTEEN

Kennedy

I couldn't wait to step out of that apartment and into some fresh air. That damn apartment smelled like fried food, stinking pussy, and stale piss. And that was where my husband was shacking up. I mean, how the fuck was he going to leave our mini mansion to come to this old torn-down-ass apartment? The more I thought about it, the more I realized this man didn't have any sort of ambition. He really lowered his standards when he left my ass to fool around with this little bitch. Her hair wasn't done. Her feet were ashy with peeled nail polish. I couldn't stand the sight of her ass one second longer.

I really didn't have a good reason for why I went to her apartment. I thought it was just that a part of me wanted to see her. I wanted to see what was so special, why my husband felt the need to fuck his marriage up. Now I saw she was a regular bitch.

I got into my car and pulled off. Even though my stomach was doing flips, I had that bitch on tape admitting that she and my husband had an affair. That was all I needed to take to the divorce lawyer. I was not playing with his ass, and I wanted him out of my life for good. I was trying to do it the right way this time. God knows I was trying.

I got back home in no time. I took the recorder out of my purse and played it. Even though that little bitch's voice irked my soul, I loved what she was saying. She had no idea how much she just helped me. Shit, it was only fair since her ass had been fucking my husband.

I heard my phone ringing. I looked at it and saw that it was Christopher. "Hello, dear."

"Hey, Miss Lady. I heard from one of my buddies that Devon was released a few hours ago."

"Are you fucking serious? H . . . how the hell did that happen?" I caught an instant headache.

"I'm not sure, but he posted bond. I just wanted to give you a heads-up just in case he tries coming to the house."

"I need to get a locksmith over here quick. Listen, I'll call you back in a minute." I hung the phone up in a rush.

I tried to google a locksmith. Then I heard my downstairs door opening. I panicked as I stormed toward the stairs. I made it halfway down the stairs when I came face-to-face with my husband.

"What the hell are you doing here?" I started to dial 911.

He reached up and knocked the phone out of my hand. "Damn! Who are you calling? This ain't no way to greet your husband, darling."

"I'm not your fucking darling! I want you to get all of your shit and get out of my house!" I yelled.

"Baby, c'mon! This is me, your husband. Whatever it is that you think I've done, please forgive me. These bitches don't mean shit to me. I promise they don't." He grabbed my arm and pleaded.

I snatched my arm away, almost losing my balance. "You must not have heard me the first time. Let me say this again. Get yo' old broke-dick ass out of my fucking house before I call the police. I fucking hate you. I wish the bitch who had you had aborted yo' ass because, if she did, I wouldn't be going through this shit right now." I lashed out and tried to push past him.

"Baby, please listen to me. I swear, I really need you. I don't love these bitches. You're the only one—"

"What the hell are you saying, boo? Why are you begging this bitch when she left yo' ass in jail?" I heard a voice say.

I took a step down on the stairs to see who this whore was in my house.

"What the hell are you doing in here? I told you to stay in the car," he said with clenched teeth.

"Wow! You not only violated me, but yo' bitch ass had the fucking nerve to bring your whore up in my damn house."

"Whore? Bitch, you got me all the way fucked up. Bring your old ass down here so I can show you what this whore can do," the little, skinny, gorilla-looking bitch said as she took a step forward.

"Man, shut up and go back to the car. You're only making this situation worse!" he yelled as he pushed her back.

"I 'on't know who you think you're talking to, but I'm not this bitch or my fucking sister. You can come on with me, or you can stay in here, begging this old, dry-pussy bitch to be with you. I'm gone."

"Man, I swear, I'm so sorry. She ain't nobody but a friend. That's all."

I looked at him, gathered enough saliva, positioned myself to face him, and then spat dead in his face. "Now get yo' dumb ass out of my shit."

"Bitch! What did you just do that for?" he said, wiping the spit off his face while calling me every curse word that came to his mind.

"Ha-ha, you're pitiful," I said. I looked at him with disgust and shook my head before I walked upstairs.

I slammed my door and then locked it. I sat behind the door. I wasn't sure what he might do, and the fucked-up thing was that I didn't have my cell phone with me. All I could do was hope and pray that this man would get his ass out of my house.

CHAPTER NINETEEN

Shari

I was too fucking heated right now. I couldn't believe
I walked in on that nigga begging that bitch to be with
him. I didn't care if he was married to this bitch. That shit
was kind of hilarious at first though. That old bitch was
no competition. I backed out of the parking space at full
speed. My emotions were running high. I was almost out
of the subdivision when I heard my phone ringing. I had
a feeling it was Devon's ass, and I ignored it at first. Why
the fuck would he be calling me when he just carried me
in front of his bitch? The phone continued going off, so
I reached over and snatched it up off the seat. "Yo, what
the fuck do you want?"

"Man, where you at? I came outside, and you were
gone."

"Really, nigga? You thought I was going to sit around
and wait for you to finish kissing up to that senior-citi-
zen-ass bitch?"

"Shari, baby, please turn around and get me." He
sounded pitiful.

I hung the phone up on him. I thought about leaving
his ass where he was at, but then I remembered this
nigga didn't pay me my money as of yet. I busted a
U-turn in the street and headed back to his house. I was
still heated and really wanted to rip that bitch's head off.

I never had a bitch disrespect me like that who didn't get their ass whipped. I pulled up at the house and saw him standing outside, fuming. He got in the car and slammed the door.

"Damn, don't break my damn door off."

"Chill, B. I'm too fucking mad right now to even entertain your bullshit."

"My bullshit? Nigga, you're the one who brought all this drama in my life. Before I met you, my life was Gucci. Not only do I have to deal with your supposed baby mama, but now I've got to deal with your grandma-slash-wife. Nigga, I ain't with all of this. You can just pay me my money and get the fuck on with yo' life."

He didn't respond. Instead, he just stared through the window. I kind of felt bad that I went off like that, but I was fucking pissed off. Without saying another word, I just cut on Plies's latest CD and totally zoned out all of the bullshit that just went on.

I lay beside him while he slept like he had no cares in the world. I, on the other hand, couldn't sleep. I had too much shit on my mind. I knew that if I wanted him for myself, I needed to get my sister and his wife out of the way. All sorts of evil thoughts crossed my mind. I just had to figure out a way to execute them and have him see things my way.

The nigga's tongue was sharp as a razor, his dick game was one hundred, and he had a few dollars, so those were all great reasons why I was determined to be his bitch, at least for now. I was willing to fight for him, but my number one motive was to see my sister's face when she found out that her ex and I were actually together.

I got up early and decided to cook him breakfast. After the stressful day that he had yesterday, I was going to make sure today was not a repeat. I knew that in order to lock him in, I had to be his calm in all of the storm he was going through. While those two bitches were yelling and screaming at him, I was prepared to feed him, suck him, and fuck him well.

I was in the kitchen, cooking in my underwear and bra, when I felt his soft lips on my neck.

"Good morning, beautiful," his raspy voice whispered in my ear.

I smiled and turned around to face him. "Good morning, lover." I planted a big, wet kiss on his lips.

"Damn, babe, I could get used to waking up to this every morning." He kissed me while he cupped my butt cheeks with his hands.

"Well, you know, if you play your cards right, all this could be yours, daddy." I kissed him passionately.

"Mm-hmm, well, in that case, I believe this ass is officially mine."

I wanted to ask him what he was going to do with his bitches, but I didn't want to spoil the moment. "Well, sit down. Let me feed my man." I laughed.

We sat there talking about him getting a lawyer to beat his case. Just the thought of how my sister did him really angered me. "I hate that you have to go through this."

"Don't worry yourself, bae. I'm a street nigga, so this ain't my first time dealing with the law. As long as I've got a good lawyer, I know I can beat this."

"Well, babe, you know you're not in this alone. I'm riding with you until the wheels fall off."

"That's what I'm talking about. Anyway, go put on some clothes. I've got to go to the Galleria in White Plains."

"Okay, let me go get a quick shower."

I took our plates and put them in the sink. He was on his phone, texting, so I walked out of the kitchen. I knew that if his ass was going to the mall, he had to buy me a few outfits too. *Let's see if Devon is really about this life.*

He bought himself a couple of outfits, drawers, and socks. He was very generous. We went into Macy's, and he told me to get whatever I wanted, so I grabbed two Michael Kors purses and a Michael Kors watch that I had wanted for a year now. He paid, and we were walking out hand in hand with him carrying the bags in his other hand.

"Devon, is that you? How are you doing?" a well-dressed lady greeted him as we walked out.

"Hey, Darlene, how are you?" He seemed very uneasy.

"I haven't seen or heard from you and Kennedy in a while. Just the other day, I was telling Jacob that I was going to phone Kennedy to see if y'all wanted to do dinner one of these nights."

I felt very awkward standing there, listening to this conversation.

"Oh, my, where are my manners? Hello, young lady. My name is Darlene. I'm friends with your brother and his wife." She put her hand out to shake mine, but I just stared at her.

"Darlene, I've got to go." He walked off before she could respond. "I'm sorry, babe. That meddling old bitch is one of Kennedy's friends."

Just the mention of that bitch's name put a bitter taste in my mouth. "I'm not worried about none of that. You're with me, and that's all that matters."

He kissed my hand and squeezed it tighter. That kind of gave me the assurance that he really wanted to be with me. But somehow, I couldn't ease my mind of the words I heard him saying to his wife yesterday.

CHAPTER TWENTY

Shari

"Babe, you know I'm falling for you hard, right?" Devon said as he started planting love kisses all over my hardened nipples.

"And do you know I've already fallen for you headfirst?" I kissed him.

"Well, you know I don't want to walk away from all that money that Kennedy has. I earned that shit, and I want what is rightfully mine." He used his tongue and licked my breast.

I was loving the feeling he was giving me, but this damn conversation was out of place. "What are you trying to say, babe?"

"I was just thinking . . . Maybe I'm just being a fool."

"What were you thinking? That we should just kill that bitch so you can get everything, and then we can live happily ever after?"

"Damn, baby, you're ruthless, but I love your idea more." He sucked on my nipple aggressively while he ground on my pussy. He grabbed me by my neck, followed by him putting his long tongue down my throat.

Our kissing intensified. My breathing became heavy, and my pussy juice dripped down my leg. I didn't know if I was horny as hell, if it was Devon's aggressiveness, or if it was the fact that we were talking about killing his bitch. Whatever it was, my pussy was craving some attention.

"Fuck me now," I begged as my hands traveled to his pants, ripping off his button. His manhood stood at attention, resting between his zipper and stabbing my belly button.

My pussy was starving for his chocolate thunder. My fingers slipped through his boxers, releasing the beast.

"Fuck me now, Devon," I begged again, wanting to feel his tool inside my womb.

He released his hands from my neck and tugged at his pants, finally kicking them off. He gently eased inside of me and pulled me closer to him. "Baby, I'm serious. I want to kill that bitch so you won't ever have to share me again."

"We need to do this. I will get a knife and cut that bitch's throat." Just the thought of looking at that dead bitch gave me a boost of energy. I gyrated my waist to the rhythm of his strokes.

"Nah, that would be too bloody. I'm a street nigga, and shooting a bitch is easier and won't leave any DNA. We have to be smart about this if we are going to do it." He pushed his way deeper into my soul with his dick.

I sank my fingernails deeper into him as I considered not just one murder but also the murder of my beloved sister, Amoy Simpson. When it was all said and done, I would be the only bitch standing!

CHAPTER TWENTY-ONE

Amoy

I was worried that something crazy was going on with my little sister. Her behavior had definitely gotten out of control over the last few weeks. We were so close growing up, but now it seemed like we were not close anymore. I could admit that, after I started dating Devon, I didn't spend as much time with her as I used to. I'd been calling her phone for a few days and texting her, but she wasn't responding. I knew I snapped on her at the hospital, but we made up.

My phone started ringing, and I looked at the caller ID but didn't recognize the number. I still picked it up, hoping it wasn't Devon's ass. "Hello."

"Amoy?"

"This is she. Who is this?"

"This is Kaysia."

"Kaysia, my sister's bestie? What? Did something happen to my sister?" I asked nervously.

"No, nothing happened to her."

"Okay, so what's up? I haven't heard from you in a while."

"I need to talk to you, but you have to promise me that you're not gonna say anything to your sister."

I was thrown off by her statement. My mind started racing. *What is really going on, and why is this girl calling me?*

"Kaysia, you know me and my sister don't have any secrets. If you have something to tell me and you don't want me to tell my sister, then this ain't a good thing to tell me."

"Listen, Amoy, your sister doesn't really fuck with you. Matter of fact, she really hates yo—"

"Girl, I've got to go. I don't know what kind of game you're trying to play, but—"

"She's been sleeping wit' your baby daddy, Devon."

What the fuck did this bitch just say? I know I didn't hear her right. "What did you just say?" I started sweating as I felt my temperature rising.

"I said, your little sister is fucking your baby daddyyyyyy." She dragged her words.

"What the fuck are you talking about? My sister doesn't even know him." I started to get angry with this little bitch.

"Girl, whatever! Why don't you go on over to her house? That nigga might just be over there as we speak."

"Girl, I'm getting off this phone. I don't know what sort of drama you and my sister have, but y'all need to leave me out of it." I pressed end on that ass.

I scooted down on the carpet by the couch and hung my head. I was trying to digest everything that I had just heard on the phone, but my thoughts were jumbled together. I grabbed my cell and called my sister's phone. I prayed she answered so I could let her know what lies this crazy bitch was spreading. Even though a part of me was curious, that was my little sister, and I refused to believe anything foul about her.

I decided to get my baby dressed. I was going to see her so we could talk, and then I was going to whoop that bitch Kaysia's ass myself. I didn't play that shit. It took me no time to dress my son and put him in his car seat. It was kind of warm outside, so I turned the AC on to cool him off a little. The entire ride to my sister's house, I was thinking about how friends could make up lies about other friends when they had beef.

I pulled up at my sister's complex. I got out and looked around. I didn't see Devon's car, and furthermore, he was still locked up. I walked up the two flights of stairs and rang the doorbell. The car seat was heavy, so I rested it on the ground.

No one answered the door, so I pressed on it continuously.

"Who the fuck is ringing my shit like they've lost their fucking mind?" my sister said as she opened the door.

"Hey, it's only me and your nephew." I smiled.

She stood there, looking at me like I had a humungous head.

"You all right? You're not gonna say, 'Come in, sissy'?" I joked.

"Now is not a g—"

"Bae, who is that at the door?" I heard a voice I knew all too well.

"Who is that?" I asked.

"Nobody. Just go, all right? I'll call you later."

I didn't respond. I picked up my baby in his car seat and used all my strength to push past that bitch!

Betrayal, shock, and fucking pissed were only a few of the emotions that flooded my soul! I blinked twice to look at the nigga standing in front of me. I tried to speak, but something blocked my throat.

"What the fuck is De . . . Devon doing in your house?" I struggled, trying to get the words out. I turned around and looked at my little sister's face. Tears welled up in my eyes as I faced the friendly monster standing in front of me. "God, please take this wheel," I whispered because my mind was speeding, and I wasn't thinking rationally.

I felt a lump in my throat as I tried to find the words to say to my little sister. *The one I took care of my entire life . . . How could she do this to me? Me, her big sister and protector . . .* I sold my pussy when I was younger to help buy food for her ass when she was hungry. I bought soap so she was able to wash her dirty ass, and this was how she repaid me?

"Sis, this is not what it seems," this snake-ass bitch had the nerve to say to me.

"Yo, what the fuck you mean, bitch? I just heard my nigga . . . fuck that, the father of your nephew, call you 'babe,' and you're telling me this is not what it seems? My dear, loving sister, please explain this shit to me." I rested my baby's car seat on the ground because I was ready to rip this little bitch's head off.

"Man, come on, B. You've got my seed and shit right here. Just go ahead on home. Your sister told you it's not what you think, but yet, you're up in here, trying to start some fucking drama."

I turned my head to face this fuck nigga. I took a few steps toward him. "Really, Devon, you're defending this little bitch? Okay, since you're speaking up and shit, tell me how long you've been fucking with this bitch?"

"Man, go ahead with all that. I'll be over there later on."

"You're a bitch just like this ho. You're not even man enough to claim this ho in front of me." I then turned to this bitch and looked at her with disgust written all on my face. "This is what you wanted? My leftovers, a no-good-ass nigga with a fucking wife? You're not even the second bitch but the third bitch. I swear, I should beat your motherfucking ass for even trying me." I lunged toward this bitch.

"I just told your motherfucking ass that you need to take my son and go the fuck home. I mean, what kind of example are you setting for him?"

"Nigga, quit claiming that little bastard. I told your ass you need a DNA test 'cause my lovely sister here doesn't know who the fuck her baby daddy is."

"Is this true, Amoy? Is he some other nigga's seed?" Devon turned around to face me.

I couldn't believe what this bitch just opened her mouth to say. I was really stuck and at a loss for words. I was angry, but I was more hurt. It was like broken glass was digging into an open wound. As much as I wanted to pretend that this was a stranger, it wasn't. This was my blood, my little sister, who was doing this to me.

"You know what? Fuck you and this bitch. I swear my motherfucking son don't need you any motherfucking way."

"Nah, fuck that. Is this my son or not? What the fuck is your sister talking about?" He grabbed my arm tightly.

"Let go of my fucking arm unless you're trying to get a new fucking charge," I snapped at him and snatched my arm away. I turned around, grabbed my baby's seat, opened the door, and stormed out of there as fast as my legs would carry me.

I strapped my son into his car seat while I tried my hardest to control my emotions. I got into my seat and put my seat belt on. My hands trembled as I put them on the steering wheel. I wasted no time getting out of there. As soon as I pulled off, the tears rushed out of my eyes like a dam that was broken. I was shocked and hurt . . . not so much behind that nigga but behind that little bitch back there who called herself my sister.

Who the fuck raised this bitch? Then reality hit me. Our mama was trifling as fuck, and she was the one responsible for raising this little bitch. How could I expect any different? The shit caught me off guard though. How could I be so blind and miss the signs, or did I see them but was too blind to believe them? My mind was clouded, and my emotions were running wild. I tried to stop the tears, but they wouldn't stop. The more that I thought about what had just popped off, the angrier I got.

Fuck that nigga, but my little sister . . . How could she let dick come between us? Not just any dick but a nigga who was married? A nigga who could possibly be the father to her blood?

I busted a U-turn in the middle of the street. I was furious, and I needed some fucking answers. I had a strong feeling that this crackhead bitch knew about this all along, and there was only one way to find out. Tears continued pouring down my face as my heart continued to break.

I got out of my car and got my baby out of his seat. That damn car seat was too heavy to carry up the stairs. I sped up the stairs while holding my baby close to me. My adrenaline was rushing, which gave me a new wave of energy. I banged loudly on her door while I waited impatiently.

"Who the fuck is banging on my door like that?" she yelled.

"Mama, it's me. Amoy. Open the door."

"What the fuck you want? Last time I was all kinds of hoes and shit."

I saw I was going to get nowhere with this bitch if I went at her aggressively. "I brought your grandson to see you. You know you ain't seen him." I waited for a response.

Seconds later, I heard the bolts of the door moving. She opened the door.

I pushed past her and entered her apartment. "So did you know Shari was fucking my baby daddy?"

"Say what? Is this what you came over here for?" She looked at me.

"Answer me, bitch. Did you know your whorish daughter was fucking my son's father? Did you put her up to it?"

"Listen to me, you little bitch. I don't give a fuck if you're holding my grandbaby. I will tear that ass up. Don't come up in my shit, accusing me of anything. You know yo' ass been jealous of Shari ever since I brought her home from the hospital. I never understood why until now."

"Jealous of her? Bitch, I took care of her ass because your crackhead ass was out fucking and sucking on any nigga who could support your crack and dope habit. But you don't remember that shit. Bitch, you know I'm tired of sparing your fucking feelings. I should've known you weren't shit when you stayed wit' the nigga who fucked yo' daughters. What kind of fucking mother are you? Wait, I know. You're a sorry piece of shit. I promise I wish you were dead, bitch. Matter of fact, I can't wait for your ass to be dead so I can spit on your fucking grave."

"Ha-ha, you've been dead to me. I should've aborted yo' ass when that sperm donor begged me to. And just for the record, Richard didn't rape you like you claimed. Yo' little fast ass wanted that dick. Matter of fact, you were jealous of me getting that good dick every night. So you threw yo' little dumb ass all over him. You're just mad 'cause he fucked you and didn't want anything else to do with your dirty ass."

"Fuck you," I said in a cold tone.

I looked that bitch up and down. It was a waste of my time to even be here around her. I shook my head and then turned around and walked out. She was so strung out and looked pitiful. The door slammed behind me. I could still hear that bitch yelling and screaming. I didn't look back. I exited the building and walked to my car. I strapped my baby back into his seat. The good thing was that he managed to stay asleep through all the drama.

With fucking family like this, who the fuck needs enemies? This bitch should have never had kids, much less called herself a mother. I'm done with both them bitches. I swear on my seed, I thought as I pulled off.

CHAPTER TWENTY-TWO

Shari

Lord knows I was not ready for this drama that unfolded in my apartment earlier. When I opened that door, I wasn't ready to see my sister's face. I tried to get her to leave, but this bitch busted her ass up in my shit, and there it was. Her baby daddy was there in the middle of my apartment with only his boxers on.

Shit, I wasn't going to lie. After the shock disappeared, I was happy on the inside when I saw how angry that bitch was. Yes, this bitch acted like her shit didn't stink, but her nigga was caught in another woman's apartment. I would do anything to find out what was going through her mind.

This bitch should've just grabbed her little bastard and left. Instead, her dumb ass stuck around, trying to come at me. So being the proud bitch I was, I gave it to her ass. Her eyes popped out when I told the nigga that wasn't his seed. What the fuck did she expect? I was going to let my nigga take care of a baby who possibly wasn't his?

After she left, I walked over and locked my door. All that fucking drama was not necessary. She acted like this was the first time a nigga done cheated on her ass. That was what her dumb ass got for believing in these niggas.

"So you're married? This old stupid bitch has no idea that I know this already." I burst out laughing.

"She thought she was telling you some shit you didn't already know. Maybe trying to get you to leave me alone."

For some strange reason, I was kind of heated that he was still married to that bitch and he had a smirk on his face. I stared at him and was kind of irritated. I was going to trip out on that nigga, show him how much of a savage I really was. I quickly caught myself. I wasn't into the drama. I was the chick who provided him with the calm in this crazy world. Truth was, I didn't give a fuck that he was fucking my sister, so why the fuck would I care that he was married to a bitch only on paper? Bitches really didn't know me, but they would soon.

"A'ight, babe. I'm so sorry this bitch popped up like that."

"Nah, bae, you're good. I'm the one who's sorry. I didn't mean to bring no drama to your house. I know she's your sister and all, and I would never want to come between y'all's relationship. I understand if you 'on't want to fuck wit' a nigga anymore."

"Say what? Yo, fuck that bitch. Blood don't make us family. You're my fucking family. I regret that you didn't move out of the way so I could show that bitch these hands. She will soon realize that I'm no longer a little-ass girl but a grown-ass woman fucking her nigga," I said in a cold tone.

"Well, fuck her for real. Come on, let daddy show you how much he appreciates you." He grabbed my hand and pulled me toward the bedroom.

Devon and I fucked for about an hour. That nigga ate my pussy and my asshole like he was famished. I thought I was freaky. Shit, this nigga beat me at being a freak. I wasn't complaining though. I loved it.

After we finished fucking, we took a shower, and I cooked us some French fries and chicken nuggets. See, I wasn't going to front like I was a big-time cook. Shit, who the fuck was there to teach me to cook? Both of them bitches were too busy being whores, but shit, he wasn't complaining. Matter of fact, he ate that shit like it was the best meal he'd ever had.

"Ay, bae, I'm about to make a few runs."

I whipped my head around so damn fast. "Where you going?"

"About to handle some business. You know money goin' to get low, so I need to get back in these streets."

My face lit up when he said that. I was happy that baby boy knew that pussy wasn't free, and if he wanted to fuck with me, he needed to have some fucking money. Shit, like Kanye West said, "I ain't saying I'm a gold digger, but I ain't messin' wit' no broke nigga."

"Okay, bae. Just be careful out there. You know you're out on bond."

"I know, yo. I'm good though."

After he got dressed, he kissed me on the cheek and left. I locked the door behind him. I decided to do the dishes so I could be free the rest of the evening. As I washed the dishes, my mind ran back on the situation that popped off earlier. I was confused why my sister popped up over here out of the blue. How did she suspect that I was fucking with her baby daddy?

I racked my brain, trying to come up with these answers. Only three people knew about our relationship. That was me, Devon, and that bitch Kaysia. That was when it hit me. That bitch and I got into it a few days ago because she was jealous of my relationship with Devon.

"You dirty bitch," I said out loud.

I cut off the water and dried my hands. I walked off into my room to retrieve my cell phone. My hands trembled as I pulled that bitch's number up and hit the call button.

"Hello."

"Bitch, who the fuck did you tell I was fucking with Devon?"

"First off, bitch, don't call my phone with no damn drama."

"Answer my fucking question, Kaysia. Did you tell my stupid-ass sister that I was fucking her baby daddy?"

"You know what, Shari? Matter of fact, I sure did. I mean, if you're woman enough to fuck her man, you should be able to take that ass whooping like a grown bitch."

"Both of you bitches are silly! I ain't met the bitch yet who can whoop my ass, but you already know that. Shit, all you did was hurt that bitch's feelings, not mine."

"You're a coldhearted-ass bitch. I can't believe I ever fucked with you, but you know karma is right around the corner, bitch."

Before I could respond, that bitch hung up in my face. I immediately tried to call back because I wasn't done addressing this dike-ass bitch. Her phone kept going to voicemail. Old scary-ass bitch and my sister would do good as friends. Both of them bitches were scary as fuck.

That bitch blew my motherfucking nerves. I couldn't believe that bitch would do me like that. She was my nigga, my road dawg. Damn, this bitch let jealousy come between our friendship. *Oh, well, fuck that ho now.*

I grabbed a bag of weed I had in my purse. I quickly rolled it up and took a few drags. I needed to calm myself down. These bitches had no idea that I wasn't your average bitch, and I would snap on their asses.

Kennedy Guthrie

I woke up bright and early. I had an appointment to see a divorce lawyer. Yes, you heard me right, a fucking divorce lawyer. At first, I thought about working it out with my two-timing husband, but the more I thought about his behavior, the more I realized that I couldn't control this nigga and his cheating ways. Not only was he cheating, but he had the audacity to bring a little bastard into this world. Yeah, the nigga denied it, but I didn't believe a word that came out of his flipping mouth. I was even more upset that he brought that bitch into my house. That nigga had no respect at all for me, and it was showing in his actions.

I parked my car and got out. My heart was heavy. No sense for me to pretend that I was happy about doing this. I'd already lost one husband, and now I was about to walk away from another. *My luck with men . . .*

I breathed a long sigh of relief and walked into the building. "Good morning. I'm here to see Attorney Bajan."

"Good morning, and your name please?"

"Kennedy Guthrie."

"Have a seat please, and I'll let him know you're here."

I took a seat in the corner. I was trying my best not to think about Devon and his bad behavior.

"Mrs. Guthrie, he's ready to see you now. The first door on the right." She pointed in that direction.

I knocked on the door before I entered.

"Mrs. Guthrie, nice to meet you. Sit down."

"Nice meeting you also."

"All righty, let's get down to business. I know we spoke briefly over the phone, but can you tell me a little more about your husband and what brings you to this point?"

I started airing out our dirty laundry to this stranger. At times, I paused as I thought about the roller-coaster ride that this nigga had taken me on lately.

"Wow! It seems like you've been through hell with him. Okay, do you have any emails, text messages, pictures, receipts? Anything that can help your case against him?

We can file the divorce based on adultery. Do you all have any children?"

"No, we didn't."

"Good. Does your husband have any off-shore accounts, real estate, or businesses that you know about?"

"That bastard has nothing. He came into this relationship with nothing but the drawers on his ass. Please excuse my language."

"No, you're fine. I am concerned that the court will grant him half of your estate."

"Say what? I'm not giving his ass shit. I done took care of this bastard, and now you're telling me I might have to give up my shit that my late husband left me?"

"No, not the things you had before the marriage, but everything that was acquired during the marriage. I'm pretty sure he'll be getting a lawyer also who will be asking for spousal support since you're the one who supported him."

"Bullshit! I'll be damned if I'm going to keep taking care of a grown-ass man who is slinging dick all over town. Excuse my French." I stood up. My blood was boiling as I digested what this man was saying to me.

"I'm only letting you know what to expect under New York's law."

"So you mean to tell me that this nigga can run around town, slinging dick from bitch to bitch, and I need to pay him? Over my dead body," I said before I took a seat.

"I'm your attorney, and I'm here to fight for you. I'm only telling you these things so you can know what to expect. Divorce proceedings can get downright messy sometimes. I just want you to be prepared."

I sat there, thinking. I wondered if there was a way I could get away with murder. I mean, this wasn't the first time that I'd killed a no-good-ass nigga, but the question was, could I pull it off again?

"Mrs. Guthrie." His voice startled me, bringing me back to reality.

"Yes, I'm sorry."

"I was asking if you want me to go ahead and start the divorce proceedings?"

"Uh, umm. You know what? Give me a few days. Let me reconsider this. It might be cheaper to stay married."

"Sure, take all the time you need. I'm going to keep your file so when you're ready we can jump right on it."

"Thank you so much. I'll be in touch soon."

"Great. Have a good day."

I didn't know what my crazy ass was thinking, but I hauled ass out of there. I got in my car and sat down for a few minutes before pulling off. See, it wasn't that I didn't want to divorce him. I just wanted to weigh my options first. There was no way that I was giving his two-timing ass a dime of my goddamn money.

I decided to invite Christopher over for dinner. He had been so good to me lately, and whenever I called, he was always there. I knew he was in love with me. He just wasn't my type. I guess you could say that he was a little more on the conservative side. That didn't stop me from using him to do whatever it was that I wanted.

I decided to throw a roast in the oven. I also cooked rice with broccoli, and I baked a chocolate cake. I sure missed throwing down in the kitchen, but since I was home by myself, there was no reason for me to cook every day.

Tonight was different though. I planned on enjoying the evening with Christopher in every way possible. After the dinner was cooked, I checked the time. It was a quarter past seven. Dinner was at 8:00 p.m., so I had time to jump in the shower and get myself together before he got here.

The entire time that I was bathing, I tried my hardest not to think about Devon. Just thinking about him and how he disrespected me only made me hate him. All kinds of wicked thoughts were running through my head. I shook the thoughts away and washed off with cold water. Yes, you heard me right. I learned a long time ago that hot water wrinkled the skin, and there was no way I wanted to walk around with saggy-looking skin. I didn't give a damn how old I was.

I got out of the shower, dried off, and put the new Oil of Olay lotion on my body. I glanced in the mirror. I looked damn good for my age. I ran my hands across my breasts, which were sitting up pretty. I damn sure could give these young bitches a run for their money. Not only that, but I knew my pussy was still tight and could grip a dick tight. That husband of mine was a damn fool, because how could he walk away from all of this? I took one last glance and then slipped on my silk evening dress that I picked out just for this night. I then sprayed a little perfume around my ears. Now I was ready to entertain this man.

I dished the food out and waited for him. Before I could sit down, I heard the doorbell ringing. *This man is always on time,* I thought before I got up to go answer the door.

I opened the door, and his fine ass was standing there with a red rose in his hand.

"Hey there, beautiful. This is for you." He handed me the rose.

"Well, thank you, sir." I took it.

He stepped inside, and I locked the door behind us. "Damn, it smells good up in here. What the hell you got going on up in here?" he asked and walked toward the dining room.

"I hope you're hungry, love."

He sat down at the table, and I put a bottle of red wine and a bowl of ice in front of him.

"I know you're tired of me saying this, but, woman, you can cook your ass off. Man, I wish I had a woman to cook these kinds of meals for me every night. Shit, I would never eat out."

"Well, you never know. If you play your cards right, you might just have these meals every night," I hinted.

"Talk to me, lady. What you saying?" He placed the fork down on the plate.

"Christopher, stop the nonsense. Eat up your food. We have plenty of time to talk about that."

"So how did it go with the lawyer? Did you show him all the pics that I gave to you?"

He caught me off guard with that question.

"Yes, I went to see the lawyer, but I didn't retain him as of yet."

"I thought you were ready to get the ball rolling on the divorce."

"I am, but after he mentioned that the bastard might get half of my money, I had a change of heart."

"Change of heart?"

"Relax, Christopher. I just had a change of heart, just for now."

"Oh, okay."

I could tell he was a little bothered by what I said because his demeanor changed.

"I didn't invite you over to talk about that dog. Tonight is purely about us." I got up from my side and walked over to him. I started massaging his shoulders. I then started kissing his neck.

"Woman, don't you start something you can't finish," he said and took a sip of his wine.

"I'm a grown-ass woman, and if I see something that I want, then I'm definitely going to go after it." I continued kissing his neck while I started unbuttoning his collared shirt.

He put the glass down and got up from the chair. He stood up, grabbed my hands, and pulled me toward him. He locked his lips on mine and started kissing me. He wasted no time in picking me up and carrying me to the couch. He was a bit aggressive, but who was I to complain? He put me down and took my silk dress off, leaving my breasts out in the open. He laid me on my back on the couch as he knelt down beside me, taking his hands and massaging my breasts. He then took one and placed it in his mouth. My body started to react to this man in a different way. He took his time, using his tongue to twirl around my nipple. He then reached down with his other hand and slid his two middle fingers into my pussy, which was soaking wet. I twitched as he worked my middle with his fingers. This man was working magic with my body without actually sexing me.

"Oweiii," I moaned out as I ground on his fingers.

"Damn, baby. I want you," he whispered in my ear.

"So what you waiting on?"

I guessed that was all he needed to hear because he started kissing my stomach and licking my navel. He then inhaled my pussy before he used his tongue to lick my clit. He then started kissing my pussy passionately. My body started shivering as I tried to control my emotions.

"Please, babes, fuck me," I screamed out to him.

He didn't pay me any mind. Instead, he sucked my clit like he was a pro on eating pussy. My legs started shivering as juice flooded out of my body and onto his face. He didn't move a muscle. Instead, he used his tongue and licked all of my juices up. He then got up and took his pants off, revealing his hard dick. For a man of his build, I was looking for a halfway decent dick. Wrong. It was a little on the small side, even though it was hard. I quickly took my eyes off it and turned my focus on him. He eased inside of me.

"Aweeee," I moaned out to give him a boost.

"Damn, baby, this pussy is good," he said as he dug deeper inside of me. He took my right leg and lifted it in the air. He then thrust in and out of my slippery pussy. The dick might not have been that big, but Christopher knew how to work the pussy. He was no Devon in bed, but he could definitely satisfy me for now, and I'd have him exactly where I wanted him.

"Damn, baby, I love you," he blurted out, shocking the hell out of me.

I didn't respond. Shit, I didn't know what the hell to say. I liked him, but as far as love, I couldn't say it back. He gripped me tighter as his veins got larger, and he started thrusting harder. I knew then that he was about to bust. His cum shot up in my pussy like a straight shooter. He lay there for a few minutes before getting up. I lay on my back, trying to catch my breath.

After we took a shower together, we decided to chill together for the evening. We drank more wine and just chatted about every- and anything. It was definitely a breath of fresh air and a change from all the drama that was going on.

CHAPTER TWENTY-THREE

Amoy

After crying for days and trying to get some under-standing of everything that went down, I finally managed to get myself together a little so that I could clean up this place. The only reason that I didn't swallow these pills were because of my son. Every time I looked at him, I thanked God for bringing him in my life, but it also saddened me that he was born in all this chaos. He was made out of love, or was he?

I heard my phone ringing. I put the broom down and rushed to the room to get it. I had no idea why I was killing myself to answer the phone when no one called me to see how my son and I were doing. I grabbed the phone and realized that it was Devon. *What the fuck does this bitch-ass nigga want?* I thought as I turned around to walk back out of the room. The phone continued ringing back-to-back. I was getting irritated. I couldn't wait to change my fucking number so his bum ass could leave me the fuck alone.

"Hello," I said in an aggressive tone.

"You ain't see me calling you?"

"Yeah, and? What the fuck you calling me for, fuck nigga?"

"Yo, watch your mouth, B. I know you're pissed off with a nigga, but just hear me out, yo."

"Hear you out? I think I heard you loud and clear that day when you were up in my sister's crib in your drawers." I ended the call without waiting on a response.

Tears gathered in my eyes. What the fuck did this nigga think he was doing by calling me? He disrespected me in the worst form, and now he was on my fucking phone, trying to talk to me. I threw the fucking phone down on the bed and stormed out of the room.

I went straight to my bathroom and grabbed one of the Percocet pills that I had gotten for pain but had been popping lately. For some strange reason, it helped me get through this rough time. I washed it down with a can of Sprite that I grabbed out of the fridge. I waited a few minutes, and then the pill started taking its effect, which stabilized my mood. I was feeling more confident now that I was floating. That phone call still had me on the edge. I just prayed that the nigga didn't show his face over here because I would hate to get him locked up.

I finished cleaning up my place. Later on, when my baby woke, I wrapped him up, and we went to the Laundromat to wash some clothes. I'd been slacking lately, and I'd allowed the clothes to pile up on me.

I was standing outside, waiting on a taxi, when the girl Kaysia walked by. It had been a minute since I'd seen her. I was hoping the bitch would continue walking, but I wasn't that lucky.

Kennedy

It had been days since I had seen or heard from my two-timing-ass husband. Truth was, at first, I wasn't too worried 'cause I knew his trifling ass would be back home soon. My husband was used to a woman catering to him, and since I wasn't doing that at the moment, I guessed he was lying up with one of those ghetto-talking bitches.

Ever since I visited the lawyer, I had been thinking hard on what I was going to do. *Well, I could just get a divorce and risk his ass getting half of my damn money, or I could—*

My thoughts were interrupted by the ringing of my telephone. I chuckled as I got up off the couch and ran to the phone.

"Hey, you." It was Christopher.

"Hey, darling. How are you doing today?"

"I'm feeling much better now that I got to talk with you."

"Is that so? You know exactly what to say to make a woman feel all warm inside."

"Well, that's a good thing. Do you feel like going out to grab a bite?"

"Christopher, just because I gave you the pussy in private doesn't mean we're going to be parading all around town. I'm still a married woman, and I don't want to give that nigga any ammunition to bring to his lawyer."

"I guess you're right. I really enjoy your company, so I guess I got a little above myself. Forgive me, sweet lady."

"No problem, dear. You can stop by tomorrow. I can cook your favorite meal."

"Sounds like a date. Well, let me get back to doing what I do best—following people around."

"All right, dear."

I knew Christopher's ass was catching feelings, and even though I wished he weren't, it was a good thing that he was because he could be beneficial to me in the long run.

I heard my phone ringing again. I really hoped it wasn't Christopher again. I looked at the caller ID and realized that it was that cheating-ass husband of mine. I thought about not answering it, but I had second thoughts. "What do you want?"

"Kennedy, I just need to talk to you."

"I have nothing to say to you. Frankly, I wish yo' ass was dead somewhere and the fucking crows were feasting on your body parts."

"Damn, yo, that's cold. You're saying this to the man who loves and cares about you."

"Love? How dare you mention you and love in the same sentence? Did you forget all the fucked-up shit you did to me? You even went as far as carrying a bastard in this world. Matter of fact, I'm done talking to you."

"Kennedy, Kennedy, please don't hang up, babe. I just need you to talk to me face-to-face one time. I promise I just want to talk."

"Ha-ha. The last time I saw you, you were chasing after one of those bimbos. What happened to her? She found out you were a fraud, or she ran off with a man with more money than you? Ha-ha, my dear husband. It seems like you're shit out of luck."

I didn't wait for a response. Instead, I hung the phone up in his face. The nerve of this man. Who the fuck did he think I was? Some little-ass girl who was wet in the ass? I got up off the bed and walked to the kitchen. I decided to fix a strong drink, one that could numb this pain that I was feeling.

I checked the time. It was a little past twelve. I pulled up into the parking lot at the Olive Garden. I was having lunch with the ladies. It had been a minute since we got together like this, and I was looking forward to mingling with them and catching up. I parked, got out, and walked into the restaurant.

"Yes, may I help you?"

"Kennedy, we're over here," Dorothy said as she waved.

"Yes, hello. I'm with those two ladies."

I walked over to Dorothy, who was standing by the bar area, and we hugged and kissed. We walked over to the table where Cecile was sitting.

"Kennedy, my love. Don't you look radiant?" She got up and kissed me on the cheek. We hugged and then took our seats.

"Ladies, it's my pleasure to be here. Wow, it's been a while."

"Uh-huh, it's only been a while because you fell head over heels over that young hunk and threw us to the side. By the way, how is married life treating you?"

"Married life is just fine. Everything is just fine," I lied.

"Are you sure? Because I heard from a close friend of ours that he was parading around town with a younger woman. She said he looked shocked when she asked about you."

"Dorothy, I said everything is just fine. Now drop it."

"I'm sorry, Kennedy. I just want you to know we are here for you if you need us. We women have to stick together."

"Hello, ladies. Are y'all ready to order?" the waitress said, interrupting us. I was happy she did because I wasn't feeling this conversation. Maybe it was because I was living a damn lie and I was too embarrassed.

After our meal came, we ate, laughed, and fooled around just like old times. It really felt good to be out and not worrying about all the chaos that was taking place in my life.

"Okay, ladies, we need to do this again soon." I hugged them both and walked off to my car. As I pulled off, I couldn't help but think about what Dorothy said about my husband. See, this shit angered me. It was one thing to be slinging that dick in private, but it was a whole different level of disrespect when he was out and about with his whores, knowing damn well I was well known in this damn county.

After I got home, I took out a pack of oxtails. Even though my nerves were bad and I had already eaten, I remembered that I promised Christopher I was going to cook for him. I was a woman of my word, so I put my feelings to the side and threw down in the kitchen.

After I finished cooking, I took a shower and decided to lie down for a few. I was feeling drained and needed a quick nap before he got here.

"You are gonna pay for what you did to me. I promise that. You have everyone around here fooled, like you're this grieving widow, but sooner or later, you will be exposed for the fraud you are."

"Travis, is that you?" I jumped up and looked around. I didn't see anyone. That was when it hit me that I was sleeping and I had a dream about Travis, my late husband. What the hell did that mean? This was the first time since he died that I had a dream about him. It seemed so real as I replayed the cold words he said to me.

I got up off the bed and rushed to the bathroom. I brushed my teeth and washed my face. "Travis, you devil, I wasn't scared of you when you were alive, and I damn sure ain't scared of your ghost. You better go to hell before I kill yo' ass again." I wiped my face and put on some cocoa butter.

I wasn't going to lie. That shit scared the hell out of me. He had been dead for years. Why did he feel the need to pop up in my dreams now? Was he trying to send me a sign or something? Hmmm, all kinds of crazy thoughts ran through my mind. I made a mental note to call the lead detective who had handled my husband's case. It had been a minute since we spoke.

I walked in the kitchen and poured a glass of gin. I wasted no time swallowing the hot liquor. I cringed as it burned my chest, but I continued drinking. "Kennedy, it's nothing. Calm down," I said to myself.

I heard the doorbell ringing, and I jumped. That was when I remembered that Christopher was coming over for dinner. After that dream that I had, I really didn't feel like entertaining, but the food was finished and my guest was here, so there was no use in cancelling on him.

"Hello there, gorgeous," he said and walked into the house.

"Hello there. I fell asleep, so I need to warm up the food. Do you want something to drink?"

"What you got?"

"Hmmm. Let's see. I've got gin, vodka, wine, and I have a few beers."

"Let me get vodka on the rocks."

"Coming right up."

After I made his drink, I walked in the kitchen to warm the food. I was tending to the oxtails on the stove when I felt someone breathing down my back. I jumped again, but he grabbed me.

"I didn't mean to scare you. You seem a little frightened. Are you okay?"

"Yes, just making sure I don't burn the oxtails."

He held me, and it felt kind of good. My nerves were all over the place, and the alcohol helped to calm me down a little but not all the way. He started kissing my neck while massaging my breast.

"You better stop before you start something that you can't finish," I teased, pretending like I didn't like it, but honestly I loved it. "Go sit down so I can dish this food out," I demanded.

"Yes, ma'am." He kissed me on the back of my neck before he walked off.

I brought the plates to the table. I sat across from him while he blessed the food. I was about to start eating when the loud ding from the doorbell startled me. Christopher looked over at me. "Are you expecting a visitor?"

"Not that I know of."

I got up from the table and walked toward the door. Before I could ask who it was, the person sat on the doorbell, just ringing it.

"Who the hell is it?" I said as I popped the door wide open.

"Hello, wife. It's your husband." Devon stood there, laughing, like he was a fucking fool.

"What are you doing here? I told you I have nothing to say to you."

"Whose car is that in the driveway?"

"None of your damn business. Now go on."

"I'm not going anywhere. Whose car is it, Kennedy? What? You got another nigga up in our house? You're cheating?" He bombarded me with questions.

Before I could respond, he pushed past me, flinging the door wider, and almost knocked me to the ground. "Who is in here, Kennedy? Come on out, nigga."

I saw when Christopher stood up and walked toward Devon.

"Yo, my nigga, what the fuck you doing up in here? Do you know this is my house and my bitch?"

"The lady of the house invited me over, and you might want to watch your mouth. This is a queen, not a female dog."

"Nigga, fuck all that you're talking. Old Malcolm X–ass nigga. This is my bitch and my house, which mean you're trespassing."

"You need to stop now! Christopher is my good friend, and we're having dinner. Matter of fact, you shouldn't be here. You don't live here anymore."

"I ain't going anywhere. I know the law. You can't just put me out, wife," he said sarcastically.

"Kennedy, what do you want to do? Do you want me to put this fool out?" Christopher asked in a very serious tone.

I knew then that things could really get serious up in here. "Christopher, you know what? I'm sorry that you had to encounter this. Go ahead and go home."

"Yes, pussy nigga. Go ahead and go home. This is my bitch, so stay the fuck away from her. You heard?"

"Ha-ha, you're a young, silly nigga. You're lucky the lady didn't give me the word to body your ass right here on her floor. See you around." Christopher winked at him before he walked through the door.

"Fuck you, nigga," Devon yelled, but Christopher was long gone.

"What the fuck you call yourself doing?" I turned to face this bastard.

"You fucking that nigga?"

"Matter of fact, I am. You think you can be out here running around and slinging that dick all over town, and I'm supposed to sit in here lonely and shit? Wrong. I have needs, and he satisfies them."

"Really, Kennedy? I should fucking smack the fuck out of you right now. How dare you bring another nigga up in our house? Our bed?"

"Darling, this is my pussy, my goddamn house, and my bed. You came in this marriage with the clothes on your back, and you will leave with just that—the clothes on your back."

"I already told your ass I ain't going nowhere. So you better call that fuck nigga and let him know that whatever y'all had going on is over."

"You're a fucking joke. I will get you out of my house one way or another," I said before I stormed to my bedroom and locked my door.

It was time to put my plan into action.

CHAPTER TWENTY-FOUR

Amoy

It was Friday night, and I was bored out of my damn mind. I remembered the days when I was free and could hang out and do what I wanted to do. Not these days. All I had was my baby boy and myself. It wasn't all bad, though, because I loved spending time with him and welcomed the way he made me feel.

I was lying on the couch, catching up on an episode of *Deadly Wives* on the ID channel. I heard my cell phone ringing, so I picked it up. It was Marquise. I rolled my eyes, wondering what the hell he wanted. I had not heard from him since the day that shit popped off between him and Devon. "Hey, stranger."

"Ay, yo, what's good, ma?"

"Nothing. I didn't know you remembered my number," I said sarcastically.

"Girl, chill out wit' all that. Is that chump over there?"

"Ain't nobody over here but me and my baby."

"That's good 'cause I'm about to pass through in a minute."

"Okay."

I didn't ask him why or anything. I mean, I still loved him even though we hadn't fucked with each other in a minute. Sometimes I wished that I hadn't fucked up with him, but guess what? There was no need for me to cry over spilled milk.

I must have dozed off, because I heard a loud banging at the door. It was so loud that it scared the hell out of me. I got up, cut the light on, and walked over to the door. I saw that it was Marquise, so I opened the door.

"Yo, what's good?" He walked inside.

I locked the door behind us, and he walked over to me. "Damn, can a nigga get a hug?"

"Of course. You know you can."

"That's what I'm talking about." He laughed and pulled me closer to him.

His masculine smell leaked through his pores, hitting my nose. I tried to ease out of his grip, but he pulled me in closer and gripped my butt cheeks with his hands. Part of me wanted to pull away, but the other part welcomed this little bit of attention I was getting.

After we finished hugging, he walked over to the couch and sat down. "Where's little man at?"

"Taking a nap. He ran me ragged today. Shit, my ass was sleeping before you called."

"Damn. That's what I came over here for. I want to talk to you."

"About what?" He had my full attention.

"Do you think li'l man is really mine?"

I sat there quiet for a few minutes, thinking of ways to put my words together without coming off as a slut. "To be honest, Marquise, I really don't know whose child he is. I slept with you right before I slept with old boy. I didn't know I was pregnant until a few weeks after."

"Damn, B. I ain't never consider you to be that kind—"

"That kind of what?" I cut him off and stared him down with an attitude.

"Nah, ma. I ain't mean no disrespect to you, but it's kind of careless that you're fucking niggas without protection. You dig?"

"You're acting like I ran around here just fucking random niggas without condoms. Before you start judging me, make sure your shit is clean for real. If I can remember right, you were the one slinging dick around here."

"Amoy, I understand you're upset at what I just said, but this ain't about me for real."

The tears welled up in my eyes. I couldn't believe this nigga was coming at me like that. I should've kept my mouth shut.

"Man, don't do that. You know damn well I didn't mean no harm by what I just said. We're supposed to be able to talk to each other about how we're feeling. I mean, when I first found out you were pregnant, I asked you if he was mine. You blurted out no, only for you to tell me after he was born that there was a possibility that he was mine. I mean, that shit bothered the fuck outta me. I ain't got no other seed out there, and if he's mine, I want to be in his life. I ain't never had no pops, so I know what it's like to be out here without one." He choked up.

"I'm sorry if I hurt you. I just don't know who his father is, and I didn't know how to tell you."

"So did you tell that other nigga he might not be the daddy, or are you still letting him think he's the daddy?"

"I had told my sister, and she told him the other day. I found out he and my sister have been fucking around, so I don't fuck with him anymore. Plus, we have a case going on."

"What kind of case?"

"Him putting his hands on me."

"What the fuck, yo? What happened to the burner I gave you? You letting niggas put their hands on you and shit? Man, you need to boss up real fast."

I wasn't proud to tell him this, and the way he was reacting, I probably should've kept it to myself. "Listen, Marquise, I never pretended like I was perfect. Shit, my life's been pure hell since the day I was born, but I'm not sitting around moping. I'll admit it—I made some bad decisions, and I'm trying my best to clean them up, but it's not easy."

He reached over and wrapped his arms around me. I laid my head on his shoulder and let it all out.

"Yo, e'erything goin' to be a'ight. I promise you that, B. I mean, you deserve so much more than this bullshit for real. I know I didn't make it no better when I cheated on you over and over. I wish I didn't, but it is what it is."

I heard his words loud and clear, but I didn't know what to believe anymore. I had a feeling that I was never going to experience happiness.

I opened my eyes and stretched my arms out. My hand bumped into something, and that was when it hit me. I was not in my bed alone. Last night, after our long talk, we started drinking and smoking. I remembered that we started kissing. I dragged my memory to see what else I remembered.

I looked down. I was butt-ass naked. I looked over at him. His ass was naked also. I knew then that we got it in, and I was tired as hell. I just prayed to God that he didn't cum in me 'cause I wasn't on the pill and I wasn't ready to have another baby this soon. I was already struggling with raising one.

I jumped out of bed and reached for my robe, which was hanging on the closet door. First, I went to check on little man. He seemed to be just getting up.

"Good morning, Mommy's Pooh," I said as I picked him up. I kissed him on the forehead. After I changed him, I made him a bottle and put him in his playpen. I washed my face and put on a pair of panties.

I sat in the living room, watching my baby and thinking about what went down last night. Lord, I still had feelings for that boy, but I also remembered the reasons why I left him alone. He was a real nigga who made sure I had everything that I needed, but his ass couldn't keep his dick in his pants. I had busted a few of these bitches in the head over this nigga. After a while, the shit got old, and I decided that, even though I loved him, I deserved better.

Lord, now here I was, waking up with this nigga in my bed. My feelings were all over the place, feelings that I'd buried deep inside.

"Yo, why you ain't wake me up?" he said as he walked up on me.

"Oh, my bad. You were sleeping so peacefully that I didn't want to disturb you."

"Nah, I 'on't usually sleep this late. You know a nigga's got to be out here in these streets."

"Yeah," was all I whispered. I was feeling all kinds of emotions. Maybe it was a mistake giving him the pussy because now I wanted to pour my soul out to him.

"Hey there, little man." He walked over to the playpen and gently took my son out.

I watched as he examined him while he pretended like he was only playing with him.

"He kind of resembles me. What you think?"

I looked at both of them side by side. I did see the resemblance, but I was cautious. I didn't want him to get all attached and then the test came back and he wasn't the father.

He sat him down on the carpet and started playing with him. This was the first time a man really took time out to pay attention to my son. Devon's ass never gave him the time of day. Tears welled up in my eyes as emotions took over. I was really wishing he was the father because, even though he had whorish ways, I still believed he would be a great father. "God, please let him be the father," I whispered under my breath.

After he finished playing with Jamal—I started calling him by his middle name after Devon put his hands on me—he placed him back in the playpen, and then he stood up.

"Listen, B, I've got some business to go handle. I'ma hit you up later. Do you need anything before I go?"

"Nah, I'm straight," I lied. I could definitely use a few dollars, but I wasn't going to be desperate.

"A'ight, I'ma holla at y'all."

He unlocked the door and left. I stood by the door for a minute. I felt like a part of me had just left. I knew I was tripping. Just because we fucked didn't mean we were getting back together. I tried to put him out of my mind because I didn't want to get disappointed.

Shari

I left the house early to go register for school. Yes, a bitch was sexy and bougie, but I needed an education to back that shit up. See, I wasn't no regular bitch, and my plan ever since I was young was to become a massage therapist. After I finished filling out the paperwork and went to see financial aid, I headed back to Mount Vernon.

Earlier, when I left, Devon was still asleep. I was going to wake him up because the nigga needed a damn job or his ass needed to get out there and sling some rocks. Every day, I had to listen to him brag about how he was the nigga in the streets, but he changed. I didn't know what kind of bitch he thought I was, but if a nigga didn't have any money, I damn sure wasn't fucking with him. This pussy was too damn good to be throwing it away on broke, useless niggas.

I pulled up at the house and realized his car wasn't there. *Well, I hope his ass is out getting some money,* I thought as I parked.

I got out of the car and grabbed my stuff. I walked up the stairs and opened my door. The stench of old food hit my nose. *Damn, this nigga couldn't even take out the garbage.* That shit gave me an instant attitude. It got even worse when I entered the kitchen and saw that he cooked and left all the plates in the sink for the fucking maid to wash. I was furious at this dude. I grabbed my cell phone out of my purse and called him. The phone just rang out. I hit redial, and the same thing happened again. This was very strange. Not one time since we'd been fucking with each other had I called him and he didn't pick up.

Maybe I was getting worked up for nothing. He did tell me he was going to be back out in the streets. I figured he was caught up handling business. I calmed myself down a little bit.

I ended up ordering some wings and pizza for dinner. I rolled a blunt and grabbed a beer out of the fridge. This shit was nasty as fuck, but it was the only thing to drink, and I didn't feel like running out to the store right now. I grabbed my phone and hit Devon's phone again. This time, the phone went straight to voicemail. This time, I was angrier than before because it was well past 11:00 p.m. and I hadn't heard from this nigga all day. I thought about calling the jails and the hospitals but decided against it. That nigga knew my fucking number and never had a problem using it before. What the fuck did he think, I was going to be up and chasing behind his ass?

After drinking about three beers and smoking the blunt, I started feeling horny. Shit, I wished he were home to give me the dick, but he wasn't, so his loss. I scanned through my contact list to see who the fuck was available to come through. I stopped on the nigga DJ's name. He was a big-time stick-up kid from the Bronx. We went to Evander Childs High School together, and we fucked a few times. I stopped fucking around with him 'cause that nigga was living recklessly, getting chased by the police a few times and had niggas shooting up his car and shit. I was too damn cute to be dead in somebody's morgue. My past memories of him didn't stop me from calling his number though.

I lay on my back, playing with my pussy while the phone rang.

"Yoooo," he answered.

"Hey, babes. How you doing?"

"Damn, B, you know you were on my mind the other day."

"I hope it was the good fuck that I gave you the last time that you're thinking about," I said sexually.

"You know you got that sugar pussy, babes. So what's good though?"

"I was just feeling horny, so I'm trying to see if you want to slide through."

"Damn, bae. You know a nigga can't turn down no good pussy. Text me your address. I'll slide through real quick and beat up the pussy for you real quick."

"A'ight, boo. I'll see you in a few."

After I hung the phone up, I texted him the address. I knew I was being reckless by inviting him over here, but this was my shit, and I didn't give a fuck for real. I went to take a quick shower so I could freshen up the pussy before he got here.

I lay on my bed, waiting on him to come through. I decided to jump on Facebook to see what was going on. All these niggas and bitches did was lie and fake, trying to impress bitches and other niggas. There was no drama going on on my timeline. I put my sister's name in. I was about to see what was going on on her page.

Add Friend.

So this silly bitch unfriended me? Wow, she must have thought that I was going to roll over and die because she didn't want to be friends on social media. *Bitch, I don't give a fuck that we are family. I still took your whole man and don't give a fuck. I should send that ho a request just to be funny.*

That thought was interrupted when I heard my doorbell ringing. It could be Devon or it could be DJ. I hoped it was DJ. I was trying to fuck. I walked over and peeped out. I saw that it was DJ. I quickly opened the door and let him in.

"What's good, baby girl?"

"Just here, trying to live," I said as I sashayed to the living room.

"Damn, B, that ass got fatter than the last time that I saw you."

"Really? The pussy got wetter, too. Come on. Let me show you."

By the time he got to where I was, I was already butt-ass naked. DJ was a freaky-ass nigga, and I was a nasty-ass female, so together we knew exactly what we wanted. I wasted no time. I dropped to my knees, taking all that big black dick into my mouth. I slobbered all over it and then slowly licked it off. He grabbed the back of my head and brought it closer to his dick. I started deep throating it. It felt very good when I felt it touching the back of my throat. Some bitches often gagged doing this technique, but I was a bad bitch, and I'd built my tolerance up.

He fucked my throat for a good ten minutes, and then he exploded in my mouth. I didn't move an inch. I swallowed every drop of his protein shake and then used my tongue to lick up the remaining milk.

"Come here, B." He pulled me up. He took a seat on the couch and pulled me on top of him. "Ride this dick, yo," he commanded.

He didn't have to tell me twice. I parted my legs and slid down on his already-hard dick. This nigga was definitely blessed with size, but I still tried my best to maneuver. After my pussy got super wet, the dick slipped all the way in. I placed my hand on his shoulder, stuck my butt out, and rode that dick like I was a porn star.

"Damn, B. Take your time. You tryin'a break a nigga's dick head off?"

"Nah, babe. This dick is just so fucking good. You have no idea. Aweee," I moaned out.

The dick was good, but that wasn't the reason why I was bouncing that hard on it. I was taking all my frustrations out on the dick. My mind was all over the place, wondering where the fuck Devon was and why he was not here.

"Damn, B, I'm about to cum. Are you on the pill?" he said as he pulled me down and gripped me tightly.

"Stop. Let me up, yo. I ain't on no damn pill," I said as I tried to get out of his grip.

Seconds later, his juice squirted all up in my pussy. He then let me up, and I jumped off.

"What the fuck did you do that for? I ain't tryin'a have no damn baby." I lashed out in an aggressive tone.

"Chill out, yo. My sperm count is low 'cause of all this weed I smoke. I can't make no damn baby."

"Boy, shut the fuck up. That shit is a lie that niggas make up."

"Nah, I'm for real. But just in case something did go wrong, hit me up. I've got the abortion money."

"You better 'cause I'm not ready to be no damn mommy."

To be honest, it wasn't that I wasn't ready to be a mother. I just didn't want to have a baby by him.

After we finished fucking, we ended up taking a shower and fucked again. This time, he did pull out. After we were finished, we got out and got dressed. I was drained as hell, so I flopped down on the couch.

"You good, B?"

"Yeah, you done wore my ass out."

"Shit, ain't that what you wanted? For me to come over here and beat the pussy up?"

"Ha-ha, you right."

"A'ight, yo, I've got to bounce. Hit me up when you need me to slide through again."

"Okay, cool."

I sat there as he opened the door and left. I was drained and couldn't move at the moment.

I jumped out of my sleep. I looked around and realized that I was still on the couch. I was so tired last night that my ass didn't move a muscle. I searched around for my phone. I didn't see it, so I got up and walked to the bedroom. It was still on the charger from last night. I grabbed it, hoping to see a ton of missed calls or texts from Devon. To my disappointment, there were no missed calls or texts from him. Not one goddamn phone call. This was getting serious. I ran over to the closet where he kept his clothes, and everything was still there. I stood there scratching my head, trying to figure out what the fuck was going on.

I called his phone again, and there was still no answer, so I shot him a message.

Hey, not sure what's going on, but I have not heard from you since yesterday. Please let me know something.

I waited a few minutes to see if I would get a text back, but nothing came through. I started feeling desperate. This was the reason why I didn't fall in love with niggas. I didn't like this desperate feeling. I searched through my phone, where I had his wife's number programmed. I didn't give a fuck. I needed to know what was going on.

The phone started ringing, and I thought about hanging up.

"Hello," the old bitch answered.

"Good morning. Can I speak to Devon?"

"Hmmm. May I ask who this is?"

"Listen, bitch, does it matter who it is? Is he there?"

"Little girl, get your filthy ass off my phone. You're calling my phone, looking for my husband, so I assume he done slung a little dick your way and now you can't find him. Next time you decide to give up your pussy so freely, you may want to make sure he doesn't belong to another woman."

I was ready to roast this bitch, but she hung up in my face. I tried calling back, but she didn't pick up. "Aargh, you scary bitch," I yelled out.

I still didn't get the answer I needed. *Where the fuck are you, Devon?* I decided to get dressed and leave. I was so angry that my vision was blurred. The honking of a horn from a big rig caught my attention. I swerved to the side in order to prevent running into the truck's path. After I swerved, I sort of regretted it. I should've just let the truck hit me and end it all. Who was going to miss me? No fucking body. Well, maybe Mama, but that bitch might be so high that she probably wouldn't realize that I was gone.

I continued driving. This time, I tried to stay focused. I pulled up at my sister's apartment complex. I pulled up two spaces down and glanced around. I didn't see his car. I noticed her car in her parking space. I circled around twice to make sure I didn't miss anything. I was convinced that he wasn't there, so I pulled off.

I tried racking my brain over where he might be, but nothing came to mind.

Kennedy

"Lord, please bless this little ho who called my phone this morning because she knows not what she has done. In Jesus' name, I pray." I got up off my knees.

I walked over to the guest room, where this bum was staying, and knocked.

"Come in," he yelled out.

I busted the door open. He was lying on top of his cover, butt-ass naked, with his dick hard as hell. It seemed like the nigga was beating off.

"I'm going to tell you this one damn time. Get your little hoes under wrap and don't let them call my damn phone looking for you again."

He threw the covers over himself and sat up in bed. "Man, what the fuck you talkin' 'bout? It's too early for you to be here bitching and shit. C'mon, man, can a nigga breathe a little?"

"You know what, Devon? The more I fucking see what kind of joke you really are, the more I despise yo' sorry ass. Oh, and by the way, I heard one of the ladies bumped into you while you were parading your little bitch around town. How low would you stoop trying to embarrass me?"

"That bitch is lying. Ain't nobody see me doing shit wit' no bitch. I told you from day one that them bitches are mad that you have a man in your life and they ain't got nobody to fuck them."

"You sound silly as hell if you think I would believe shit that's coming out of your mouth. You better clear that shit up before I snap on you and them hoes. I don't think any of y'all know what deadly game y'all are playing. Trust me, I don't play fair."

I shot his ass an evil look and rushed out of the room. This couldn't be the man I fell for. Shit, he didn't even look the same. It looked like he was famished and on some kind of drugs.

I walked back into my room and dialed Christopher's number. "Good morning, beautiful," his raspy voice echoed.

"Good morning, Christopher. I need to send you a number. I need a name to go with it."

"Oh, Lord, who's in trouble now?" he chuckled.

"Hmmm, a young slut who has no business calling my phone."

"Well, my dear, I will have that info for you in a few."

"A'ight, dear."

I hung up feeling pleased. As soon as Christopher got back with me, I'd be paying that rude bitch a visit.

CHAPTER TWENTY-FIVE

Amoy

Marquise was over, visiting us again. His visits were more frequent, and he had been buying groceries, Pampers, and wipes, and he had even bought my baby two pairs of Jordans. I kept reminding him that, since he wasn't sure he was the father, he should stop buying all these things. He didn't listen to me. Every time he walked through the door, he had bags in his hands.

They were both still asleep when I decided to sneak out of the room and make some breakfast. I quickly tidied up the living room and started cooking. I had the music turned down, but it was loud enough for me to hear it. I was definitely jamming this morning to Pandora. I didn't know what we were doing. I just knew that I was loving it.

"Good morning, beautiful." He kissed me on my neck, scaring the hell out of me. I jumped.

"Good morning." I wasn't too sure what to call him.

"Damn, that's what I'm talking about. Baby girl's up, making her daddy breakfast."

He slid his hands up under my nightgown, caressing my breasts. There was something about this nigga's hands that did something to me.

"Boy, stop playing before you make me burn these darn pancakes." I giggled but was enjoying the way he massaged my breasts.

"Man, fuck them pancakes. I'm trying to get in them drawers real quick."

He took the fork out of my hand, took two pancakes out of the frying pan, and cut the stove off. He picked me up and placed me on the countertop. He took my nightgown over my head, leaving me naked. I was already wet, and my pussy was yearning for his dick. He pulled me down toward him and slid up in me.

"Awee." I gasped as he ripped through my love hole.

"Damn, this pussy's wet and tight, ma," he whispered in my ear as he dug deeper and deeper in.

I hugged him and braced myself for the pain that came along with getting fucked good. "Awee, baby, I love you. Please fuck me. Please fuck me," I pleaded with him.

He heard my cries. He parted my legs and threw the dick on me. I started shaking. I sank my fingers deep in his back and yelled out, "Yes, daddy. Fuck meeee." I then exploded all over his dick. He continued throwing the dick until his veins started getting bigger. I knew then that he was about to bust. "Please pull out," I said as I continued twerking on his dick.

"Nah, you good."

I didn't have time to ask him what he meant. His juice exploded all up in me. I jumped down, and the juice ran down my leg.

I ran to the bathroom to take a quick shower. "God, why did I let this nigga cum up in me?" I whispered.

After I finished bathing, I got out and quickly got dressed. I walked in the kitchen. He was in there, finishing up breakfast. I smiled at him and just walked off to go check on my baby. I stood over my son's bed, just looking at him. I really wished this was his father because this could be my little family. I let out a long sigh and walked back out of the room. Before I walked back into the kitchen, I heard him on his phone.

"Yo, I told you I'ma come through in a little while," he said. "A'ight, man, I'm gone."

He hung the phone up, and I walked into the kitchen. I grabbed one of my son's bottles so I could make him some formula with cereal.

"You a'ight?"

"Yeah, I'm good."

"You ain't get in trouble wit' your chick, right?" I quizzed.

"Man, cut it out. I ain't got no damn girl," he said with an attitude.

I decided to drop it because, clearly, he was bothered by that phone call.

After he finished cooking pancakes, eggs, and sausage, we sat at the table, eating. I was kind of feeling some type of way about how he spoke to me a few minutes ago. I took a sip of my orange juice.

He reached over and snatched my arm. "Ay, listen, I'm sorry for snapping a little while ago, man."

"It's cool. I was out of line," I lied.

"Man, cut it out, yo. I know when you're bothered."

"Why should I be bothered? It ain't like you're my nigga or we on some serious shit."

"So you ain't tryin'a fuck wit' a nigga?"

"You ain't say anything about us getting back together."

"Yo, B, I've always loved you. One night, I was out and about. I was high and drunk, and I was in my feelings. I asked God what was I doing wrong and why couldn't I find a good woman. I mean, I make good money, but what's that if I don't have no one to enjoy life with? I was searching for answers. That's when it hit me that she was right in front of me all along."

I looked at him. "Hmm, who you talking about?"

"You, silly. From the day that we met, I knew you were my soulmate, but I was young and stupid and was still into trying to fuck a lot of bitches."

I sat there, listening to what he was saying. Why had I heard this statement before? I knew niggas said the darnedest things when they were trying to convince women that they were worth a try. Part of me believed him, but the other part remembered all the shit that I went through with that asshole. I was still hurting inside even though I tried to hide it. I knew mentally that I wasn't ready for another relationship this fast when I still had unfinished emotions floating around.

"You know I've always loved you, but I remember how you used to cheat and lie to cover it up. How I used to call your phone and you would ignore me. You hurt me badly. How do I know this time is different?"

"You don't know. All I've got is my word, ma. I can only show you from this day on that I'm one hunnit wit' you if you give our love another chance."

"Are you here because of love or is it because you think Jamal might be your son?" I looked him dead in the eyes.

"I'm here because of you. Yeah, I'm hoping he's mine, but for real, B, even if the test turns out that he's that fuck nigga's seed, I still want to be with you. I want a family with you. I'm tired of these streets, and I plan on getting out in a year's time."

I wanted to say that this was all bullshit he was spitting, but I saw the sincerity in his eyes. Behind all that hardness, I saw the good part of him. And it was in that same moment that I fell back in love with him.

The loud crying of my baby interrupted our little heart-to-heart talk. "I think someone feels left out," he said.

We both burst out laughing. I got up from the table and went to his room.

"Hey, Mommy's Pooh." I picked him up.

As I changed his diaper, I took an extra look at his features. To be honest, I couldn't call it one way or the other. I could only pray for it to work out in our favor.

***

An hour later, Marquise left, and it was back to li'l man and me. I cut on kid cartoons for him while I grabbed my computer. I decided that it was time for me to get back in the work field. Money was tight after that asshole stopped giving money to us, and I got a letter that rent was due. I guessed his ass stopped paying that, also. I knew that if I asked Marquise, he would help me, but I preferred to figure it out for myself. I didn't want to start depending on niggas too much after all that I'd been through. I was responsible for providing for me and my little man. I also looked up beauty school. I was a beast at braiding hair, but I really wanted a license so I could do more than that, possibly open my own shop one day.

I heard my cell phone ringing, so I grabbed it up without looking at the caller ID. "Hello."

"Is Devon over there?"

I removed the phone from my ear to look at the number. I was correct. It was my slut-ass sister on my damn phone. "Bitch, are you crazy? Don't you ever call my phone asking for that bum ass nigga. Ha-ha, he must be over the next bitch's house. You might want to call her number," I said sarcastically and hung my phone up.

The nerve of that ho. I swore that little bitch knocked her head when she was a baby because she wasn't wrapped too damn tight. What the fuck she thought? He was going to leave me for her and then be faithful to her? That bum had a whole wife.

Oh, Lord. I shook that negative energy off and went back to what I was doing before this stupid-ass bitch interrupted me. As a matter of fact, I grabbed my phone back up and pulled her number up. I went ahead and blocked that ass. It saddened me that I had to do that, but that bitch was disrespectful and was dead to me just like her fucking mama.

After I finished filling out applications, I pulled up information on how to get a paternity test done. I'd been putting it off long enough.

Shari

I swore I felt like I was losing my mind. *What the fuck did I do to his ass for him to carry it this raw with me?* I asked myself as I took several pulls off the weed I copped earlier. I had called the bitch he was married to and the bitch he supposedly had a baby with, and both of these bitches carried it. I knew what it was. Their asses were just jealous 'cause he didn't want them. But wait—if he wasn't with them, where the fuck was he? Was he with another bitch I wasn't aware of? I had too many damn questions and no damn answers. It had been three days and I hadn't received one text or phone call. I really thought he and I were on the same page, but I guessed not. I took several more pulls and started coughing. "Damn, bitch, take yo' time," I said out loud to myself.

I heard my phone ringing, and I jumped to pick it up. I accidentally dropped the blunt. *Fuck,* I thought as I picked it up hurriedly before it burned my couch. Shit, I had to fuck a nigga a few times to get the money to buy my living room set. By the time I got to the phone, it had stopped ringing. It was Mama's number. I was disappointed because I was really praying it was Devon. I flopped back down on the couch. *Man, what the fuck this lady want right now?*

I dialed back her number. I lay on my back, staring up at the ceiling. "Yeah."

"Hey, baby. Why you ain't pick up the phone?"

"Ma, it don't matter why I ain't pick up. I called you back, right?" I was annoyed, not really with her but with what I was dealing with.

"Damn, who pissed you off? This wouldn't have nothing to do with that boy?"

"Ma, what boy are you talking about?" I was ready to hang up on her ass for real.

"The boy your sister said you took from her."

"When the fuck she told you this?"

"Watch yo' goddamn mouth. You done lost your mind."

"Ma, I'm grown as hell, and in case you haven't noticed, I have my own place, so I can cuss as much as I want to."

"Mm-hmm, you still my damn baby."

"Ma, when did she tell you that?"

"Girl, I don't know. One day she popped up over here, talking 'bout I was in on it. I cussed her little pissy ass out. She knows better than to put me in some shit. Your pussy is yours, and you're free to screw whoever you want."

"That chick's funny. If he were hers, I couldn't take him. Anyway, she needs to go find out who her real baby daddy is."

"Say what? That boy not her baby daddy?"

"Nah, you know yo' daughter a ho. She better keep my motherfucking name out of her mouth before I run up on that ass."

"Hmm, well, I just want to know if you had a few dollars to spare."

"I knew that was the only reason why you called me. Where is that nigga you have laid up over there? He does know ain't nothing free in this world, not even pussy."

"He don't get paid until Friday, and I just need a few dollars to keep me over until then."

"So you can buy drugs?"

"Shari, come on now. I ain't got nothing to smoke in a while. Your mama is trying to clean up her life. Watch, you goin' to be proud of your mama."

"Listen, I've got to go. Come by later and get it."

"All right, baby. Mama loves you."

I hung the phone up without responding. I loved my mama to death. I just wished she would leave that nigga and the drugs alone. I told her numerous times that I would help her get into rehab, and a few times she agreed until that nigga got into her ear, telling her she could go cold turkey. If you asked me, his nasty ass loved keeping her high so she could depend on him.

I must've dozed off, because banging on the door woke me up. I jumped up and ran to the door.

"Damn, Ma, why the fuck you banging on my door like you're the police?"

"Sorry, baby. I was calling you to let you know I was on the way, but you didn't pick up."

"Maybe 'cause my ass was sleeping."

I walked off to grab my purse. I shouldn't have told her I was going to give her shit. I grabbed $40 out of my purse. I walked back into the living room. I saw her all up in my fridge, looking around. "Why you up in my shit?"

"I'm hungry as hell, but it looks like you ain't been to the store lately."

"Close my fridge. Here goes forty dollars. Please spend it wisely 'cause I ain't got no more to spare."

She snatched the money out of my hand, and her eyes lit up. "God bless you, baby. Mama loves you."

She walked through the door, and I locked it. I walked over to the window and saw as she got into a car and handed the money to a man who was driving. I closed my curtains and shook my head.

I was tired of sitting around here hoping this nigga would show up. I needed to get back out there and start playing these niggas for their money. I really didn't know what in the hell had gotten into me with this nigga, because I had never been so gone over no dick. Shit, to be honest, I kind of loved pussy more than dick. Maybe I needed to get back on that shit. That was when Kaysia ran through my mind. I still couldn't believe that bitch snitched on me to my sister. *Old jealous-ass ho.*

I was definitely starving, and Mama was right. A bitch hadn't been to the grocery store in days. I decided to order some Chinese food. That little place over on Sanford Boulevard had food off the chain. After I placed the order, I decided to take a quick shower before they came.

I was feeling horny as fuck, so while the water beat my skin, I started to play with my pussy. I felt so good fucking myself that I started working my fingers harder, and I ground my pussy down on my fingers.

"Awe, baby, damn this feels so good," I moaned out as I started going faster. My temperature rose, and I started getting hot. "Oh, shit, aweee, oweiiii." I exploded all over my fingers. I got lightheaded, so I held on to the wall for support. Even though I was weak, that shit felt damn good. I put my fingers between my legs and then licked it off. "Shit, bitch, you taste damn good, too," I said out loud as I resumed washing myself off.

As soon as I got out of the tub, I heard a loud banging on the door. *Who the fuck is that?* I wrapped the towel around me and walked to the door. The knocking was getting louder, and I was ready to curse out whoever it was. "Who is it?" I yelled.

"It's Devon," he yelled.

My heart skipped a few beats. I didn't know what I wanted to do. Did I want to let him in or just not answer the door? Truth was, I was happy to see him, and even though he had made me mad, I was weak for him.

"Yeah, what do you want?" I opened the door and asked him.

"What the fuck you doing, coming to the door in just a towel? What, you got a nigga up in here?" He pushed past me and started looking around.

I locked the door and stood there, looking at this madman walking through the house, looking in closets and under the bed.

"For a nigga who's been gone for more than a week, you've got some fucking nerve coming up in here acting like you run shit."

"Yo, what the fuck is that s'posed to mean? What? You got another nigga now?"

"You know what, Devon? You're fucking ridiculous. You know you're in the wrong, so you run up in here, acting like you own me. Nah, nigga, the minute you pulled that little disappearing act, this pussy was up for gra—"

Before I could finish my sentence, this nigga lunged forward and grabbed my neck with one hand, forcing me up into the wall. "Bitch, you better not play with me. Yo, you just don't know, B." He squeezed my neck.

"Boy, get your ass off of me. You must think I'm that stupid-ass sister of mine or the bitch you married. I will get your wig knocked off, nigga. Trust me."

I felt the blows connecting, and all I could do was put my hands up, hoping that they wouldn't reach my face.

"Bitch, you should've listened to yo' dumb-ass sister. I beat bitches." He kept throwing blows on top of blows.

I wanted to scream out, but I couldn't because I was scared it would only infuriate him more. The tears slid down my face as he finally let me go.

"You really put your hands on me?" I looked him dead in the eyes as the tears continued flowing.

"Bitch, you deserved that shit. Oh, yeah, why the fuck you calling Kennedy's phone and shit? Didn't I tell you not to bother that bitch? See, I was trying to be with you, to make you my wife when I get this divorce, but you're hardheaded. You're not goin' to stop until I fucking leave you alone for good."

"Get out of my house, nigga. I swear it's fucking over."

"Bitch, I ain't going nowhere. Matter of fact, go clean yourself up so I can take yo' ass shopping. I've got a few bands to burn on yo' ass."

I stood there looking at him and realized that he was dead serious. I reluctantly walked off into my room. I glanced at my face in the mirror and realized that my face was swollen, especially by my eyes. I was angry but more hurt.

After I applied some MAC makeup, I was able to hide the bruises and cover up the swelling a little bit. I wasn't in the mood to get dolled up, so I grabbed a pair of my Pink sweatpants from Victoria's Secret and a tank top.

I walked out into the living room where he was looking at his phone. I thought about getting a pot of hot water and throwing it on his ass.

"You ready, babes?"

"Yeah," I barely whispered.

We got into his car, and he pulled off. I thought he was going to take me to Bay Plaza, but I realized once he got on the Bronx Expressway that we were going downtown.

We spent hours shopping in the Village in Manhattan. I got two purses out of the Michael Kors store and a few pairs of jeans and some shirts out of the True Religion store. I wasn't goin' to lie. The more money he spent, the quicker I was forgiving him.

"I'm tired now," I said to him after we exited Victoria's Secret.

"You sure, ma? Today is your day."

"Yeah, I'm tired and hungry."

"Yeah, I feel you. My belly's touching my back."

After we made it to the car, he placed the bags into the trunk, and we got in and pulled off.

"Ay yo, I want to apologize about earlier. Man, I don't know what came over me. I think it's because I'm in love with you."

Wait, did I hear this nigga right? Did he say he was in love with me?

"Don't be looking like that. You heard me right. I'm in love with you, B."

I sat quietly, trying to put my words together. I didn't want to say anything that might anger him and bring out his bad side. "Where were you all these days?"

"Listen, I'ma keep it one hundred with you. I was over at Kennedy's house."

I turned to face him, trying my best not to explode. "Over at Kennedy's house? So you're back with that bitch?"

"Hell nah, I ain't back wit' her ass. I thought we talked about this before. I want what's rightfully mine—half if not everything that the bitch has."

"That was way before I fell for you. I really don't give a fuck about that bitch and her money."

"Yeah, I hear you. You're saying that 'cause you ain't the one who had to fuck that dry pussy bitch e'ery night. Controlled by that bitch. I had to be a fucking puppet for this bitch for years. I deserve all that damn money."

I realized he was serious and there was nothing I could say that was going to convince him differently. "So you're back living with her? I'm confused as fuck right now."

He reached over and grabbed my hand. "Listen, babes, I just need to do this for a little while. I'm going to see a lawyer this week. I'm filing for a divorce, so I need to make sure that bitch doesn't have anything on me."

"Mm-hmm."

"Please believe me. Picture us living in a big house out in White Plains. With money in the bank, lots of money. You know how you love designer clothes. Baby, I know this bitch. She doesn't like drama, so she's goin' to settle for whatever I'm asking for. I need you to ride with me on this, babes. We're in this together." He squeezed my hand.

The wheels were spinning in my head, especially when he talked about the big house up in White Plains. I could definitely see me living among the elite. Fuck that ho. I deserved to be living royally. It didn't take much convincing. I was with him on this. "So does that include fucking her?"

"Hell nah. I 'on't want that dry-ass pussy that keeps rubbing on my dick like rubber. Matter of fact, I've got my own room."

"I just don't want to share that dick."

"Babes, you know that you own this dick. Can't no other bitch out here say I'm fucking them."

I didn't say anything. I really didn't believe him, but I didn't want to let him know that I had doubts.

After we got to the house, he bathed me and fucked me good. I threw the pussy on him extra because I wasn't sure what was going on, but I knew that he would miss this fuck that I gave him.

It was getting late and I was drained, so I decided to get ready for bed. I noticed that he was behaving fidgety. "Babes, I'm going to lie down. You coming?"

"Nah, I'm about to bounce."

"You serious?" I looked at him.

"Yeah, B. I told you that I've got to pretend like I'm back with this bitch. Yo, don't start tripping, man. Just look at the bigger picture. We goin' to be rich, babe."

"I hear you." I let out a long sigh and looked at him. I saw that, no matter what I said, it wasn't going to change his mind, so I laid my head on my pillow, feeling helpless.

"A'ight, yo. I'ma hit you later."

"Okay. Just lock the door behind you."

I was feeling irritated as fuck. This nigga beat my ass, and now he was going back to his little bitch. *What kind of fool does he think I am?* I wondered while a tear fell from my eye.

CHAPTER TWENTY-SIX

Amoy

The court date for Devon and me was steadily approaching. That must have been the reason why his ass kept calling me. I thought about blocking his number but decided to do it after I found out the paternity test results. I swore I'd be happy when this nigga was finally out of my fucking life.

The thought had not left my mind when I heard knocking at the door. I knew it wasn't Marquise because I had just spoken to him and he was on his way to Queens. I peeked through the peephole and saw two well-dressed females standing there. They looked like they were detectives, but what the fuck would the police want from me? Marquise ran through my mind. I didn't have time to figure the shit out because they started calling my name. I unlocked the deadbolt and opened the door.

"May I help you?"

"Are you Amoy Simpson?"

"Yes, and you are?"

"My name is Miss Warren, and I'm with New York State's child protective services."

"Okay, and what do you want with me?"

Out of the corner of my eye, I noticed two officers standing there. I started panicking. What the fuck did CPS and the fucking police want with me? Shit, didn't that have to do with kids and shit?

"May we come in?"

"Uh, I don't . . . Yeah, sure." I was confused and nervous.

The ladies stepped in, along with the two officers. "Okay, so our office got a report that you have a minor child who was being abused and neglected. In that report, it was also mentioned that there were illegal activities going on in your apartment, including weapons possession and the dealing of drugs."

"Say what? Who made that report? That shit is a lie," I blurted out.

"It's our office policy that, whenever we get a report about any kind of abuse against a child, we have to investigate the accusations."

"You know what, lady? I don't know what kind of fucking games y'all playing, but I have one fucking child, and he is sitting right there in his swing, and he ain't getting no type of abuse. As far as drugs and guns, do I look like I'm in these fucking streets?"

"You need to calm down. We are only doing our job," the white officer said.

"Look at my baby." I pointed to my son. "He ain't dirty. He ain't hungry, and he ain't got one damn scratch or mark on him."

Both bitches walked over to my baby and were looking at him and writing some shit on their notepads. "Ma'am, is it okay if we take a look around?"

I was going to say yes, but then I remembered that the gun that Marquise gave me was under my mattress. "This is my apartment, and unless you have a warrant, nah, you can't snoop up in here."

"Fair enough, but you know this could help your case with CPS."

"I ain't got no damn case. Somebody's lying to y'all asses."

"Well, fair enough, but know this, if we do come back with a warrant and find anything illegal here, I am personally going to drag your ass to jail, and your son will be placed in CPS custody."

"Get out of my apartment."

"Have a good day, ma'am." The two officers walked out, but the CPS women stayed.

One said, "I need to get some information from you. Miss Simpson, are you employed?"

"Nah, bitch. I don't work, but does that mean I abuse my fucking child?"

"You need to calm down, talking like this in front of the child."

I rolled my eyes at that ho and tried to calm my nerves.

"All right, Miss Simpson. We're done here. You will hear from us after we have concluded our investigation."

I didn't say a damn word. As soon as they exited my shit, I slammed the door behind them. To be honest, I acted all hard in front of them, but I was tearing up on the inside. I walked over to my son and took him out of the swing. I held him close to my chest as the tears started to flow like Dunn's River Falls in Jamaica. I took a seat on the couch as I trembled.

Who the fuck would call these people and do such a horrible thing? Who hates me that fucking much? My stupid-ass mama or my conniving-ass sister? I needed to know, 'cause when I found out, both them bitches were going to feel these hands. I grabbed my phone and unblocked Shari's number.

"Yo, what the fuck you want, bitch?"

"Did you call CPS on me?"

"Ha-ha, nah, you silly bitch. Did they take the little bastard away though?"

"You're a stupid ho. You know something crazy? How did I ever love and care for you? Treated you like you meant the world to me? You're right, little bitch. I should've left you for dead."

Those were the coldest words I'd ever had to say to the person I was supposed to care for the most, but you know what? This time I didn't feel sorry. As a matter of fact, I was feeling damn good because I knew there was no way I would ever let her back in my life again.

I went through my phone and blocked her number again. I then hopped onto Facebook and blocked her there, too. *RIP, little bitch!*

Later that night, Marquise came through. I was getting used to this in-house dick. It was more than that though. It was the way that he cared for me and my son. It was like he accepted him even though we weren't sure he was the father.

"Yo, babe, is something bothering you?" he asked as I leaned my head on his shoulder as he played his Xbox One.

I raised my head and let out a long sigh. "Somebody called CPS on me."

"What?" He paused the game and gave me his full attention.

"The people came here today, talking 'bout how I abused and neglected my child. They also said I have drugs and guns around him."

"Man, why you ain't call me?"

"I know you in them streets. I didn't want to disturb you."

"Man, fuck these streets. You're my woman, and any-thing that has to do wit' you is more important than anything. Did they say who did that shit?"

"Nah. The police even asked me if they could search the apartment. I told his ass hell nah."

"You did right, baby. Unless they've got a warrant, they can't just come up in here. By the way, where is that hammer I gave you?"

"In my room, under the bed."

"A'ight, cool. I'ma take it up outta here. You never know what they've got up their sleeves. I 'on't want you to get involved in no bullshit."

"Yeah, I feel you."

"So what they goin' to do?"

"I don't know. I know it's a lie. I think my mama or my sister got something to do wit' it though."

"You think so? I was thinking it was that fuck nigga. You know these niggas nowadays be acting just like bitches."

Until he said that, I really didn't think it was Devon, but seeing how he was behaving lately, I wouldn't put it past him.

We talked for a little while and then smoked a few blunts together. I was feeling blessed that he was back in my life. I couldn't help but wonder how long this fairy tale was going to last, because I felt like I was cursed from the day I exited that crackhead bitch's bad-luck pussy.

"Bae, you ready?" Marquise yelled.

It was my court day. He told me the night before that he was definitely going with me 'cause he knew Devon was going to be present. I looked at myself in the mirror and walked out to the living room where he and Jamal were waiting.

"'Bout damn time, B."

"Boy, hush. You know I had to make sure my hair was on point."

"Yeah, whatever. Let's go."

We walked out the door, and I locked the door behind us. I was kind of nervous, but after the beating that nigga put on me, there was no way I was going to miss his court date.

"Yo, you goin' to be straight. I love you, girl," he said as he reached over and grabbed my sweaty hand.

"Love you too." This was the first time that I said it back to him.

We got to the courthouse a few minutes before nine. He parked and we walked in. I looked around me, but I didn't see Devon, which was great because I didn't want a confrontation between him and Marquise. We entered the courtroom, and there they were, that nigga and my dumb-ass sister sitting beside him. My blood started boiling just seeing them together. Marquise must've felt it, too, because he placed his arm around me.

"Come sit over here, bae."

I saw when my sister whispered something in Devon's ear, and he turned around and stared at us. Marquise smirked at him. He smiled in return, but it wasn't one of those friendly smiles. It was more like a devilish grin.

The bailiff entered the courtroom, and that broke up the drama that was brewing.

"All rise. The Honorable Judge Hudson presiding."

My body was present, but my mind wasn't as I remembered the day that nigga beat the hell out of me. I was here for his trial and to make sure I told my side of the story.

To my surprise, the coward decided to plead guilty. I couldn't believe I heard right. Instead of facing me on the stand, this bitch-ass nigga entered a guilty plea in exchange for a little bit of time. Who the fuck decided this shit? Why wasn't I notified of this ahead of time? God knew I wouldn't have wasted my time by coming here today. The judge set a date for his sentencing, and just like that, it was over. I waited to speak to the DA.

"Hello, Miss Simpson."

"Why did you accept that plea?" I confronted the DA who was handling the case.

"This was a hard case to prove. It was your word against his, and with your sister willing to testify that you told her it was someone else, if we had gone to trial, there was a possibility that he could've walked. With the plea bargain, I will be asking for prison time, up to eighteen months."

"Eighteen months? Lady, did you look at the pictures? Did you see how bad he beat me? But y'all don't care 'cause it didn't happen to y'all. What does it take? That nigga killing me for y'all to take me serious? Because he's dangerous as hell, and he is allowed to walk these streets," I lashed out.

"I understand you fully, Miss Simpson. Even with the plea, he will get some prison time, and now you can secure a permanent restraining order against him."

I looked at that bitch and shook my head. Whose side was she on anyway? I had a feeling that all of these motherfuckers were buddy-buddy.

"Let's go," I turned and said to Marquise.

He picked up my son, and we left that bitch standing there looking like a damn fool.

We were about to go up the stairs when I heard Devon's voice.

"Now you got this nigga carrying my son and shit?"

I turned around to face this nigga. "Your son? The one you don't even know. Have you even bought a Pamper or, fuck that, a McDonald's Happy Meal? Yes, this nigga can carry him 'cause guess why? He tucks him in at night. He buys him Pampers, sneakers, and clothes. He makes sure he eats."

"You're a stupid-ass ho."

Marquise put little man down and took a few steps down. I jumped in front of him. "Nah, what you doing? You see where we at? This nigga ain't worth it. Trust me, he's pussy, just like the bitch he's standing beside."

"Ha-ha, you're funny. Bitch, you know I'll beat that ass. I done told bae not to trust your nasty, pussy-selling ass."

I stood there laughing in that bitch's face. Another place or time, I would've torn her little young ass up.

"Yo, son, this the second time this ho saved you. The next time, you won't be that lucky," Devon said, winking at Marquise and then walking off.

The walk to the car was quiet. I was furious that this bitch kept on trying me. I just wanted one chance, just one, to show her she wasn't built like that.

After I strapped Jamal in his seat, I got in, and he pulled off. "Yo, B. I know that nigga might be Jamal's father and shit, but I'ma have to dead that nigga. He done threatened my life more than once. I 'on't take no threat lightly, and I'll bust a cap in a nigga before he gets at me first."

"I'm sorry that I brought you into my drama."

"Man, cut that shit out. You ain't did nothing but give the pussy to a lame-ass nigga."

"Yeah, if only I knew how he was goin' to turn out."

"And I know that's yo' sister and shit, but that li'l bitch needs her ass beat."

"Man, I swear I'm still shocked that she's carrying it like that. I don't really care though. Fuck her." I meant every word of that.

"Listen, boo, we need to get that test done. I'm going to set an appointment."

"What test?"

"The paternity test."

"Oh, a'ight. Yeah, go ahead and do that." I whispered under my breath, "God, please don't let my baby be Devon's son."

Kennedy

This nigga had the nerve to ask me if I could go to court with him. Nah, his exact words were, "It would be a good look if my wife went to court with me." So you mean to tell me that this nigga beat up his side bitch and he wanted me, Kennedy, to make a fool out of myself by going to court with him? Ha-ha. I almost choked laughing at that ridiculous idea.

I noticed him sitting at my kitchen table when I walked in from getting groceries. I tried my best to ignore him as I spotted him staring at me.

"So you ain't goin' to ask me what happened in court today?"

"Why should I? That's your business," I said as I washed the grapes in vinegar and water.

"Damn, Kennedy, why are you so cold toward me? I mean, a nigga knows he fucked up, but I'm home now, and I told you that I regret ever fooling around on you."

"So you think that you disrespected your vows and made a fucking, illegitimate bastard and, because you say you're sorry, we should forget all about that and move on?"

"What else can I do? Name it. I'll do whatever you want me to do, and I done told you that bitch's lying. That ain't my damn baby. She's broke and trying to get money up out of me."

"Money? Hmmm." I was about to say, "Nigga, you're broke as hell," but I decided to keep my mouth shut.

He got off his stool and walked over to me. "Listen, Kennedy, baby. You're my wife, my soulmate, my best friend. I'm a man, and I fucked up, but please don't hold this against me. This is what that bitch wants. She wants you to leave me, thinking I'll be back over there. Yo, B. I love you, and if I can't have you, then I don't want to be fucking alive." He grabbed my hand and fell to his knees. "Please, baby, forgive me. I can be the man you want me to be if you just show me."

"You look fucking weak right now, and you know how much I despise weak-ass men."

"I don't care how the fuck I look right now. I fucking love you, and I don't care if I look like a bitch."

He stood up and started rubbing on me. God knew I was trying to back up, but this nigga and his hands always managed to keep me hostage.

They say that breakup and make-up sex was the best. It had been months since I gave him the pussy, and no lie, my love hole was missing his ass, or more like his dick, like a motherfucker. His chocolate body was very enticing in that wife beater. He palmed the bottom of my ass as he stuck his tongue down my throat. My brain was telling me to push his trifling ass off me, but my pussy and my heart were in cahoots.

"Ugh, don't touch me, Devon," I snapped with an attitude.

I guessed he said, "Fuck that shit she's talking," because he wrapped his arms around my waist and pressed his hard dick against my body.

"Kennedy, babe, don't act like that," he whispered into my ear, followed by a kiss.

"Stop, Devonnn, you know that's my spot," I whined like a baby.

He continued to kiss around my ear, and then he slid his fingers down my shorts, into my wetness.

"Sssss, stop it," I moaned.

There was no way I was going to stop him. My pussy was so moist and wet, and his dick was yearning for my sweet, chocolate pussy. He licked his finger, tasting my juices while he stared in my eyes. I unzipped his pants and slid his dick out of his boxers. I was truly missing Devon's sex, no matter how many side bitches he had. I was battling with different emotions. I sure hated his ass for the shit he did to me, and then I was loving the way he was finessing my body.

"Stop it, Devon. You know I hate your ass right about now."

He totally ignored my pleas. He slid my panties to the side and squeezed his dick into my wetness, lifting me up and wrapping my legs around his waist. "Oh, shit, babe. I miss you so much," he whispered in my ear as he sank his manhood deeper inside of me, penetrating into my goodies.

"Sssss, I hate you so damn much," I moaned. He carried me while he was still inside of me. He put me down and slid out. He then turned me around on the couch. My back was arched perfectly as he gripped my shoulders to keep me from running from the dick.

"I hate you. I fuckin' hate you," I moaned louder and louder, at the same time backing it up on his dick.

He didn't ease up any as he applied pressure. I finally decided to stop fighting the feeling and loosen up. He started slapping my ass. "You hate me, huh?" He slapped my ass harder and jammed every inch of his dick into my pussy. His balls smacked against my ass with each thrust he took.

"I love you, Devon. I fucking love you." I sang a new tune while I felt his dick go in and out of my wetness. He continued slapping my ass, and I screamed out in ecstasy.

"Oh, shit, Kennedy. Oooooh, shit," he groaned.

My pussy muscles gripped his dick. I threw the pussy back like a champ, and I was definitely the most valuable player. His veins got bigger. He grabbed me aggressively, and seconds later, his dick was spitting out cum like a sprinkler.

After he pulled out, I hurriedly ran up the stairs. I couldn't believe that I allowed this to happen. But wait, I actually liked it, so why was I feeling like this? *Kennedy, get out of your feelings,* my inner voice scolded.

I got off the bed and decided to take a shower. I was slipping, though, because I should've made him use a condom. I was too old to be having a burning pussy.

After I took my shower, I decided to finish unpacking my groceries. Shit, the ice cream that I bought was left on the counter and had melted. I threw it in the trash and wiped the counter off. I thought about throwing something in the oven, but to be honest, after getting fucked that good, all my energy was gone. I had to remind myself that I was no longer in my twenties.

I didn't see Devon after we had sex. I assumed that he was in his room, trying to recuperate from beating up this pussy.

After warming up some Progresso Clam Chowder, I decided to lie down and relax. I grabbed the remote, trying to catch an episode of *Criminal Minds* on A&E. Before I could rest my head on the pillow, my phone started ringing.

"Hello."

"Hey there, beautiful." Christopher's voice caught me off guard.

"Hey, you. How you doing?"

"I got that info you requested the other day."

I took a second, trying to remember what info he was supposed to get for me. It quickly flashed in my head. "Oh, shit. I totally forgot about that."

"Yeah, I was tied up on another case. That's why I didn't get with you sooner."

"So are you going to email it to me?"

"I was thinking about dropping by so I can make sweet love to your mind and soul. You know I can make that thing wet," he chuckled.

All of a sudden, I didn't feel too good. "No, Chris, I need to take a rain check. I'm a little bit under the weather."

"I can come over and make you some homemade soup," he persisted.

"Christopher, no. I'm just going to sleep."

"All right. I'll email you the information."

"Thank you, Chris."

I hung up the phone, sort of feeling bad that I was so short with him. But there was no way I could invite him over, knowing Devon was here. I thought I'd made a big mistake when I allowed him to fuck me the other day.

I am too tired to stress over all this shit right now. Tomorrow I'll figure out a way to make it up to Christopher, I thought before I dozed off.

Shari

The last couple of days, I'd noticed that when I peed, it started burning. At first, I thought it was only because Devon and I had sex and he tore my ass up as usual. But this morning, we didn't have sex, and when I went to pee, the pain had become unbearable to the point where I couldn't move. On top of that, a foul smell was coming out of my pussy when I stuck my finger in there.

I got dressed and decided to go to the clinic on Fourth Street. As I sat there waiting to be called, I couldn't help but wonder what the hell was going on. I was a bitch who loved getting head, so I tried my best to keep my shit on point at all times. *Devon . . . Fuck, I totally forgot about old boy I fucked the other day. Shit, I didn't make that nigga wear a condom. Oh, fuck.*

"Miss Simpson." The nurse finally called my name after about forty-five minutes of waiting. I followed her into the room. "What brings you in today?"

"I need to do some tests. I think I've got something."

"Please be more specific."

"I think I've got some sort of STD."

"What symptoms are you experiencing?"

"Burning and painful urination and . . . oh, yeah, a fishy smell."

"Are you sexually active, and how many partners do you have?"

"Listen, lady, I've only got one. Okay?" I was getting irritated with all these damn questions. As a matter of fact, my ass really didn't want to be here.

"Put this gown on and remove everything from the waist down. The doctor will be in shortly. Here's a cup. Pee in it and put it in the window."

Soon after she left the room, I quickly took my clothes off. I was ready for this process to be over with quickly. Ten minutes later, the doctor walked in, and I told his ass the same shit I told the nurse. He placed me on the bed and examined me. He also took samples to send to the lab.

"Miss Simpson, it seems like you have gonorrhea. I am sending off the samples to the lab, and those tests won't be back for a few days. I'm going to give you a single dose of two hundred and fifty milligrams of intramuscular Ceftriaxone and one gram of oral Azithromycin. Please advise your partner so he can also get tested and treated. Until this is cleared up, please refrain from having sexual intercourse. Also, your pregnancy test came back positive."

"What?" I looked at him.

"Congrats on your pregnancy. It's best for you to follow up with your doctor to start getting prenatal care."

I wasn't really paying attention to what the fuck he was saying. I was going straight to the abortion clinic ASAP.

After I left their office, I hurried to my car. I was tight as fuck because I knew one of these niggas gave this shit to me. Which one of them was the million-dollar question. I wanted to call both of them, but if I called the wrong one, it would be proven that I was fucking around. My head started hurting. I hoped I didn't give this shit to Devon, or it could possibly be his ass who gave that shit to me. I needed a way to find out who gave this shit to me.

As far as being pregnant, I could tell Devon that I was pregnant, and we could have our own little family since Amoy's baby wasn't really his in the first place. I smiled as I thought about how freaking brilliant that idea was.

I stopped by the grocery store to pick up some chicken breasts. I looked up a recipe on YouTube, and I was going to try it. Shit, it wouldn't be a five-star meal, but hey, with this good news that I was about to give him, shit, he couldn't help but be grateful that a bitch was trying.

I got my items, paid, and walked out. I dialed Devon's number to let him know I was cooking, but his phone went straight to voicemail. Here this nigga was with this bullshit. I threw the phone on the passenger seat and cut the music on. I was trying my best not to get irritated because I knew what he was trying to get done. I just wished he would just kill the bitch and get it over with already.

CHAPTER TWENTY-SEVEN

Amoy

"Dear God, I know I haven't been the best, but I come to you as humbly as I possibly can. God, I need to ask you this one favor. Please let Marquise be the father of my son. I know I should've been more careful, but if you're going to punish someone, please punish me for my sins and not my baby. My baby needs a father who can provide and teach him to be a man. God, please, I'm begging you." I got off my knees and wiped the tears away from my eyes. I swore I needed this one miracle.

"Listen, bae, I know you're nervous and shit, but we need to know this." He squeezed my hand as we walked to the building. A week ago, I scheduled for us to go in and get the test done.

We had to wait a few weeks to get the results back, and those were the worst couple of weeks of my life. I kept wondering how I was going to deal with this nigga, Devon, if he turned out to be my son's father and, most importantly, how the relationship between Marquise and my son was going to be if Jamal wasn't his child.

I knew he said he would still be here, but at this moment, that was all talk. I guessed that was the bed that I made.

***

I finally got a call back from a salon in the Bronx. I would be braiding hair and doing the shampooing. It wasn't much right now, but it would help me to make a few coins while I got into beauty school. I knew Marquise was spending his money, but shit, I wasn't sure how long it would last. I was excited as hell to share this news with him.

I pulled up and parked in my parking space. Before I could run into the apartment, I noticed the mail lady pulling up, so I turned back around. I had no idea why because all I ever received was damn bills, and it was sure bill time again. "Miss Pam, you got anything for me?" I asked as I approached the mail lady.

"Hmm, let's see." She dug through her mail. "Yup. Here you go." She handed me three pieces of mail.

"Thank you."

I took them and walked off. I noticed the big envelope, so I decided to open it up first. I stopped dead in my tracks.

You're excluded as the biological father of Devon Jamal Guthrie Jr. The probability of paternity is 0 percent.

I read it over and over, and it was still saying the same thing. My head started feeling dizzy. How could this be? *God, no!* I leaned on my front door as I tried to digest this bullshit. A few minutes later, I wiped my tears and opened the door.

"Hey, bae." Marquise greeted me as soon as I walked in the door.

I noticed he was sitting there playing a video game with little man sitting on his lap, pretending like he was playing also. I couldn't find the words to say anything. Instead, I flopped down beside him on the couch.

"You a'ight, bae?"

I shoved the paper at him.

"What's this?" he quizzed.

Before I could respond, he had already started reading. He took little man off his leg and paused the game. He stood up, took another look at the paper, and walked off. I got up and followed him into the hallway.

"Man, how the fuck could this be? They wrong, bae. They fucking wrong. That nigga ain't no damn father. I am, B," he yelled as he hit the wall.

I didn't know what to say to him. I was hurting just as much as him or even more. I wrapped my arms around him as I felt a tear drop on my arm.

"Babe, listen, I'm so sorry. I didn't mean for this to happen," I said while tears started to flow.

"That nigga don't know shit about him. He's too busy to even check on him. How the fuck he a father, huh?"

"I know, baby. I'm just as shocked as you." I hugged him tighter.

He turned around to face me. He pulled me closer and hugged me. "Listen, B. I don't give a fuck what them white people shit say. This my motherfucking son, and I ain't goin' nowhere."

We hugged each other, crying, until we both heard little man. "Mama."

Marquise let me go and picked Jamal up. "Yo, you're my son, and that's law," he said to my son and hugged him tight.

It broke my heart to see this man in so much pain. As a matter of fact, this was my first time seeing him this emotional. He was always this hard street nigga, but right now, I was definitely seeing another side of him. A side that was calmer and genuine.

Now that I knew he wasn't the father, I knew the only other option was Devon. It hurt my stomach just to think that his blood was running through my son's veins. I thought about not telling him, but I wasn't that type of person, and I wouldn't dare keep him away from his child. I was hoping the bum would give up his rights, but knowing him, it was all about control, and he would not give me the satisfaction.

After we calmed down from the shock, we decided to order something to eat. Jamal ate, and I gave him a bath. We watched cartoons with him, but before the cartoon was over, he was knocked out. I took him to his room and tucked him in. I returned to the living room to chill with Marquise. I knew we were both feeling fucked up behind the results, but there wasn't anything that I could really do about it.

We ended up getting fucked up after smoking blunt after blunt and drinking Grey Goose. That night, we didn't have sex. Instead, he just held me as we both got lost in our thoughts.

After I dropped Jamal at day care and Marquise left for the day, I decided to give Devon a call.

"Yo, what the fuck you callin' my line fo'?" his arrogant ass answered.

"Boy, whatever. I did the paternity test on Jamal. Marquise ain't the father, so that leaves you as the only other option."

"Bitch, you're silly as fuck. So you mean to tell me this whole time you had me believing I was the father, and now you're telling me you had to do a test. You're a bigger ho than I thought."

"You know what? I was so praying that you weren't his father because you're a no-good-ass nigga. All I want from you is for you to sign over your fucking rights so I don't ever have to deal with you again," I lashed out.

"Bitch, I ain't signing shit. Fuck you. Matter of fact, I will be taking your ass to court for full custody. There's no way I'ma let you raise my son around that bitch-ass nigga. And oh, yeah, ho, you need to find somewhere else to lay your head. I want you out of my shit."

"Your shit?"

"Yeah, bitch. Did you forget that I was the one who got it for you in the first place? Ungrateful-ass ho."

I hung up on his ass while steaming with anger. This nigga deserved to die for real. I sat on the bed, trying to calm myself down. I had no idea how the fuck I allowed myself to even fuck this bitch-ass nigga. I dialed Marquise's number.

"Hey, babes. You a'ight?"

"No, I'm not. I swear I hate Devon's ass," I cried into the phone.

"Why? What that fuck nigga did? Did he do something to hurt you?" He bombarded me with questions.

"I called his ass to tell him that I thought he was the father, and that nigga went off, calling me all kinds of names. Then he's talking about he goin' to take me to court for full custody. I swear, boo, if he comes near my child, I'ma kill his ass."

"Babe, listen to me. That pussy nigga ain't goin' to do shit. He's just trying to scare you. Man, if that nigga ever does anything to hurt you, I'ma bury his ass."

"I just need to move for real and get away from him."

"Yeah, I feel you, bae. But ay, I'm out here in these streets. I'ma hit you back later."

"Okay, love you."

"Love you, bae."

I hung the phone up and lay back on the bed. I needed to move out of this place ASAP. I didn't have all of the money, so I planned on asking Marquise for help later.

Kennedy

I checked my email and saw what Christopher sent to me. It was a picture and an address. I sat there, staring at the bitch who called my number looking for my husband. It was crazy because she resembled the bitch I visited before. As a matter of fact, they could pass for twins. What kind of crazy joke was this? Was this the same bitch? I grabbed my phone and called Christopher.

"Hello there, pretty lady."

"Christopher, this picture you sent me . . . are you sure this is the person?"

"Yes, I'm one hundred percent sure. I followed her around for a few days, and I also caught a few pics of your husband going in and out of her apartment. Is something wrong?"

"Nah, maybe I'm just tripping. But there's a slight resemblance between the bitch who has the baby and this one."

"I thought the same thing at first, and after digging around, I found out they're sisters."

"You're fucking lying, Christopher," I yelled out.

"No, ma'am. I'm pretty sure they are. The one with the baby is the oldest."

"What a dog. You mean to tell me my husband is fucking two sisters and has a baby by one? Wow, fucking amazing."

"I told you his ass has been busy."

"I see. Anyway, I will call you later. I just had to make sure I wasn't tripping."

"All righty. Talk to you later."

After we hung up, I put the address in my phone. I grabbed my purse and headed out the door. I knew that maybe I should leave this alone, but I refused to. I needed to know every little bit of dirt this nigga was doing. I walked downstairs, where he was in the living room, playing music.

"I'm heading out for a little while," I yelled over the music.

"Where you off to? Do you need me to go with you?"

"No, I'm just running down to the bank. I'll be back in a few. Maybe we can grab something to eat at Fridays later."

"A'ight, babes. Sounds like a plan. Be careful out there, and remember I love you." He came over and kissed me.

I smiled at him as I hurried out the door. I got in the car and pulled off. I was on a mission.

I pulled up to the apartment complex, parked, and walked to the building. I realized that I had to walk up the damn stairs. *Fuck,* I thought as I started climbing these damn stairs.

I reached the apartment and knocked. I had no idea what I was going to say to get in here.

"Who is it?" she yelled.

"It's Kennedy." I decided not to beat around the bush.

There were a few seconds of silence, and then I heard the locks unlocking, and the door flew wide open. "Look at what we've got here." She stood there, one hand on her waist and the other holding the door.

"I see you remember who I am, and since we're both grown, how about I step inside?"

She moved out of the way and used her hand to motion me to step inside.

"So what can I do for you? Isn't your husband back home with you?"

"Yes, that two-timing-ass bastard is back at the house. As far as with me, I doubt that."

"Well, what the fuck you want with me?"

"What I want from you is for you to tell me how long you've been screwing my husband."

"Don't you think you should be asking your husband these questions?"

"Listen to me, little bitch. We both know the nigga is a dog. Matter of fact, isn't he fucking your sister also? Oops, did you know about that?"

"Listen, Kennedy, or whatever your fucking name is, I don't give a fuck if that nigga's fucking you, my sister, or a goddamn dog. All I care about is when he's fucking me."

"Nonsense! You're putting up this hard facade, but I see through it. Matter of fact, I've been through this kind of shit before. You know, when you love a man and, in your heart, you're hoping that he'll leave all those other women he's sleeping with. I've been there, so I feel your pain, but, baby girl, it's all empty promises."

"Bitch, you think you know me, huh? I'm nothing like you or my motherfucking sister. Matter of fact, you're the one who married him, not me. So while you're over here preaching to me like you're a fucking saint, shouldn't you be worried about who your husband is fucking right now? 'Cause guess what? I ain't worried."

"Ha-ha, little girl. One thing I've learned in my years of dealing with men is that if he's going to cheat, he's going to do it, and there's nothing me or the next woman can do to stop him. See, the difference between you and me is that I don't need that cheating-ass bastard, so like a sick puppy, he will always run back to me."

"Yeah, right. I might not be old and wrinkled like yo' ass, but trust me, I do know that you're worried about that nigga 'cause if yo' ass weren't, you would be lying up comfortably in yo' big-ass house and not standing in my living room trying to convince me that you don't want him."

"You know what's wrong with us women? Instead of us sticking together and stopping these cheating-ass niggas, we lie for them, give them pussy, and let them dog us out. You're still young, and you've got a long way to go. It might not be today, but karma's going to bite you in the ass. That nigga ain't shit, and you will find out in due time."

"Listen, I don't want to hear shit you've got to say. From my understanding, the nigga's back over there with you. So go on home, put that old, wrinkled-ass pussy on him, and make him happy. I don't have shit else to say to you, so please lose my fucking address. Oh, by the way, how do you know where I live?"

"How would I get it? You're the smart dummy. I'll let myself out."

I took one last look at the bitch and walked to the door. I unlocked it and let myself out. I was disgusted with Devon and how he disrespected me.

Shari

I was past irritated that this bitch showed up where the fuck I lived at. How the fuck did she know where I laid my head at, and why would she think it was cool to pop up at my shit just because we were fucking the same nigga? As soon as I saw her pull off, I grabbed my phone.

The phone rang a few times and then went straight to voicemail. I didn't ease up any. I kept redialing the number.

"Yo, man, what the fuck you blowing me up for like you're dying or something?"

"Shit, nigga, I know you see me calling you," I said, sounding irritated.

"Man, you know I'm at the crib, and I can't be on the phone like that in the daytime. I don't want ol' girl to think that I'm on no bullshit."

"Hmm, that's strange."

"What's strange?"

"You claiming that you're at home, and you're worried about that bitch hearing you on the phone, but her ass just left here."

"Say what? Who just left there?"

"Mm-hmm. Nigga, you're too funny. You know what? Go ahead and play them damn games by yourself."

I didn't wait for a response. I just hung the phone up. That nigga sat there telling a whole lie, not knowing that bitch was just over here. I didn't know what to make of this dude. One second, it seemed like he loved me and we were going to work it out, but as soon as I started believing in him, he'd do something that made me question how solid he really was.

"Hello. Man, what you want?" I answered the third time he called back.

"I'm on the way over, B." This time he hung up before I could respond.

I just shook my head and threw the phone down. *Oh, now he wants to fly over here 'cause his bitch was here. Tell you about his flip-flop ass,* I thought as I cut the TV on. I was gone all day and didn't get a chance to watch *Paternity Court.* Shit, I might be having my own case of paternity court going on.

"Open the door, man." I heard him yelling and banging.

I opened the door and looked at him like he'd lost his fucking mind. "Yo, you do know I've got neighbors. Why are you out here behaving like this?"

"Man, you shoulda opened this shit when I first knocked."

I was going to argue, but I remembered what took place the last time that we got into it. I wasn't trying to get my ass beat again. I took a seat on the couch, pretending like I was still watching television.

"Yo, why'd you hang the phone up when I was trying to talk to you?"

"Because, boy, all you do is lie, lie, lie. I mean, I'm tired of all the bullshit you're dishing out. I mean, I know what the fuck you say you're doing, but your actions are screaming differently."

"Man, c'mon, B. Do I have to keep going over the same damn thing? So what did Kennedy say to you?"

"Nah, the question is, why did you give this bitch my address?"

"Man, what? I ain't give nobody yo' damn address and definitely not her."

"I don't know what kind of games y'all playing, but y'all need to keep that shit over there at y'all house."

"Yo, B, I'm dead-ass serious. I didn't give her your address or discuss you with her. So what the fuck she say?" He seemed agitated.

"Why don't you ask her? I mean, you her husband and shit. Remember, I'm just the side bitch."

"Yo, B, cut it, man. You know what? I don't need this shit. Maybe y'all two can get together and suck on each other's pussy. I'm out."

"You're so fucking disrespectful. I swear."

"Disrespectful? You keep playing kiddie games and shit. Like you want me to beg you. Nah, B. I'm a grown-ass man, and I ain't got time for y'all childish games. I'm out."

I really thought he was bluffing or trying my hand to see if I would fold. Shit got real when he opened the door and walked out. I jumped off the couch and ran out the door after him. "Devon, wait. You can't go." I grabbed the back of his shirt.

"Man, get off me," he said and tried to get away from me.

"Please don't go. I'm pregnant."

He stopped suddenly and turned around to face me. "You what?"

"I'm pregnant, bae."

"Man, it ain't mine."

I let go of his shirt. "What the fuck you mean it ain't yours? You're the only nigga I been fucking."

"Man, you know what? I'm sorry, babe. You just caught me off guard." He stepped closer and hugged me.

Yeah, that's more like it.

"Come inside. Let me talk to you." He grabbed my hand and led me inside.

I knew he would see things my way once I told him I was pregnant. He took a seat on the couch. "Come here. Sit right here."

I took a seat on his lap. He took my hands into his hands. "You pregnant for real?"

"Yes, I went to the doctor today."

"Damn, babe. How far along are you?"

"I'm not sure. I need to follow up with my primary care doctor."

"For what? You having an abortion, right?"

I jumped off that nigga's leg and stood over him. "What the fuck you just ask me?"

"I mean, c'mon, you know what I'm trying to do. I can't be having no more babies popping out."

"No more babies? So now you're claiming my sister's little bastard?"

"You ain't heard?"

"Heard what?"

"The paternity test came back that the other nigga ain't the daddy."

"And what? You think you're automatically the daddy? I can't believe you're so naive. That bitch was a pussy-selling whore. Anybody can be the damn daddy, but here you are thinking you're special 'cause she said you're the daddy."

"Damn, B. You sound bitter as fuck. How do you want to be my woman but you're not willing to accept my seed?"

"Boy, I hate that bitch, and I hate anything that is part of her, including that fucking baby. You can go ahead and play daddy. That ain't got nothing to do with our relationship. I'm fucking you, not your child."

"Yo, this been on my mind for a long time, so I'm curious. Were you always this hateful toward your sister, or you just developed this?"

"Hate? Nah, let me correct you. I despise this bitch. You know, when I was younger, I looked up to that bitch. Matter of fact, I wanted to be like that bitch. But the older I got, I realized how selfish that bitch was. She only cared for herself, so I started developing my hate for her."

"Damn, B, that's deep. I wish I had known that y'all were sisters—"

"What? You wouldn't have fucked with me, nigga?" I cut him off before he got to talking stupid.

"I'm just saying y'all need to mend y'all relationship."

"So now you give a fuck? Ha-ha, you're a funny nigga. If you care so fucking much, you would've left, but you didn't. So guess what? Yo' ass ain't no good either. I don't give a fuck about all this that you're talking 'bout. I got my own shit to worry about."

"A'ight, man. Chill out wit' all this. We need to figure out what we're goin' to do."

"Nah, I know what I'm doing. The question is what you goin' to do?"

"You're not thinking rationally right now. You're going off emotions."

"Really, Devon? Why you don't just kill the bitch? It's much easier than you playing house and shit. Yo' ass might still lose. That bitch ain't no fool."

"Yeah, I've been thinking 'bout that, too. I just know I'm the first person they're gonna look at if something was to happen to her, and considering my track record . . ."

"Man, if we go ahead and plan this shit out, trust me, they can't tie you to anything. Plus, I'll be yo' alibi. See, they know you were fucking my sister, not me."

"Well, let's think this out clearly. It would be good to get this out of my life permanently and still get all of her fucking money. That bitch is damn near a millionaire."

"Yes, now you're talking, babe. We're goin' to be some rich motherfuckers. We can push that bitch down the stairs and make it seem like her old ass fell, or we can find somebody to shoot that bitch in the head." I giggled.

"Like I said, I can't do it because I'm going to be the first suspect on their list. But I know a few niggas who are hungry and will definitely take that bitch out for the right price. I'ma do some thinking. Listen, don't ever text me or talk about this on the phone. You know that's how niggas be getting caught up in some bullshit."

"Trust me, I know. I watch a lot of shows on the ID channel."

"A'ight, cool. I've got to get back to the house and play husband. I love you, yo. In the meantime, you need to think about getting an abortion. C'mon, babe, we've still got our whole lives ahead of us, and if a baby is involved, they might say that's why I killed her. Trust me, I know how these motherfuckers operate."

He stood up and grabbed me toward him. "Listen, yo, you're my woman, so quit getting in your feelings and shit. I ain't goin' nowhere, just like yo' ass ain't goin' nowhere. You hear me?"

"Yeah, I hear you," I said nonchalantly.

He started kissing me passionately. I placed my hands around his neck and kissed him back. I wasn't listening to none of that nonsense he was spitting. I was more worried about the money that we were going to get after this bitch died.

CHAPTER TWENTY-EIGHT

Kennedy

"Doctor, I know what you just said, but I'm telling you you're wrong. There's no way I've got no damn gonorrhea. Do you see my age? I ain't had that shit in my twenties, so I know damn well there's no way I've got it now."

"Mrs. Guthrie, I examined you, and I listened to you tell me the symptoms you're feeling, and this is what it sounds like. You said you're sexually active, so it could possibly be from your partner."

"Doctor, listen, how long does it take for those other tests to come back?"

"Three or four days at the most. If there's anything, you will receive a call from us for you to come in. In the meantime, I'm going to give you a single shot of an antibiotic called Ceftriaxone, along with a second oral antibiotic called Doxycycline. Please don't have sex while you're being treated, and you might want to tell your partner so he can get tested also. If he doesn't get treatment, he'll just reinfect you."

I didn't say much. Instead, I just laid my head back on the examining table. I was at a loss for words, and to be honest, what was I going to say? I was a fucking fool.

After I left the doctor's office, I headed straight home. I was too fucking pissed to say the least. I fucked two men. One used a condom and one didn't, so there was no reason for me to guess which one of them had a burning dick. I shook my head. I was disgusted as hell. Never had I ever had to go in no doctor's office, telling them my pussy was on fire until now. I was doing a hundred miles per hour, trying to get home.

I pulled into the driveway and quickly turned the car off. I grabbed my purse and rushed up the stairs. I was so mad that I forgot to check if his car was parked in the front. First, I looked in my room. He wasn't there, so I rushed to his room. I tried to bust in, but the door was locked.

I started banging on the door with my fist. I wanted to break this shit off the hinges. "Open this fucking door, Devon," I yelled out.

"Damn, bae, I didn't hear you come in. What's going on?"

"What's going on? Your dirty-dick ass done gave me a fucking STD."

"What the hell you talking 'bout, Kennedy? I ain't gave you shit."

I took the paper out of my purse and threw it at him. "See there. I've got gonorrhea, and you're the only man I'm sleeping with."

"You sure about that? Remember I was gone for a while, and you had that other nigga all up in here. Maybe his ass gave that shit to you, 'cause I ain't got shit. My dick is perfectly fine," he chuckled.

"You know, I really thought we had a chance, but you're not even man enough to admit when you're wrong. I know you gave me this shit because you're nasty, and you were running up in them hoes without a condom."

"Kennedy, baby, I swear I'm a changed man. I told you if you gave me another chance, I would not cheat anymore, and I mean that. I'll go get tested tomorrow, but I doubt that I have anything."

I looked at him, shook my head, and walked away. I wanted to throw his ass out, but that wouldn't make sense. I had a plan.

I was lying down in my room, just thinking about life. I needed a change of scenery. Lately, I'd been thinking about relocating to Florida. My oldest sister, Flora, lived in Fort Lauderdale, and for years she had been asking me to move down there. I was a New York girl and never thought of leaving. But what was really here for me? Nothing, not after all the shit that I'd been through for the last few months. I was ready to sell these houses and buy me a house in Florida. Truth was, I wasn't getting any younger and needed to start thinking about my golden years.

The ringing of my cell phone interrupted my thoughts. I reached over and grabbed it up. I really wasn't in the mood to talk to anyone right now. "Hello."

"Hey there, beautiful."

"Hey there."

"I'm calling you to invite you to my house for dinner. I never showed you, but your boy knows his way around the kitchen."

"I 'on't know. You know what? What time is dinner?" I thought about turning him down, but what the hell? I was feeling depressed and needed to get out of the house.

"Dinner is at seven sharp. That will give you some time to get all fancy. You know how you do," he chuckled.

"Okay. Text me the address so I can put it in my GPS, and I'll see you at seven."

I lay back down on the bed, second-guessing myself. I grabbed the phone to cancel, but before I could press the call button, I hung the phone up. I took a quick shower and got dressed in a pair of slacks and a nice shirt. I applied a little face powder and lipstick and put my long mane into a bun. I kept it simple and classy.

As I pulled out of the driveway, I looked up and saw Devon looking out of the corner of the bedroom curtain. I cut the music up and sped off down the street. Christopher stayed over by the Village of Pelham, a nice, affluent neighborhood. The houses were huge and looked like they were well cared for. *How does a PI afford this kind of living?* I thought as the GPS notified me that I had reached my destination. I made a right turn at the Victorian-style home. Before I could park, he walked out of the house, smiling from ear to ear. I parked and got out of the car. We exchanged hugs, and he walked into his house, and I followed.

"Welcome to my home. Make yourself as comfortable as you want."

"This is nice, Christopher."

"Well, thank you, my love. The dining room is this way. I cooked lamb, potatoes, and asparagus."

"Wow! A man with taste. You never cease to amaze me at all."

"Well, when a man sees a woman he wants, he will go out of his way to make sure she's comfortable at all times."

I just smiled because I was still in pain, but I couldn't let it show.

"Okay, I have gin, Jamaica overproof rum, and Baileys."

"Let me find out you've been studying me. Baileys is my favorite, so can I get a glass of that please?"

He placed a large bottle of Baileys in front of me, along with a bowl of ice. Soon after, dinner was served.

"I have to tell you that this is the most tender lamb I've ever eaten."

"Well, thank you. I was kind of nervous, but I seasoned it yesterday and let it marinate."

"Well, you did that, sir."

"Well, if you insist," he chuckled.

After dinner was over, we moved to the living room, where we watched a few movies.

"Tell me, Christopher, you ever thought about killing someone?"

"Hmmm. I hope it's not me," he laughed.

"No, I'm serious. Has someone ever done something to you so bad that you just snapped and wanted to blow their fucking head off?"

"Well, no, but I felt like I wanted to kill my ex-wife. That woman dragged me through the mud. When she was done, I felt broken."

"Well, I did . . ."

"You did what?"

"I killed someone before."

"Ha-ha, this Baileys is really taking a toll on you. Now you're telling fascinating stories."

"I'm serious. You know I told you my husband was killed. I killed him. That bastard cheated and cheated with everything that had a pussy, and I begged him and begged him to stop, but he laughed at me. He even told me one night that my pussy was too dry and the young bitches gave him life. How was I supposed to feel after that? My husband telling me that he wanted other bitches? I tell you what I did. I got me a gun, and I blew his fucking brains out. I bet you he ain't fucking nothing else now. That dick is dead!" I chuckled.

"Wow! That's a story there. Are you for real?"

"Yes, I'm for real. See, Christopher, I keep telling you I'm not no little helpless woman. I know how to defend myself."

"I'm at a loss for words. So how did you get away with it?"

"That was the easy part. I'd been planning his murder for about a year, so I created an alibi, and I made sure someone else found his body. When the police came, I almost fainted. I was so distraught over the death of my husband, I had to be hospitalized for days."

"And the gun?"

"No, no, I can't tell you all of that. If I do, I might have to kill you, too."

"You're right. I don't want to end up like his ass. He's one unlucky fella. I just hope you were careful enough. You know there's no statute of limitation on murder."

"I ain't worried. Every so often, I call the station to see if there's any leads on the murder case of my husband, and each time, the detective on the case tells me there's still no news. Sometimes, I want to laugh at how dumb they really are."

"Well, my love, on that note, let's drink to one of the smartest women of all time."

It felt good getting that off my chest. It had been years that I'd walked around with all of that bottled up inside. I took a big gulp of the Baileys. I cringed as it burned my stomach lining. I couldn't tell Christopher I was on the verge of murdering another sorry-ass bastard.

"You're in no shape to drive home. So either I drive you home or you spend the night in my guest room," Christopher said.

"Christopher, I'm not drunk, just a little tipsy," I said before I fell on the couch.

CHAPTER TWENTY-NINE

Amoy

When it rained, it poured. I got an eviction notice today. I knew Devon's ass was being spiteful. His ass could've waited until I found somewhere else to live. What the fuck was I going to do? I applied for Section 8 a year ago, but the waiting list was long as fuck. I knew bitches who had been waiting for three years and still hadn't been approved. This stress was getting to be too damn much.

I thought about moving to the Bronx. At least those apartments were a tad bit cheaper, but they were way smaller. I had a few dollars saved up from working, but it wasn't enough for no two bedrooms when I had to pay first, last, and security deposit.

We sat at the table, eating dinner. I tried to put on my best face, but the stress of getting evicted was weighing heavily on me.

"Bae, what's going on wit' you? You seem a little distant. You good?"

I took a long sigh. I was trying to hide everything from him, but time was winding down, and I could no longer hide it. "I'm getting put out of here."

"What you mean?" He gave me his full attention.

"I didn't tell you, but Devon was the one who got me this place. He told me he was paying the rent, so I wasn't wor—"

"What the fuck you mean you had this nigga paying for this and you have me over here? Man, what kind of foul shit you on?" he yelled.

"It wasn't like that. Once me and you started back fucking with each other, I wanted to move, but I didn't have the money."

"I ain't tryin'a hear that shit, B. You know damn well we ain't hurting for no paper. Yo, B, you on some sneaky shit, and I ain't feeling it. Yo, are you still fucking wit' that nigga?"

"No, I'm not. You know damn well what that nigga did to me. You must think I'm a weak bitch or something." I looked at him while the tears rolled down my face.

"Man, chill out wit' all that fucking crying. If we're together, you need to start being straight up with me. I can't take all these fucking secrets and shit."

"Ain't nobody keeping no damn secrets from you. It just slipped my mind."

"Well, fuck all that. You need to start looking for a new place ASAP."

"I don't have all the money to pay for everything."

"So you ain't got a nigga to hold you down? Why you acting like this, Amoy?"

"Acting like what? I didn't know you were going to help. Lately, you seem a little distant and shit. I thought it was because we found out Jamal wasn't your son."

"Man, you're tripping. I don't give a fuck if he's my blood. He's my fucking son. I'm the one he calls Dada, not that fuck nigga. And as far as me acting distant, B, you know what I do out here in these streets. I got fuck niggas tryin'a take my spot and the Feds tryin'a lock me up. My life ain't easy, B, but I love you, and I'm wit' you one hunnit. So either you're in for this ride or you're not. I've got to know you wit' me all the way 'cause this shit can get real serious real quick."

He caught me off guard. I knew he was out there in these streets, but I never knew how deep he was. To be honest, I tried to stay out of his business. Now that he put me on the spot, I was sitting here, looking stupid as fuck.

"Listen, I love you with everything in me. I am grateful that God brought us back together, so I'm riding with you all the way."

"That's good to know, 'cause I can't have no bitch around me who's not solid."

"You better watch yo' motherfucking mouth. I ain't no bitch."

"My bad, but you know what I was tryin'a say. If you're on my team, you've got to be all the way solid."

"Yeah, I got you."

He reached into his pocket and pulled out a stack of cash. He started peeling off some money. "Here, this is five stacks. It should be enough to find you a two-bed-room in a nice neighborhood. If you need more, let me know, and don't worry 'bout no furniture. We need new shit anyway."

"Aw, thank you, bae." I stood up and hugged him.

"Man, chill. You're my woman, and you should never want for anything."

I didn't say anything. I just smiled at him. I swore this dude was one of a kind. I just hoped this time he was serious about us and not just playing games.

"A'ight, I've got some things to handle. I'll hit you later."

"Okay. Love you, bae."

"Love you, B."

I locked the door behind him, feeling a lot better. I looked at the money I had in my hand. I could really get used to this type of treatment. Living the fast life in the fast lane.

I heard a knock on the door. I ran over there and opened the door. I thought he had forgotten something.

"Yo, what's good?" The smile fell from my face and turned into one big frown. "What the fuck you doing here?"

He pushed me out of the way and entered my house. I thought about running for my gun, but Marquise had taken it away just in case the police ran up in here.

"You need to leave my shit now," I demanded.

"Where my son at?"

"Why?" I folded my arms and gritted my teeth at him.

"Bitch, 'cause he's my motherfucking son. Do I need a reason to see him?"

"Get out of my shit with your disrespectful ass. If you want to see yo' son, go ahead and file them court papers so I can get some child support."

"Child support? So now yo' silly ass wants to bring the white people up in our lives?"

"Ain't that what you did when you called CPS on me, talking 'bout I abuse my son?"

"What? Now you're making up shit. Bitch, I don't deal wit' the law. I'm a street nigga. Don't you ever disrespect me like that again."

"Boy, get out of my shit. Like I said, take me to court."

"Amoy, I'm telling you this, and please take me seriously. If you or that fuck nigga ever tries to keep my seed away from me, I will bury both of y'all."

"You're a bitch-ass nigga who only knows how to put your hands on a female. Trust me, Marquise ain't scared of you, and he showed you that before. You're weaker than me, nigga, and it shows in your eyes. I can't believe that I gave you the pussy. I should've bought me a strap and fucked you in the ass e'erynight."

"Bitch, fuck you." He balled his fist up.

"Yeah, go ahead so they can lock yo' ass up again."

"That's what you want. You know, at first I felt bad that I was fucking yo' little sister, but now I admit her pussy is way tighter and wetter than yours. Shit, you should consider having a threesome with us."

"You're a lame-ass nigga. Like I said, get your bitch ass out of my shit before I call the police on you. Don't forget you didn't get sentenced yet."

I walked over to the door and opened it as wide as I could. He gritted his teeth at me as he walked out. He stopped, grinned, and then said, "Bitch, I got you."

I didn't say shit to him. Instead, I just slammed the door shut in his face. That nigga was too old to be running around here acting like that. It hurt my heart that he was the father of my child. I prayed to God his dumbness didn't rub off on my child at all. If it were all up to me, he would not be allowed to be in his life, not acting like that.

Shari

I'd been wrestling with my thoughts for a few days. Part of me wanted to have an abortion, and the other part of me wanted to keep the baby. I knew Devon said he wasn't ready to have a baby right now, but truthfully, I wasn't trying to hear that shit. I felt like if this nigga fucked with me the way he claimed, then he would accept our child without giving a fuck who found out.

I took one last glance in the mirror. My stomach wasn't showing yet, but I could see that I was getting a bit thicker. The way the True Religion jeans hugged my curves was definitely a good look. I knew one thing. If Mama didn't give me anything else in life, she gave me looks and a bad-ass shape. I just prayed that if I decided to have the baby, it wouldn't mess up my shape, 'cause a bitch couldn't afford to have no grandma body.

I grabbed my purse and my phone and headed out the door. I exited my building and stepped on the pavement, getting ready to walk to my car.

"Yo, I was just coming to see you." I heard a male voice yell from behind me. I turned around quickly to see if the person was talking to me.

"Oh, yeah, boo." I smiled when I realized it was DJ.

He didn't return the gesture. Instead, he approached me with a deadly look on his face. "Bitch, you fucking burned me," he yelled.

I quickly looked around to see if any of these nosy bitches were outside. "Lower your voice. What are you talking about?" I acted like I had no idea what he was fussing about.

"Bitch, fuck you! Yo' nasty ass done gave me a disease, knowing I had a fucking girl. Now she done broke up with my ass."

"Boy, you better get the fuck on. You must've gotten that shit from one of yo' hoes, 'cause my shit ain't burning. I just went to the doctor, and I'm good. Matter of fact, I was going to call you to let you know we have a baby on the way."

"What, bitch? A fucking baby? That shit ain't mine," he yelled even louder.

By now, I saw a few bitches gathered on the steps pretending like they were not there for the show.

"Well, I ain't goin' to argue with you. Let's just see when the baby gets here."

He lunged toward me, grabbing my throat and pushing me into my parked car. "Bitch, I just said it ain't mine." He pressed his gun against my temple.

"Get the fuck off me. You've lost your fucking mind. Do you see all these people out here?" I tried to talk some sense into him.

"Bitch, I don't give a fuck. I'll blow your fucking brains out all over this fucking street. You fucked my life up. My fucking bitch left me, and now you're talkin' 'bout you're pregnant. Ho, I ain't got shit to live for," he yelled.

You could hear the anger in that nigga's voice, and I could feel the pressure on my neck. Tears started rolling down my face as I didn't know if I wanted him to hurry up and use the gun. That way, I wouldn't suffer like this.

I heard a car approaching and started praying that one of these nosy bitches had called the police. I waited a few seconds, but my hope faded when I didn't hear anything else.

A few moments later, I heard a voice yell, "Yo, what the fuck you doing?"

"What you say, nigga? You better mind yo' motherfucking business."

"This my bitch right here, so this is my motherfucking business, nigga. Matter of fact, take your hands off her," Devon demanded.

I didn't know if I should be happy that he was here or wish I were dead because of what he might find out.

DJ took his hand from around my throat and aimed his gun at Devon. I lifted my head up and realized Devon was aiming a gun at that nigga also.

"Nigga, who the fuck are you? I'm out here handling this bitch 'cause I fucked that bitch and she burned me."

"You fucked her?" Devon quizzed.

"Yeah, this ho hit me up about a week and a half ago. She wanted me to come over and fuck. My dumb ass not thinking anything about it came through. Now my girl went to the doctor, and she got gonorrhea."

"Yo, you was fucking this nigga, B?"

"He's lying. He's just mad that he tried to fuck and I turned him down. Matter of fact, I told him that I have a nigga, and that nigga said fuck you."

"Yo, nigga, it's all good if you're wifing this ho. This bitch been a thot since junior high school, fucking and sucking e'ery nigga who had a few dollars. I'm just stupid as fuck, running up in her ass without using rubbers."

I could see the anger plastered across Devon's face. "Baby, please don't believe him. If I had anything, I would've given it to you. I swear he's just trying to break us up," I said to Devon while I started crying. I was desperate and didn't give a fuck if these bitches and niggas were staring.

"Yo, son, if you want to trust this ho, it's on you. I'm out though. Bitch, you're lucky. I'ma catch you though." He tucked his gun in his waist and walked off.

I looked at Devon as he walked off. I grabbed his arm. "Babe, please don't believe him. I swear that nigga's lying."

"Yo, let's go." He started walking up the stairs.

I dreaded going into the apartment with him, but what choice did I have? I couldn't afford to let him go, knowing he might not come back. I nervously tried to open the door. I fumbled the key in my hand. I tried again, and this time the door unlocked. He entered first, and I cautiously stepped in.

"So you're out here fucking niggas and shit." He grabbed me by my weave from behind.

"Devon, I swear that nigga's lying on me. I never fucked him, and I damn sure didn't give him no damn STD."

"Bitch, you're a fucking liar. Kennedy's ass has the same fucking thing, and guess who the fucking common denominator bitch is? You."

He took my head and pushed it into the wall. "Noooo," I screamed out in anguish.

"Bitch, who the fuck you think I am?"

"You just broke my nose," I cried. I put my hand to my face and felt the sticky substance, which I concluded was blood. He wasn't done though.

He dragged me by my weave and pushed me on the sofa. He then pointed his gun in my face. "You're a nasty ho. You know that? So who the fuck you pregnant for, this nigga?"

"I swear I never fucked him. This is your baby," I cried.

"Bitch, I told yo' ass to get a fucking abortion. You thought I was playing? I don't want that shit, and I don't want yo' trifling ass no more either."

"Please don't say that! Devon, I love you. I swear on my mama's soul I never fucked him. He's lying, babe." I tried getting up.

"Sit yo' ass down, ho. I should've known you were trifling as fuck when you still wanted me after you knew I was fucking with yo' sister."

"Devon, baby, please. You don't mean all this. This is me, yo' baby girl. You promised to never leave me."

"Man, fuck you, bitch. I should shoot yo' ass, but I ain't goin' to waste no bullet on yo' ass. Lose my motherfucking number, bitch." He hawked up some spit and spat dead between my eyes. "I wish you die, bitch."

He started to walk off, and I jumped off the couch, diving on the ground and holding on to his legs. "Please don't leave me, Devon."

"Get the fuck off me, bitch." He tried kicking me.

I held on tightly, like my life depended on it. "Devon, I love you. I swear I'll do anything for you. I swear anything."

He stood still for a minute. "Anything?"

"Yes, anything."

"Suck this dick for me."

I really thought this nigga was playing. That was, until I looked up and noticed he had taken his dick out of the gray sweatpants he was wearing. I looked at him for confirmation.

"Bitch, what are you looking at? You said you'd do anything. Fuck it then. I'm out."

"No, I'll do it," I said as I grabbed his dick.

I started licking the tip of his dick, but I almost gagged because I could tell he didn't bathe. His dick smelled like sweat and stale pussy. I tried not to smell it and just started sucking. This was the most humiliating shit, but I had to show him how much I wanted him. I massaged his balls while I sucked his dick. To be honest, my happiness depended on it, and those were the only thoughts that I had to help me get through this. I sucked harder and used my hands to massage his balls more aggressively, trying to speed up the process, silently begging God to make him cum.

"Aargh, damn. Yeah, right there," he said as he grabbed my head and pulled it in toward him.

I just breathed harder and sucked. Within minutes, he was exploding. I tried to jump back, but he had a strong hold on my head.

"Where you going, bitch? Swallow this cum."

There was no escaping, so I swallowed the cum. I used my tongue and licked it up. After I was finished, I ran to the bathroom, put my head in the toilet bowl, and vomited everything up. I tried to get up, but I still had to vomit up the breakfast that I ate earlier. I was sick to my stomach and had no energy left in my body. I took a seat by the toilet bowl and rested my head on the rim. Tears rolled down my face. I'd never felt this low in my life, and to think it was by the hands of the man who was supposed to love me.

I waited patiently to see if he was going to come check on me, but about ten minutes later, I realized that wasn't going to happen. I thought he was just sitting out there, trying to get his mind right. I got up, brushed my teeth, and rinsed with some mouthwash. I was trying to get rid of that bitter taste that came from his cum. I then walked out in the living room. I soon discovered that he was no-where in sight and my house door was wide open. I ran over to the door and looked in the hallway, but there was no one around. I walked back inside, slammed the door, and ran to the window to see if his car was still out there, but it was gone. I walked back over to the couch and grabbed my phone out of my purse. I called his number, but it went straight to voicemail. Ten tries later and the same thing was happening. I threw the phone across the room, shattering it. "Damn you, Devon. I did what you wanted," I screamed out in mental anguish.

I ran to the fridge, grabbed a beer, and started drinking. *I swear I can't live without him,* I thought as I gulped the alcohol down.

Kennedy

This was strange. I tried calling Christopher two days ago, and he had not answered or returned my calls. That was so out of character for him. At first I charged it to him being busy working on a new case, but I checked my phone and he still had not called last night. I hoped my friend was okay and hadn't gotten himself in a dangerous situation.

I went about my business, taking care of some errands and grabbing a few things out of the grocery store. I was pulling in my driveway when I noticed a black SUV following closely behind. It slowed down after it got to my gate and then it pulled off. That seemed a little suspicious, but I blew it off. I proceeded to take the things out of the car.

"Babes, I need to talk to you real quick." Devon startled me when he walked into my room.

"What is it?"

He took a seat on the edge of the bed. He looked like a man with the world on his shoulders. "You know how, years ago, we talked about adopting a child?"

"Hmm, that was before I knew you were slinging your dick around town."

"I know that, but just hear me out. I know I've been telling you that the baby that girl has ain't mine, but I need to come clean with you. I think he's mine."

"So what the fuck you telling me that for? Isn't that supposed to be between you and your bitch?"

"Kennedy, please stop! This is not easy, but I need your support on this."

I looked at that nigga like he was a fool. *Did I hear him mention "support"?*

"Listen, you're wasting your fucking time talking to me about a fucking monkey you made while cheating on me. I have no desire to nor would I ever help you or that bastard," I said in a high-pitched tone.

"I ain't asking you for no money. I've got my own shit. All I'm saying is that the bitch ain't in no position to take care of my seed, and I want to take my son from her. I was only asking you if he can come live with us for a little while."

I stood up immediately and looked at this nigga to see if he was really serious about what the fuck he just said out of his mouth. "You must have fallen down and knocked your fucking head. You think I would allow you to bring your little bastard in my house? How dare you even think about it, much less have the balls to approach me with such bullshit? You're barely living here your damn self."

"Damn, I guess our wedding vows didn't mean anything to you. We're supposed to be there for each other no matter what the situation. What happened to you weathering the storm with me? I know I fell short of being the man you want, but I've changed, but you don't give a nigga no credit. Kennedy, it's me, the man you fell for. How can you say you fuck with me one hundred but you're not willing to accept my seed?"

"That speech sounded convincing and everything, but I was never a weak bitch, and I'm too fucking old to be yo' fool. You made that bastard. You chose the bitch. It's your mess, so you clean it up on your fucking own."

He looked at me as if he was shocked. I didn't pay him no fucking mind. Instead, I picked up the remote and turned the television on, trying my hardest to tune him out.

CHAPTER THIRTY

Amoy

After searching for weeks, I finally found a two-bedroom over on Thirteenth Avenue. It was really nice, and the landlord seemed like someone I could get along with. I had two weeks before the court date, so I was trying to be gone before then.

Getting the place was one thing, but packing was another. Jamal's things were top priority, so I made sure those were packed first. Marquise insisted that I leave all the old furniture and shop for new stuff for the new apartment. He didn't say it in so many words, but I thought he didn't want anything that had to do with Devon. That was fine with me because I needed a new couch and a new dining room set.

I made sure everything was washed and folded neatly so I wouldn't have too much to do once we moved. I was on my last load of clothes when I heard a knock at the door. I peeped out the hole and realized it was two uniformed police officers. My heart suddenly dropped because the first thing that popped in my mind was child protective services. I stood there, wondering if I should open the door. I heard a couple more knocks, and then I opened the door.

"Yes, may I help you?"

"Ma'am, are you Amoy Simpson?"

"Yes, I am," I reluctantly said.

"I'm afraid that I have some bad news."

I looked at their faces, trying to figure out what the fuck they were talking about.

"Your mother was murdered this morning by her live-in boyfriend."

I looked at him, expressionless, and I had to catch myself real fast.

"Ma'am, did you hear us? Your mother was killed this morning by her live-in boyfriend. You're listed as her next of kin."

"Yeah, I heard you."

"We already have him in custody and have a full confession from him. It seems like he and your mother were fighting over drugs and money. He grabbed a knife and stabbed her in the abdomen. He did call the ambulance, but she died on her way to the hospital."

"Right now, she's at the coroner's office. We would like you to come down and identify her body."

"Umm, you might want to hit my little sister up. She can identify her."

They both turned their heads, looking at me as if they were shocked at what I'd just said to them. Shit, if they only knew how that bitch treated me, then they wouldn't be too surprised at the statement I'd just made.

"You're the next of kin listed."

"Look, no disrespect, but let me get my sister's number, and she can help y'all out," I snapped.

I turned to go back in. I grabbed my phone and gave them the number. I was ready for them to get the fuck on.

"Thank you, ma'am, and again, our condolences."

I smiled at them, waited for them to walk off, and then I slammed the door. I stood in the middle of my floor, just staring at the walls. I was feeling kind of confused.

***

It had been three days since I found out my mama was killed by the same old nasty-ass nigga who used to molest me, and from what Shari's lying ass said, he used to molest her also. When I first heard she was dead, to be honest, I really didn't give a fuck. My whole life, she treated me like I was the scum of the earth. Our last words were very disrespectful, but I never expected to hear that she was gone and definitely not murdered. Last night, I lay in bed thinking about her and how she once was when I was a young child. She wasn't all that mean before the nigga and the drugs. Tears flowed on my pillow as reality set in that I never knew my daddy, and now the woman who gave birth to me was gone also.

"Baby, did you talk to your sister?" Marquise asked as he walked into the room.

"Nah, why would I talk to that bitch?" I threw down the clothes I was folding and turned my full attention to him.

"I mean, y'all mama just passed, and from what you tell me, it's only the two of you. Now might be a good time to mend y'all relationship."

"Listen, baby, I love you, and I respect you, but don't you ever tell me that I need to mend anything with that bitch. I didn't do anything to her ass. That bitch is jealous of me for no damn reason. I have never done one damn thing to her ass."

"B, I know, but yo' mama gone, and you're the big sister. I'm pretty sure y'all both in pain."

"What time you getting in later?" I quizzed, changing the conversation.

"It'll be after midnight. Why, what's good?"

"Nothing, just want to go to this furniture place over by Baychester Avenue."

"Yeah, I did forget. What time you tryin'a go?"

"I have three heads to braid today, and then I'm done for the day. I'll call you before I finish so we can meet up."

"A'ight, cool. Just lemme know." He kissed me on the cheek and then walked out the door.

He wasn't gone a full minute when I sat on the couch. Mama's face flashed across my eyes. Tears welled up in my eyes. I felt an emptiness in the bottom of my heart. This was the first time I felt this hurt over her death. I clenched the pillow that was on the couch and buried my head in it. I cried, not caring how mad I was at her. I wished I could take back those horrible words that I said to her weeks ago. Just one more chance to let her know I loved her. I was caught up in different emotions. I loved her. Nah, I hated her for the way she treated me. I felt so alone and cold, like an abandoned child yearning for her mother's love. Only it was too late for all that.

This wasn't a good day. I was at the funeral parlor making final arrangements for my mother.

"What the fuck you think you're doing? You know damn well Mama didn't want to get cremated," my stupid-ass sister yelled as we both stood in the morgue.

"You need to lower your voice. Furthermore, she's dead and has no say in this. If I'm correct, she didn't leave a dollar to help with these expenses. I see you running your big-ass mouth, but I don't see you trying to chip in with a dollar. It's all on me, the one she despised. You were her pet and should be handling this shit."

"Bitch, whatever. You jumped yo' ass over here making plans and shit, and now you want to complain about somebody helping you. Nah, put your big-girl panties on and make it happen." She grinned in my face.

"I'm done entertaining you, little bitch. She will be cremated and that's final." I shot her ass a dirty look and walked off. This wasn't the time to deal with her little ungrateful behind.

I planned a small ceremony at the parlor because she didn't belong to any church. I invited a few people I knew she was close to in Mount Vernon, but only a handful showed up. Marquise and I sat on one side while Shari sat on the other. It was a shame the way Mama lived her life, burning bridges behind her and never making amends before she died.

After the funeral, I took the urn and brought it home. I placed it in a box and put it in the closet.

"Babe, you okay?" Marquise walked up behind me.

"Yes. Just a little hurt, you know?"

"Look, regardless of what she did to you, or how she treated you, truth is she's still yo' mama. I mean, I can't imagine losing mine."

"You know, I really appreciate you stepping in and taking care of the bill. I don't know what I would do without you these past couple of months. You've really been my rock."

"Nah, B. It's the other way 'round. You know I just be out here living reckless and shit, not giving a fuck, but the minute that we started fucking with each other again, it's like I have a whole different look on life. I love you, B, and we're in this for life."

"Aw, babe, I'm happy that you feel this way. I love you so much, and I'm happy that God gave us another chance."

His phone started ringing, and he looked down at it. "Damn, bae, you goin' to be a'ight? I've got a run to make in Queens."

"Yeah, I'm good. Gonna lie down for a little bit before I pick up Jamal from day care."

"Listen, B, we're in this together. You hear me?" He stared in my eyes.

"Yeah, I hear you, boo." I smiled so he could know that I was with him 100 percent.

"A'ight, bae. I love you. I'm out."

Before I could respond, he was out the door. I smiled as I thought about our relationship and the bond we shared. I didn't believe in fairy tales, but this one was one for the books.

Pop! Pop! Pop!

I thought I heard gunshots, or was I tripping? I ran over to my window and looked outside.

"No, help. Somebody just got shot," I heard somebody yell.

I grabbed my phone and dialed Marquise's number, but there was no response. I dashed out the door, and before I could run down the steps, I noticed the clothing. It was the same outfit that Marquise was wearing. I dashed through the crowd that was forming.

"Noooooo, baby, nooooooo. Call an ambulance please."

My baby was on the ground with two gunshot wounds in his chest. He was bleeding heavily. I gently lifted his head off the concrete and placed it on my leg. I noticed the gun in his hand. I thought about taking it and hiding it real quick. I took a quick glance around me and realized that was a very bad idea.

"Does anybody know CPR?" I yelled.

"I'm a registered nurse," an older lady said and walked over to him.

I moved out of her way, and she started working on him.

"No, God, no. Did y'all see who did this?" I turned around and asked no one in particular. No one said anything. Instead, everyone was whispering or talking on their phones.

I heard the sirens and felt a little better. "Y'all, move out the way," an EMT worker said as he dashed through with a stretcher.

I trembled as I watched them place him on the gurney and hurriedly put him in the ambulance. "Can I ride with him please? I'm his girl."

"Sure, let's go."

I watched in despair as they tried their best to keep him alive. "God, pleaseeeee don't take my baby away," I pleaded.

When the ambulance reached the hospital, I jumped out of the back and stood to the side. I saw a team of doctors rush to the ambulance, and they took him inside. I knew he was in critical condition by the way they were behaving. I ran into the hospital and tried to follow them.

"Ma'am, you're not allowed to go back there," a doctor informed me.

"Why not? That's my baby." I shot him a desperate look.

"Only doctors and nurses are allowed in the OR. He's in critical condition and needs immediate care."

I saw there was no use in debating, so I took one last look in the direction they took him, and I walked off. I walked into the waiting room and found a seat in the corner. I sat down, hanging my head in my lap. My heart was ripped apart as I constantly talked to God.

My cell phone started ringing. I wondered who the fuck would be calling me at a time like this. "Hellooo," I answered with major attitude.

"Miss Simpson, this is Miss James from Brighter Ones Day Care. You were supposed to pick Jamal up about twenty minutes ago."

"Shit. Umm, I'm so sorry."

"Is something the matter, Miss Simpson?"

"My boyfriend got shot, and I'm at the hospital with him. I'm so sorry. I'm—"

"Oh, my. Sorry to hear that. Is he going to be all right?"

"No, he's in surgery right now. It doesn't look good." I broke down crying again.

"You know what? I'm going to be here until about seven. Go ahead and see about your boyfriend. I've got the baby."

"Are you sure? 'Cause I can be there in about twenty-five minutes."

"Yes, I'm sure. I've got him. Now get off the phone and go handle your business."

"Yes, ma'am." I cracked a smile because of her in-control attitude. She had always been warm but stern.

Seconds turned into minutes, and minutes turned into hours. I paced the emergency room floor and kept asking the nurse questions. The bitch acted like she was irritated, but oh, well.

I was about to sit down when I saw his sister walk in along with two other chicks I didn't recognize. She walked up to the counter and briefly spoke with the nurse. As soon as she walked off, I approached her. "Hey, Sonja, I don't know if you remember me—"

"Yeah, I remember you. What happened to my brother? Who tried to kill him?" she asked between sobs.

"I don't know. He told me he had a run to make. He went out the door, and a few seconds later, I heard gunshots. I tried calling him, but when he didn't respond, I ran out there. That's when I realized it was him on the ground." Tears welled up in my eyes as I relived the emotions that I felt when I came out the door.

"Man, I swear my brother don't be fucking with these niggas. They better pray that he ain't seen whoever did it 'cause it's goin' to be bloodshed e'erywhere," she cried.

"Come on, Sonja. Come sit down, babes," said one of the chicks I assumed was a friend or family member.

As they walked off, the other chick stayed behind. "So you're the bitch Marquise was creeping with?"

"Creeping with? You mean we live together, and by the way, who the fuck are you?" I asked, bracing myself for the inevitable.

"Say what, ho? He don't live wit' yo' ass. He lives with me and his daughter."

His sister must've caught wind of what was taking place because she bolted to where we were standing. "Really, Kaye, my motherfucking brother is in there fighting for his life, and you're in here worried about who he's fucking with?"

"Girl, this bitch knows she ain't got no business being up here. E'erybody knows that I'm his bitch and ain't going nowhere."

"You're a silly bitch. I told yo' ass not to come up here 'cause I know you ain't got no chill. If my brother don't make it, ain't nobody going to be getting no dick. So if y'all can't keep the drama down, y'all can fucking leave."

"I'm straight." I shrugged.

I didn't wait for a response. I walked off. I thought about smoking a Black & Mild. *Shit.* I realized I didn't have my purse. My head was pounding, and my anger was elevated. This bitch had the nerve to add to what I was already going through. I wasn't worried about who he was fucking. My first concern was if he was going to make it.

I waited and waited, and there was still no word on how his surgery was coming along. I looked at the time, and it was steadily approaching 7:00 p.m. I had no choice. I walked out and headed to my car. I was tripping. My car was at home. I pulled up the Uber app and requested a cab. On my way to the day care, I prayed and cried. I just wanted to grab my son and make it back to the hospital.

After I grabbed Jamal, I rushed to the house, grabbed my car, and sped off. I stopped at McDonald's, grabbed him a Happy Meal, and then headed straight back to Mount Vernon Hospital. I parked and picked my baby up. I rushed into the hospital, hoping that I would get some good news. I walked over to his sister, but she was still waiting.

***

I must've dozed off, because I felt a slight tap on my shoulder. I jumped up immediately.

"Sorry, but my brother's out of surgery. I think you might want to see him."

I stood up and followed her. She kind of gave me a rundown of what was going on. When we reached the room, I was kind of scared to step in because I wasn't sure what to expect.

"Let me keep your son out here while you go in. He doesn't need to see his father like this," the nurse said.

"Thank you." I was going to correct her about him being Jamal's father, but she was right. That was his daddy.

I also noticed that there were two uniformed police sitting outside of his room. I knew then that they were going to charge Marquise with that gun once he recovered.

I pulled up my big-girl panties and walked in the room. I stood there, and he had wires coming from everywhere. He was purple in complexion, and his face was swollen. I leaned over and touched his hand. I really didn't know what to say. "Babe, I swear we goin' to get through this," I whispered.

"Listen, did the police come talk to you?" Sonja asked.

"Nah, only when we were at the complex."

"They better find out who the fuck did this to him."

I started wondering. That was when it dawned on me that he was in the streets heavily, and this could be a beef. The only thing was that he never mentioned that he had any kind of beef going on.

After I stayed there for a while, I realized that it was time to get my son home. At times like these, I wished that I had some type of help. "Ay, babes, I've got to go get my baby home. Please take my number and call me if there's any change. I'll be back tomorrow morning as soon as I drop him off at day care."

"Okay. Our mom is on her way up here from Atlanta."

We hugged and I left. The one lady was still in the room with Sonja when I left, but I noticed that the bitch who claimed she was Marquise's girl was nowhere to be found. I wiped my tears as I stepped on the elevator. I hated to leave him like this, but I had no choice.

I got downstairs and stepped off the elevator. I looked around to see if I saw the bitch anywhere, but I didn't. I figured she was somewhere moping around. These bitches were silly as fuck, always running up on a bitch. Shit, her best bet was to wait to confront that nigga because I wasn't going anywhere.

I stopped by Burger King to grab some nuggets. I was mentally and physically drained and had no intention of cooking tonight. I pulled up to the apartment complex. My heart was heavy. I sat in the car for a few minutes, trying to gather my thoughts before I exited the vehicle. Jamal was sleeping, so I picked him up and carried him inside.

After I put him in bed, I sat on the couch. I needed to take a shower, but I wasn't moving. My mind was on Marquise. I hoped he understood that I wanted to be there with him so badly, but I had no one to watch my son. I attempted to eat one of the nuggets, but I couldn't even chew it. I spat it out and threw the bag away. I was about to pour a glass of wine when I heard a knock on my door. I got up to see who it was. It was the police.

"Damn, were they watching my shit?" I said before I opened the door.

"Miss Simpson?"

"Yes, what's going on?"

"We want to talk to you about a shooting that took place out here earlier. It's our understanding that the gentleman was a close friend of yours, and he was just leaving your apartment."

"I don't know what to tell y'all. Yes, he's my boyfriend, and he left. Other than that, I don't know anything else."

"Well, do you know why he had a gun?"

"I never saw him with a gun before, so I wouldn't know."

"Miss Simpson, we're only trying to find out who's responsible for this crime. If you're holding back information—"

I cut his ass off. "Listen, it's been a long day. I don't know anything." I didn't wait for them to respond. Instead, I shot them a fake smile and then closed my door. I wasn't stupid. I knew they had run a background check on him, and they also knew that he was a convicted felon with a gun. I knew it was only a matter of time before they arrested him on gun charges. My plan for tomorrow morning was to find him a lawyer.

I was just about to jump in the shower when I heard another bang on my door. *Man, if these motherfuckers don't get the fuck on . . .* I was ready to curse these motherfucking police out.

"Yo, I just told y'all . . ." It wasn't the police but my nosy-ass neighbor who lived downstairs. "Oh, what do you want?" I was ready to slam the door in her face, too. This bitch was knocking on my door like we were cool or something.

"Girl, I just came to see how ol' boy was doing. I heard the shots out of my bedroom window."

"He's good. Now I'm tired and need to take a shower." I was about to lock the door.

"I think I saw who shot him."

I turned back around quickly. This bitch had my full attention and better not be playing either. "You saw who did it?"

"Well, not exactly, but minutes before your boyfriend came out, I saw a black car pull into the parking lot. My nosy ass was trying to see who came out of the car, but the person remained inside. Then as soon as the shots rang out, I watched the vehicle slowly pull off from beside your boyfriend."

"What kind of car?"

"I'm not good with cars, but I'm almost sure it looked like a Chrysler 300."

I almost fainted when she said what model car it was.

"Are you okay? Do you know who drives that car?"

"Huh, say what? Nah, I don't. I just feel sick. Must be 'cause I ain't eat all day. Did you tell the police what you just told me?"

"You know I don't fuck with the law. Shit, they killed my brother a few years ago, talkin' 'bout he was trying to run them over."

"Listen, I'm sorry to hear about your brother, but I need to make some tea or something. My stomach is killing me."

"Okay, sure. Keep me posted on ol' boy's health."

"I got you," I lied.

I locked the door and leaned my face up against it. This couldn't be. There was no way. I walked to the couch and grabbed my phone. I dialed Devon's number.

"Yo!"

"Where were you earlier?"

"Man, what kind of question is that? You ain't my bitch."

"I swear if you had anything to do with Marquise's shooting, you're gonna pay."

"Yo, bitch, you're tripping. I ain't shoot nobody. Matter of fact, don't call my phone accusing me of shit."

Before I could respond, he hung up. I had a bad feeling about him. All the threats he made popped up in my head, especially the last time I saw him. I thought about calling the police to let them know, but I had no proof, only what the neighbor told me. Hmm, I needed to think.

Kennedy

Some might say I'd lost my goddamn mind, and I probably did. Weeks after Devon kept begging me to let his little bastard stay here, I finally gave in and told him it was okay if and when he got custody. The one thing I couldn't agree to, though, was me lying on that girl. Don't get me wrong, I didn't give a fuck about that little bitch, and if you asked me, she deserved everything she had coming to her. See, these little bitches had to start realizing that not all these sweet stories these niggas fed them were true. A nigga was going to say whatever the fuck they wanted to say to get into those drawers and get to the pussy. But it was up to them not to fall for the foolery. I knew what it was though. A lot of them thought they were getting over on the next woman. Wrong. What that nigga did to his main bitch he'd end up doing twice as worse to the bitch on the side. *Oh, well, fuck them all.* All of this would soon be over.

I dried my hands and hurried up and grabbed my cell phone. I took a quick glance at the screen. I smiled as I answered quickly. "Hello there, stranger."

"Hey there, beautiful."

"Christopher, where the hell have you been? I haven't heard from you since the night that I left your house. I've called, texted, and I was tempted to stop by your house."

"Just been tied up doing some work. I had a case that required my undivided attention."

"Well, you could've shot me a text or something, you know?"

"You're right. Listen, I'll make it up to you."

"Hmmm, you better make it soon. I've been doing a lot of thinking lately. I might not be in New York much longer."

"You're moving? Where are you going?" he shouted.

"I've been thinking about moving to Florida with my sister. I think I've mentioned her to you before."

"Yes, sure. I just didn't think y'all were that close."

"We're not close, but that's my only relative. Plus, I need a change of scenery. There's nothing really in New York for me."

"You taking the husband with you?"

"Ha-ha, no way. I am going by myself."

"Oh, okay. Well, Miss Lady, you know if you want me to go with you, all you have to do is say the word."

"Ha-ha, there's no way I could possibly ask you to pack up your life and leave. Plus, I need to take time to myself. I need to refocus on my life. Travel the world a bit and just live life a little."

"Well, promise me you'll keep in touch, and I would love to see you before you leave if you don't mind."

"Well, my plan is not concrete yet. I'm in the planning stage, but I'll keep you posted."

"Okay, my love. Talk to you later."

I put the phone back down on the counter and went back to cutting my greens. I planned on cooking Sunday dinner tomorrow. Something ran across my mind as I stood at the sink, chopping away. Something about Christopher had changed. I didn't know what it was, but right after that night when I poured out my soul about my deceased husband, I noticed he was rarely around. Let me remind you that this was a man I could barely keep away, but nowadays, I couldn't seem to find him. The thought of him betraying me ran across my mind. What if he told the police about my confession? *Nonsense.* If he did, they would've kicked my door in already. So what was so different about Christopher? Maybe he found a new love. "Ha-ha, Christopher, you dirty old man," I chuckled as I washed the greens in salt water.

"Did I hear you talking to yourself, my love?"

"Oh, my mother once told me it's okay to talk to one's self as long as you didn't respond to yourself."

"Well, Mother was a wise woman. So what are you cooking?"

"Nothing, my dear. I was seasoning up some greens for Sunday dinner."

"I had a long day, babe, so I handled all my business early so I can spend quality time with you. I brought dinner home," Devon said, followed by his sexy "make my pussy wet" smile.

"Is that so? You really are a changed man. A girl could get used to this kind of treatment again."

"This is nothing, my love. I told you that once you gave me another chance, I would make you the happiest woman in the world."

I felt like throwing up, but instead, I smiled like a young schoolgirl crushing on her new lover. Truth was, Devon was a slimeball who would do whatever it took to weasel his ass back into my life.

"Dinner was delicious," I said to him as he cleaned up and packed away our leftovers.

"I've got somebody even better for your dessert." He winked at me and smiled.

"Well, on that note, let me go take a shower." I winked back at him. I rubbed his hand as I walked off.

I had no idea how long I was going to be able to play this doting wife. I knew I needed to put my plans into motion fast if I planned on getting this no-good-ass bastard out of my life.

As soon as I stepped out of the shower, Devon was standing there, naked, dick hanging like he'd been in an African Mandingo tribe or something. Yes, I said it. Y'all know how them Africans be dancing in the wilderness with those long cones covering up the goodies. LOL, an inside joke. I giggled to myself.

I grabbed what I called my Bath & Body Works "sex on a platter" lotion. As I was bent over, moisturizing my legs, I felt Devon's strong hands rubbing my ass.

"Damn, babe, you're making me horny as fuck." He stood in front of me, massaging his dick.

I couldn't say anything. He picked me up and carried me over to the bed. He bent my ass over, revealing my pussy in the back. Devon ran his soft lips on my back, slightly up from my hips.

"I miss you so much, baby." He continued kissing on my lower back.

Damn, his lips felt so soothing caressing my back. I held back my words until his tongue slithered in the crack of my ass. "Hmmmm." I let out some air and squeezed my ass tight. His warm slobber hit the crack of my ass. I braced myself because his tongue slid into my hole.

"Oooo, ahhh," I hissed in between moans. Dammit, man, this shit was feeling so great. I struggled to keep my eyes open. They were slightly closed.

Devon spread my ass wide and licked my ass as if he were licking the cake mix out of the bowl. My pussy was dripping wet. I stuck two fingers inside my pussy and worked them in and out slowly.

"Ohhhh, oooo, shit, yes." I couldn't hold back. Juice started leaking and flowing onto my fingers. I had to taste myself. Just as I thought, I tasted like passion fruit since that was all I inserted into my body.

"Stay just like that, babe." Devon wrapped his arms around my waist and pulled me closer to him. He eased his head inside the house before thrusting his way in. "Just like that, babe." He took long and hard strokes, scraping my walls. His dick was touching my entire insides.

"Yesss. Fuck me, my king," I begged.

I was feeling good. I wanted to feel his dick ripping my insides out. I loved when he took long and gentle strokes.

Each thrust felt like I was losing my breath because he was really into it.

Shit was getting intense. He pulled my hair with one hand and held my chin with the other hand. "Mmmmm." The pain was devastating. The ripping I was talking about . . . let's just say I felt his dick touching my stomach. "Yes, Devon. Oh, shit, I love this dick." I bit down on his fingers and bounced my ass on his dick. "I love this dick," I yelled, taking every inch of him.

Devon removed his wet fingers from my mouth but still kept his left hand wrapped around my hair, pulling it. I felt four fingers graze across my lower back, and then I felt his thumb jam into my ass.

"Auhhh, shit. Jesus, take the wheel," I cried out. His thumb and dick were working magic at the same time. I couldn't stop creaming on his dick and thumb. I knew this nigga was a freak, but goddamn, he was trying to turn me the fuck out, and I was loving every bit of it.

After busting my last nut, my knees buckled underneath me, I flopped onto my stomach. Devon braced both hands on my lower back and pounded my ass out until he nutted inside my goodies. Minutes later, he collapsed on top of me. We were both gasping for air and enjoying each other's company, lost in our own world, reminiscing about what just went down.

After I caught my breath and got my head level, I got up. I walked back to the bathroom and washed off real quick. I was definitely a fool for a good fuck. This was one of the best fucks that Devon had ever given me, and since he wouldn't be around for long, I might as well enjoy them while it lasted.

Shari

Blowing up the phone, hope she see me calling her.

*I whip up in the driveway, she done packed up all
my stuff.
And I'm like what the fuck? Can't even talk to her.*

I sat on the floor, playing Kevin Gates's song over and
over while dialing Devon's number over and over. There
was no response.

How could he be this cold to me? I'd just lost my
mother, and not once did he call me to say he was sorry.
How could he do this to me, the woman he loved? I
turned against my sister for him. I couldn't stop the tears
from flowing. I picked up the phone to call my mama and
quickly realized she was no longer with me. She was gone.
Mama was my world. My everything. God, how was I
supposed to live without her? "God, answer me. How can
you say you love me but take away the only person I love?"
I put the bottle of Cîroc Peach to my head and couldn't
stop drinking.

Twenty minutes later, I was drunk and high as fuck,
but instead of feeling much better, I was still feeling
lonely and angry. I gargled with mouthwash, sprayed
my body, grabbed my car keys, and got into my car. *I
shouldn't be driving, but fuck it.* I didn't have nothing to
live for anyway. My best friend was gone, and it wouldn't
be a bad idea for me to join her.

I made my way to my sister's apartment. Shit, I hadn't
seen the bitch since the day of Mama's wake, and even
then, she was still acting like a bitch toward me. I mean, I
knew I fucked her nigga, but shit, she should be thanking
me. I did get his cheating ass away from her. At least she
wasn't the one he was cheating on right now. I wiped the
tear that fell on my face.

*"Bitch, quit all this fucking crying. I didn't raise no
weak-ass bitch."* Surprisingly, I heard Mama's voice in
my head. I almost crashed when I heard that because

this was the first time since she died that I had heard her voice.

"Mama, is that you?" I looked over to the seat across from me. I didn't see her. I glanced in my mirror to the back seat and didn't see her. "C'mon, answer me, Mama. I need you. How you gonna say some shit to me and then disappear just like that?" I started crying again. I waited to hear her once again, but I didn't hear anything.

I parked and jumped out of my car. I stumbled to her door and started pounding on the door. "Open up, Amoy," I yelled.

I knew she was there because I saw her car. I wasn't leaving until she opened this damn door.

"What the fuck you doing here, bitch?" She opened the door.

I didn't respond. I used all my force, pushing the door wide open while I stumbled inside, hitting the floor. "I need to talk to you, Amoy." I tried to regain my balance without further embarrassing myself.

"Bitch, I have nothing to talk to you about. Now get yo' ass out of my shit before I throw your drunk ass out." She stood there with an angry look on her face.

"Listen, sis, I know I fucked up. I should've stopped talking to Devon once I found out he was who you were messing with. But by the time I found out, I was already in love with him. My entire life, you have always been the happy one. The one everybody praised. I was always in your shadow as Amoy's little sister."

"So what, bitch? You decided to take the same dick that I was fucking? You're fucking disgusting. How do you feel, you fucking the same nigga I fucked?"

"I'm sorry, Amoy. I swear, if I could go back and change the hands of time, I would never sleep with Devon."

"Well, ho, it's too late for your apologies and for you to pretend like you give a fuck. So why are you really here?"

"I'm pregnant! Mama is not here. You're the only one I've got," I blurted out.

"Ha-ha, you're pregnant? Why would I give a fuck? Did you forget all the fucked-up-ass names you called my child? Bitch, why in God's name would I give a fuck about that motherfucker you're carrying? If you came over here for any kind of pity, you knocked on the wrong bitch's door, because you're dead to me. Now get yo' ass out of my shit." She walked over to the door and opened it wide.

I was desperate. I didn't know what to do. This bitch wasn't trying to hear me out.

"I'm your sister. This is me, Amoy, Shari, your little sister. Mama is gone now, and we are all we got." I grabbed her arm, trying to hug her.

"Bitch, get the fuck off of me. You're the worst kind of snake. The kind that hides behind that 'sissy' shit. See, I loved you, so I was blind and didn't see the real you until it was too late. As long as I'm living, I would never fuck with you again." She grabbed my shoulder and pushed me out the door, slamming her door shut.

"Please, Amoy. I need you. I swear I'm sorryyyyy," I cried out.

"Ay, cool down on the noise," said her neighbor, opening her door.

"Bitch, shut the fuck up!" I yelled back.

After minutes of pleading and begging, I realized that she wasn't trying to open the door. I sat up and stumbled out of her building. I was crushed even more. I grabbed my phone and dialed Devon's number, but he still didn't respond.

I sat in my car and pulled out the little pack of cocaine that I had. I'd been dabbling here and there for about a year now, but lately, it had become an everyday thing for me. I put the coke in a dollar bill. I took a quick glance around to check if anyone was looking. I then snorted the white powder. It only took a few seconds for it to hit my brain. My sullen mood quickly changed as I felt powerful, like I was in control now. I was fully alert now.

I searched my phone for Kennedy's number. I knew she probably wouldn't pick up, but if she did, I planned on letting her know what the fuck her husband had been up to.

"Hello. So you're a bold bitch. Didn't I tell you not to call my phone anymore?"

"Listen, lady. I'm not calling for your husband. I'm calling to talk to you."

"Talk to me? Whatever I had to say to you, I said it the day I visited you. Now go ahead, little girl, before I end up hurting you."

"Ha-ha, that's hilarious, but I ain't worried 'bout yo' old ass hurting me. But listen, lady, I need to talk to you."

"I am done talking to you. Keep on, I'm going to get you for harassment."

"Kennedy, chill out. Your husband is planning to kill you."

"What?"

"You heard me right. Your husband is going to have you robbed and killed."

"Did you say you want to talk? When can you meet up?"

"I can meet now. You've got the address. Meet me at the crib."

"Sure thing."

I hung the phone up and pulled off. I was trying to get to the house before she got there. I was still tweaking, plus the scent of alcohol was seeping through my pores. Not that I gave a fuck, but if I wanted the bitch to believe me, then I needed to not appear like I was high or drunk.

I took a quick shower, brushed my hair into a ponytail, and brushed my teeth. I put on a pair of tights and a wife beater. I looked down and realized my stomach was showing a little bit. *Fuck.* I'd been so fucked up for the past few days that I didn't have time to worry about being pregnant. Anger crept up on me. That fucking nigga, Devon, didn't give a fuck about me or this baby. I rubbed my stomach. *Oh, well, his loss.*

Within minutes, I heard the doorbell ringing. I already knew it was her. The bitch kind of made me nervous with her old, evil ass, but tonight, she was my ally. With what I was about to tell her, she was going to love me.

I opened the door, and she walked in. "Ain't nobody follow you here, right?" I asked.

"Why would anyone follow me?"

The truth was I was still high as fuck off of the powder. I let out a long sigh, trying to control myself and hoping she wasn't smart enough to know I was high as fuck.

"So let's get to the point. You said on the phone that my husband was planning my murder?"

"Yes, yes, but before I tell you anything, I need some money."

"Ho, you're silly. Your broke ass thought you were going to extort money from me?" She laughed.

"Listen, lady, chill out wit' the name-calling, okay? I think we both know that nigga ain't worth shit. I've got some info, and you've got some money, so I think we can work something out."

"What makes you think I would pay to get information from you when I can just call the police and have them arrest your ass for forgery?"

"Forgery, police . . . You know what? You can get yo' ass out of my shit." I walked over to my door and opened it up. I was bluffing to see if this bitch was serious.

"How much money are you talking about?"

"Let say about . . . Hmm, let's see how much this information means to you. About ten grand."

"Bitch, you've lost your damn mind. The whole nigga ain't worth that fucking much."

"Take it or leave it. But what I have is juicy, real juicy." I winked at her.

"I'm gone. Don't call my fucking phone no more."

She started to walk off, but I jumped in front of her.

"Stop. Wait, give me five grand, and I'll give you everything, including the recording that I have."

"I say that's a deal. Now tell me what you know and give me the disc, and I will gladly write you a check."

"A check? I need cash. What if your check ain't good?"

"I don't know what kind of people you're used to, but I am a businesswoman. I don't go around writing bad checks. We have a deal."

It took about twenty minutes for me to tell her about Devon's plan to have her murdered. I then gave her the disc that I had recorded Devon on for security purposes. See, this nigga thought he was so fucking smart, but I was always one step ahead of him. He would learn that I was not to be fucked with.

I watched as she pulled her checkbook out and wrote the check.

"Here you go, but before I go, let me ask you a question. Why did you decide to turn against him?"

I grinned at her, looked at the check, and then responded. "That nigga ain't loyal to nobody but himself, and I'm only loyal to me. That nigga said fuck me, so I'm fucking him raw without grease."

She nodded and walked quietly out of my apartment. I quickly locked my door. I was happy she was gone. There was something about being in that bitch's presence that made my skin crawl. She came off as nice, but I could see the poison pouring out.

I looked at the check and my eyes widened. I hadn't seen this much money in a while. My account was almost drained because I'd been dipping in it to keep up with these bills and even more because I was getting high more than usual. I really needed to get this shit under control soon. I didn't want to turn out like Mama. But Mama was smoking crack. All I was doing was powder.

I grabbed the phone and called my connect. "Ay, can I come see you?"

"Yeah, I'm around the way."

"Okay, cool. I've got to stop at the bank, and then I'll be on my way."

I hung the phone up and took out the last little bit of dust I had left. I placed it on a dollar bill and started sniffing it. After the second drag, I was back on cloud nine.

Was that a knock I heard, or am I tripping? I wiped my nose and walked over to the door. *Shit, it's Devon. What is he doing here?*

I was too happy to see my man. I guessed he was missing me as much as I was missing him. I quickly opened the door. "Hey, babes," I greeted him in an upbeat mood.

He didn't respond though. He just walked past me and into the living room. I locked the door and followed him.

"You okay, babes?"

"What was Kennedy doing here?"

"Huh? Who . . . what are you talking about, Devon?"

Blap! Blap! Blap!

"Bitch, don't play with me. What the fuck was Kennedy doing up in here?"

"Devon, baby, she wasn't here, or if she was, I didn't see her."

That nigga raised the gun and slapped me a few times, knocking me to the ground. I held my face as I screamed and pleaded for mercy.

"Now what the fuck did you tell her?"

"I didn't tell her anything, Devon. I swear, baby, I would never betray you. Please, baby, don't forget that I'm pregnant."

"Bitch, I don't give a fuck 'bout that bastard or you. Bitch, I told you to leave me the fuck alone, but you didn't listen. I told yo' ass."

I balled up in a fetal position as he stomped me. I knew then that he'd come to handle business. "Please, Devon, please. I swear I didn't tell her nothing," I cried.

His anger was rising as he knelt down and started beating me in the head with the gun. I started losing consciousness. I tried to plead with him, but my mouth was hurting so bad that the words were not coming out. Everything around me started spinning, and the room got darker. I tried to stay awake, but I couldn't. Eventually, I closed my eyes, hoping that when I woke up this would all be a dream.

CHAPTER THIRTY-ONE

Kennedy

Hmm. That's strange. When I left, Devon was at the house. He said he was tired and was lying down. I knew I wasn't gone that long, but his car was gone. I pulled into the garage and got out of the car. I walked up the stairs. I searched through the house to make sure it was empty.

I then shut my room door and put the disc into my computer and played it. Tears rolled down my face as I heard my husband, another man, and that bitch discussing how my murder was supposed to take place. I knew that he was a cheater but never suspected that nigga was also a killer. His words sent chills up my spine when he described to the other man how he wanted it done. I was tearing the fuck up. I'd killed before, but this was me they were discussing.

I heard the door open, so I hurriedly cut the computer off. I pulled out the disc, put it back in the envelope, and threw it back into my purse. I grabbed the mail nearby so I could pretend like I was reading.

"Hey, love. You're back fast."

"I told you I was only making a quick run. I thought you were taking a nap."

"Shit, I was until my homeboy hit me up, and I had to go meet him."

"Devon, I hope you're not back in them streets, dealing them drugs again."

"Hell nah, babes. I told you that part of me was over. I ain't goin' to lie. I miss making all that money, but I can't risk losing you behind no foolish decision."

"I love you, Devon. I just want us to be happy."

He sat beside me on the bed. "Kennedy, after today, we will forever be happy."

"Why? What happened today that was special?"

"Nothing special happened. Listen, babes, I'm all yours forever."

I didn't respond. Instead, I just rubbed his hand.

I was up in the living room, drinking a cup of coffee and watching the morning news on ABC. The reporter came on talking about the body of a young girl found Friday evening after 7:00 p.m. She went on to say that she was brutally murdered.

"Good morning, babes," I heard Devon holler as he walked down the stairs.

"Hey, love," I yelled back.

My focus, however, was on the news and what the reporter was saying. I spat coffee all over the place when the picture of the bitch I visited that same evening flashed across the screen. "Devonnnnn," I yelled out as I stood up.

He ran into the living room. "What's wrong, babe?"

I couldn't even get the words out. I just pointed to the television. He looked and then looked back at me. "Somebody got murdered."

"Not just anybody. The little bitch you were sleeping around with," I blurted out.

"Really? Well, you know her ass was out there. It was only a matter of time before one of them niggas killed her for playing them."

"Devon, you didn't have nothing to do with this, right? This happened yesterday evening."

"Babe, you're tripping. I ain't no killer. Trust me, I was nowhere near that girl or her apartment."

His tone was cold, but it was his demeanor that grabbed my attention. I didn't believe him. I recalled that, when I came back, he wasn't home. What if he followed me? He would've known that I went to see her.

"Well, babe, now we ain't got to worry about her bothering us no more."

"You're right about that." I smiled at him.

"What's your plan for later?"

"Nothing. Do some cleaning and put a roast in the oven for dinner."

"Sounds like a plan. I'ma make some runs, and then I'll be back home to spend some quality time with the wife." He kissed me on my lips.

I sat back on the couch. If he saw her after I saw her, did she tell him that I was aware of him plotting my murder? I had too many questions with not enough answers. *Fuck, the check I wrote her.* My head started spinning.

I went ahead and canceled the check. I prayed to God the police didn't find it. I had no idea how I was going to explain why I wrote a check to my husband's side bitch who just so happened to end up murdered on the same date as the check. I thought about going over there and breaking in, but that was even crazier. I didn't kill the bitch and definitely didn't want to get caught up in no murder investigation.

I went grocery shopping and grabbed the biggest, juiciest roast. Tonight was a very special night, and I planned on preparing a big meal. After the grocery store, I stopped at the liquor store and grabbed some Grey

Goose. I saw that Devon's liquor of choice was almost gone. I grabbed me a bottle of Rémy Martin V. This was becoming one of my favorites.

After I got home, I washed and seasoned the roast and let it marinate for a while before I put it into the oven with carrots and potatoes. It didn't take long for the aroma to fill the entire house. I started drinking early, and before you knew it, I was feeling pretty good. I was in a great mood, and nothing or no one was going to stand in my way ever again. I was just setting the table when I heard Devon enter the house. *Damn, he's home early. No worries though.*

"Hey, love. Damn, woman, you've got this house smelling good."

"You need to get in the shower while I set this table."

"Yes, ma'am." He ran off upstairs.

By the time he was finished dressing, I had the candles lit and his food dished out. I placed the bottle of liquor on the table. I'd been preparing for this night for a while now. Ever since this nigga played me. I tried over and over to go about this another way, but truthfully, I just wanted this bum gone for good, out of my fucking life.

My thoughts were interrupted when he entered the dining room and took a seat across from me.

"Damn, bae, you went all the way out tonight. What a nigga do to deserve this type of royal treatment?"

I smiled at him as I took a sip of my Rémy. This fool still had no idea.

"Man, you put yo' motherfucking foot in this roast. Shit's so juicy it's just melting in my mouth."

He was just eating and smiling from ear to ear, saying all the nice words he thought I wanted to hear. I just listened and smiled.

"Devon, let me ask you something."

"What's good, babe? You a'ight?"

"It's been on my mind lately. Did you ever love me, or were you just after what I've got?"

He put the fork down and stared at me. "Yo, B, what the fuck kind of question is that? You're the only woman outside of my mama I ever loved like this. You're my motherfucking heart, yo."

"Devon, if a man loves a woman, he would never cheat on her. At least that's how I was raised. You not only disrespected me, but you dragged me around this town. You know how embarrassed I felt? Even my friends thought I was a laughingstock. I mean, what did I do to you that was so bad? I loved, fucked you, sucked your dick, licked your balls, and gave you everything, but that wasn't enough. You still cheated."

"Yo, B. Yo . . ." He was struggling to get his words out. "I . . . I can't breathe. Kenn . . . ddy." He tried to get up, but he stumbled.

"Oh, my, what's wrong, darling? Did you say you can't breathe?"

He held his throat while gasping for air. I took a seat close to him while he struggled. He looked at me with tears in his eyes. He reached out to touch me, but I moved my foot out of the way.

I then knelt down to where he lay on the tile. He was now foaming at the mouth. I rubbed his head. "See, darling, I wasn't so stupid after all. You dogged me for a while and then thought I was one of these dumb-ass bitches. Wrong. Anyway, say hi to Travis for me. Let him know this old cow is still alive and kicking." I got closer to him and placed a long kiss on his forehead.

I walked away and left him on the floor. It was only a matter of minutes before he would meet his Maker. I poured another glass of Rémy. "Cheers to husband number two." I placed the glass in the air before I swallowed the liquor. I tuned out his groaning sounds and focused on how I was going to get rid of him. I'd just taken my last sip of liquor when I heard something.

Bang! Bang! Bang! I jumped up. *What the fuck was that?* I ran to my door and realized it was the police. My heart started racing, and that was when my ass remembered that Devon's body was still on my dining room floor. I was planning to get rid of him after dark.

I figured they were here to arrest Devon for the murder of that girl. All I had to do was tell them he was not here, and they could get on their merry way. I opened the door, smiling.

"Hello there, Officers. How may I help you all?"

"We have a warrant for your arrest and also a search warrant for your house."

The officer then reached in and grabbed my arm. "Mrs. Guthrie, you're under arrest for the murder of Travis Guthrie."

"What are you talking about? I didn't murder anyone and definitely not my husband. Who is responsible for this madness? I promise, y'all have no idea what y'all are doing."

"Detective, come in here. We have a deceased male on the floor."

They looked at me before they rushed inside. One of the remaining officers led me off to the police car. So these bastards wanted to arrest me for killing a nigga years ago. What fucking evidence did they have? None. I couldn't wait for my lawyer to eat their asses up. I sat in the police car. I saw as other cars pulled up. The coroner also pulled up. I hung my head down. My dumb ass really fucked up this time. I was so caught up in all these different emotions that I didn't notice a man walk up to the car.

"Hello, Kennedy."

My eyes popped open. This couldn't be. "Christopher, what are you doing here?"

"It's Detective Walden."

"Say what? Christopher? Now is not the time for your silly jokes."

"Mrs. Guthrie, I'm not joking. My name is Detective Walden."

My mouth hung wide open. I looked at his face. He was not joking. Shit, he didn't even look the same. Alarms started going off in my head. *Detective. Oh, my God.* He was undercover, and my stupid ass confessed everything to him. That was when it hit me. After all these years, they were charging me with murder because I told this nigga I killed my husband.

"You bastard! How could you?" This was the same nigga I fucked and sucked. Oh, my God, this couldn't be . . .

He didn't say a word. He looked at me, shook his head, and walked toward the house, where the rest of the pigs were.

All I could do was cry. How could the one person I trusted betray me like that?

CHAPTER THIRTY-TWO

Amoy

I had just dropped my baby off at day care and was about to head back home so I could clean up before heading to the hospital to see Marquise. The last few days had been hell for us. It was found out that the gunshots had damaged his tissues and organs. Twice, he went into cardiac arrest. However, the doctors were very optimistic on his recovery.

For the first time, I got to meet his mom and the rest of his family. It was sad that we had to meet under these circumstances. I could see the hurt in his mom's eyes when she walked in and saw the condition her son was in.

I'd been praying daily for him, and for hours at a time I would sit with him, telling him how much I loved him. I begged God every day to protect my baby. I couldn't lose him.

My phone was ringing, but I was mopping the kitchen floor. *Whoever that is is goin' to have to wait,* I thought as I continued doing what I was doing. The phone kept ringing though. I could no longer ignore it, so I put the mop down and dashed over to the couch and grabbed it up. I had four missed calls, all from his sister's number. I panicked immediately and dialed her number back. "Hey, babes, I was—"

"You need to get up here now!" she yelled into the phone.

"Okay," was all I said before I dashed to my room. I grabbed my keys and my purse and sprinted out the door. My heart was jumping in my chest as I pulled off in a rush.

His sister's voice was that of desperation. I knew in my heart that this wasn't good. I felt the tears trying to seep out, but I used everything in me to hold them in. "God, please don't take my baby away from me." As soon as I said that, the tears poured down my face. I pressed on the gas and dashed to the hospital. I was pissed off that I had to stop at the stop signs because every little second counted.

I pulled up to the emergency entrance and parked. "Ma'am, you can't park right here. You're blocking the entrance," a parking attendant said.

"Get the fuck out of my way," I said as I dashed into the lobby.

I had no time to wait on the elevator, so I ran up the stairs. My feet were moving, but it seemed like I wasn't going fast enough. My chest started tightening up on me, but I didn't let that slow me down. Finally, I got to the ICU. I dashed to his room.

"Ma'am, no one is allowed in that room right now but the immediate family," said the policeman who was guarding his door. He was definitely new and not the regular one who had been there.

"She's family. Let her in."

I ran in the room, and I saw the doctors, nurses, and his family standing over him. I looked at them and pushed toward him.

His sister grabbed me. "He's gone. My brother is gone," she yelled as she held me in a bear hug.

I looked at her like she was a foreign object. "He ain't gone. My baby's right there. C'mon . . . Tell them, baby." I tried to break loose. "Let me go. Let me get to my baby," I yelled at the top of my lungs.

I used all my strength and broke free from her. I dashed over to him and threw my body on him, holding his face. "Baby, c'mon, wake up. I know you're just playing. Wake up, Marquise. Noooooooooooooooooo," I screamed from the bottom of my lungs.

When it rained, it poured. After I left the hospital, on my way home, I got a phone call from the police telling me that my sister was dead. She was found murdered. After I hung the phone up, I pulled over to the side of the road, and I cried. I had no idea if I was crying because she was dead or I was relieved that she would no longer be a nuisance to me. They said God didn't give you more than you could bear, but shit, God must have known by now that I couldn't bear any more. I lost three people back-to-back. How was I supposed to carry on like this?

After I got myself together, I pulled back on the road. It was late, and I needed to get my baby home.

I couldn't sleep because I was so used to him being on the other side of the bed. I kept reaching over just like I used to do. Only this time he didn't reach back and pull me closer. I had no idea how I was going to live without him. I grabbed the pillow and hugged it close to me, inhaling his strong scent that was all over the pillow.

God, I can't live without him, I really can't. I could still hear him telling me how much he loved me. Who would be so wicked to take my baby's life away? Whoever it was, they were going to pay. I grabbed my cell phone and dialed Devon's number. As I sat there waiting for his bitch ass to answer, I had no doubt that he was responsible for what happened to Marquise. He didn't answer. Instead, his phone just rang out until the voicemail came on.

"Listen up, you little bitch-ass nigga. I know you're the one who shot my man. But don't worry. Lady Karma's going to visit yo' ass, and when she does, I hope you're fucking ready. I hope you die a slow fucking death. I fucking hate you with everything in me." I hung the phone up and threw it onto the bed.

"God, please take this pain that I'm feeling away from me. I can't live like this, God," I cried out as I collapsed on the floor.